LITTLE WHISPERS

A NOVEL BY GLEN KRISCH

LITTLE WHISPERS

PROLOGUE

MENOMONEE FALLS, WISCONSIN, 1995

Melody Underhill clutched a stack of books as she left the library, taking two stairs at a time. The frigid wind gave her an immediate shiver after the long hours she'd spent in the library's warmth since school ended. She was alone, but that was her existence pretty much 24/7. It didn't bother her to walk home by herself.

"You sure you don't want to phone your mom to pick you up?" Mrs. Foley called out from behind her. At the sidewalk, Melody turned and found the grandmotherly head librarian standing in the doorway.

"She works late. It's not a big deal. My house is, like, five blocks away."

Her mother was most likely home, most likely high, most likely "entertaining" some biker dude she'd met at The Pour House, her favorite seedy bar off the highway north of town. Mrs. Foley didn't need to know those sordid details to understand Melody was fine on her own.

"I'll give you a lift if you give me five minutes to lock up."

"That's silly," Melody replied. "I'll be home in five minutes."

Mrs. Foley didn't look convinced. She absently straightened her dark wig, as if it chafed her so late in the day. "Okay, dear. See you Saturday?"

"Yes, ma'am," Melody said, and waved from under her mound of books.

Mrs. Foley waved back before locking the door.

Melody didn't exactly want to go home, not with the many

unseemly possibilities she might encounter there, but she couldn't wait to crack the spine on the new Lauren Bacall biography. She hoped to slip inside her bedroom unnoticed, dive onto her bed, and read until her eyes dried out. She hadn't mentioned to anyone that her dream was to become a confident, headstrong actress like Bacall.

She had begun to hum a nonsensical tune when she noticed the streetlights casting globes of light between long stretches of darkness. She couldn't believe she'd lost track of time, although it happened daily; the stories of lives different than her own provided an escape.

Fearing her mom's wrath, Melody's heart quickened. Her mom was easy to set off, and violence often followed.

As she neared the next intersection, a van parallel-parked into one of the islands of darkness between lampposts. Dark paint, tinted windows. She would've never seen it—would have walked right on by without a second thought—but a glimmer of streetlight reflecting off the chrome bumper caught her eye.

The hair on the nape of her neck prickled and she stopped humming. The night had become unwaveringly quiet. Something felt wrong, off-kilter. She felt it to her marrow.

She'd rather walk barefoot over broken glass than pass that van. She would head back to the library, she decided, loop around the block, and add a minute or two to her walk home. No big deal. She was already *way* late and *way* beyond hope of escaping her mom's anger, but it wouldn't matter as long as she got home safely.

The revving of the engine goosed her pace. The van's headlights turned on, blinding her for a split second. The vehicle veered from the curb, inched forward and cut a sharp left. Headlights panned the chilly street as the van made an illegal U-turn before disappearing up the block.

Melody chuckled at her overreaction, even though her heart still thudded in her chest. Maybe it *hadn't* been an overreaction. Maybe it had been instinct. Whatever. All she knew was that she was now heading the wrong direction for home.

When she reached the library's steps once again, the shadow of a large maple tree expanded, but it wasn't darkness shifting in the

6

limited light. A man wearing a tweed coat and thick-framed glasses had stepped out of the shadows. His well-groomed white beard nearly glowed in the darkness. He blocked her path.

"I'm sorry, young lady," the man said, startled by her sudden appearance.

"Excuse me." She gripped her books, getting ready to run.

"But of course." The man tipped an imaginary hat and trotted across the street.

Melody let out a pent-up breath and picked up her pace, *so* ready to put this night and her jumpy nerves behind her. She turned at the next street corner, glancing over her shoulder.

She didn't notice the van until it was too late. No more than three feet away, the sliding door gaped open like a hungry mouth.

It couldn't possibly be …

She dropped her books, to double back toward the library, to scream bloody murder, but something struck her temple, hard, sending stars cartwheeling across her vision. And then she plummeted through a deep well of infernal night, a warm wetness trailing down her temple, across her cheek, to her lips.

Her body thumped onto a coarse blanket strewn across the floor of the van. She writhed wildly to get away. She only succeeded in clearing her body from the doorframe of the van when a man climbed inside after her and slammed the door shut, blanketing them in murky darkness. Melody's attacker yanked her arms behind her and pressed his knee into her lower back.

After the knock against her skull, she had little will left to fight, and felt disconnected from her limbs. Her fading vision throbbed to the beat of her heart, consciousness retreating.

She tried to say something, to shout, but no words came out.

She felt numb. So incredibly tired.

"*Shhh* … Oh, don't you say a word, Melody."

Adrenaline stripped away some of the grogginess.

He knew her name, which surprised her as much as his tone. He was calm, which threw her for a loop. She was used to her mom's full-on rage. This man's lack of anger, his relaxed grace, only sharpened her fear.

She felt a surge of panic.

If he can do this without even raising his voice ...

"Please," she managed through streaming tears.

"Shhh ..." the man repeated. He pressed a rough finger to her lips, silencing her. "Words will only make things worse. There is no excuse for your devilry. No explaining your sins ... so don't even bother."

He touched her hair, the tips of his fingers tracing from her slight widow's peak to where her hair fell midway down her back. He stroked her shoulders gently, somehow affectionately. This illicit contact made him exhale in a fitful spasm.

"Glorious," he whispered.

Melody sobbed, unable to control herself, even if it set him off and brought out his demons. Certainly, only demons fueled this man's intentions.

And what are his intentions?

She cast the thought away, not wanting to consider the possibilities.

He seized her hair in a firm grasp and she cried out.

"We have much to learn," he said, barely audible, again under control. "About each other. About weakness. About absolution and redemption."

"P-please ..." she managed, dazed, lost in shadows both real and illusory.

Dim streetlights lit the van's tinted windows. Cool autumn wind whistled against glass. The city slumbered, unaware.

"No words, Melody. There will be no words."

She remained silent, biding her time. Only later would she realize she'd missed her one last opportunity, however slight the possibility.

He helped her to sit, knees pulled to her chest.

"Good girl. Now wrap your arms around your knees."

She complied, feeling powerless to do otherwise.

"That's my girl."

Melody's eyes had somewhat adjusted to the gloom. She could see him now, and he wasn't scary at all. If anything, he was both striking and young: dark brown hair cropped military short, eyes so blue she couldn't help but stare into them.

He unfurled the end of a wide roll of industrial plastic wrap, tucked the end between her knobby knees.

"Squeeze and don't let go."

She pressed her knees together as he yanked slack from the roll and wrapped it around her. With each successive pass around her body, the plastic held her ever more tightly. The plastic shrieked as it shed its spool to add layers to her confinement, making it difficult to breathe beyond shallow pants. He mummified her from feet to shoulders in a few short minutes.

"Not … not my face?" she said, hopeful.

"I wouldn't do that to you." The man smiled. "But I will need to put *this* over your mouth." He held a length of fabric before her eyes. "Remember, no words? I can't risk you shouting when it's not appropriate. I'd like to trust you, but we just met. You understand, don't you?"

Melody nodded, almost relieved. He wouldn't gag her if he was planning to kill her; she would already be dead if that's what he wanted, or so she hoped.

He lifted the fabric over her head, grinning. He could be reaching out to place a necklace around the neck of his girlfriend.

"Open," he said, and dangled the fabric against her lips.

She complied.

After cinching the fabric taut across her open mouth, he tied a double-knot behind her head. The gag had a chemical taste, the odor dizzying. Her eyes wanted to close and fluttered as she fought to keep them open. It would be so easy to let go, to stop struggling …

"That's it, Melody. My sweet girl. Relax."

He wrapped the plastic around her some more, cocooning her to her chin. When finished, he cut the end of the plastic with a box cutter and tucked the edge under one of the many layers. Both her mind and body were warm, sweaty, *heavy*—like hot molasses drawn slowly through a straw.

Her eyes closed and only opened again after she felt him lifting her into his arms. With deliberate care, he settled her onto her side. He had placed her *inside* something, a small box.

A coffin?

Her mind raced, but she was helpless but to play her part in his sick game.

The man combed his fingers through her hair, tucked a lock behind her ear. He leaned over and brushed his lips against her cheek.

"Soon, Melody," he whispered, his lips touching her ear. "Soon, we will learn."

The man closed whatever confined space she now occupied and yanked on a metal zipper. A thin seam of meager light knitted together as he pulled, the sides joining like a rapidly healing wound.

And then the light was gone, for good most likely.

A suitcase?

She was unable to question anymore, and well past the point of fighting for her life. Her eyes closed for good as she fell into a dreamless abyss.

Melody chased after unconsciousness like a moth chasing a flame.

CHAPTER 1

WESTERN MICHIGAN, PRESENT DAY

Clara Forrester straightened the hem of her blue pleated skirt as she waited for the next spelling word.

"Okay … the next word is …" her mom said, turning around in the front passenger's seat of their Volvo. She glanced at the papers in her lap. "*Precipice.*"

"Definition, please," Clara said automatically, even though she already knew the answer.

"A cliff with a vertical, nearly vertical, or overhanging face. A situation of great peril. Pres-*uh*-pis."

Clara pursed her lips and internalized the word, her unfocused gaze drifting toward the ceiling. She mouthed the phonetics of the word, hearing their every nuance and texture, their every etymological wrinkle.

Pres-*uh*-pis.

"P-r-e-c … i-p … i-c-e. Pres-*uh*-pis."

"Correct," her mom said.

"Good job, sweetie-pie," her dad said, steering up a winding incline.

Clara smiled on the inside, not allowing it to reach her stern façade, already eager for the next word. The windshield shifted from the road's bare expanse to splashes of vibrant spring foliage: petals in a variety of purples, lemon yellows, virginal whites, leaves and seedlings in every shade of green. The western Michigan woods enveloped them, as if their car were the only one remaining in an empty world. The engine hummed rhythmically. Clara straightened the cuffs of her gray cardigan, rested her hands in her lap, ready.

"Okay," her mom said, checking her papers, "the next word is—"

"Krista," her dad cut in, "when exactly is the National Spelling Bee?"

"You know as well as I do."

"August something-or-other, right?" her dad said. "That's months away."

"It's August 12th, Daddy." Clara waited impatiently for the next word. "That's two months and three days from now."

Her mom sighed. "Yes, it's a long time away, but there are thousands of words to cover, and thousands of kids working just as hard."

"Look outside the window," he said, not exactly changing the subject but reframing it.

"What? Why?" her mom said.

This was one of his favorite tactics to get people to see things his way.

Clara didn't care; she wanted the next word, wanted to drink it in, to dominate it and make it her own.

"Just look. And I mean both of you." Her dad took his eyes off the road until she caved.

Her mom rolled her eyes. "Okay, I'm looking."

"Clara?" His dark green eyes met hers in the rear-view mirror.

Clara scowled as the landscape blurred by in a colorful torrent. The hills were thick with ancient oak, maple, and beech trees. This wilderness was a foreign geography for a kid raised in a condominium on Chicago's Gold Coast.

"It's my strong opinion children should spend their idle time staring out windows," her dad said.

"But—" her mom cut in, but her dad stopped her with a raised index finger.

"Thousands of kids are in this competition, right?" he asked.

"And the finalists are all practicing their lists. Every one of them."

"Clara finished in the top fifty last year—"

"Forty-third," Clara clarified.

"Forty-third. As an eleven-year-old. I say that's incredible. Don't you, dear?"

Her mom fidgeted with her seatbelt. "Yes … yes, I do, but—"

"No buts. Clara, you are officially off the clock. No more words for the duration of this little trip. Enjoy the view. With how busy we all are, we don't get out to the country too often. Stare off into space. Let your mind wander. Be a kid."

"If I have to."

Her dad chuckled. "Well, you do."

Clara harrumphed and stared out the window to prove her dad wrong. She could let her mind wander. She could be a kid … if she tried hard enough.

Her mom gave her a quick glance and patted his hand before whispering, "Sometimes, I have to admit … you're right. Sometimes we need to take the time to just *breathe*."

"Can I get that in writing?" he said and laughed, the sound like glue binding their family.

"What? Like a legally-binding agreement? Sure, counselor. I'll get my lawyer to throw something together."

"But *I* am your lawyer," he said.

"Sounds like a conflict of interest."

She kissed her fingertips and pressed them to his cheek, a gesture guaranteed to bring a smile to Clara's normally stoic face.

He steered the Volvo down roads winding through impenetrable woodlands. "And what about … you know?" he whispered, trailing off.

"What about?"

"I know this visit is stressing you out big-time. It's been so long since you've been to the summer house."

Clara tensed, her eyes skimming the beautiful wilderness.

"It *has* been a long time," her mom said. "Since the summer I turned twelve. After all that happened, I'd always stayed back in Grand Rapids with Nan."

Clara waited for her to continue, but she seemed exhausted of words. Clara considered what she'd learned. Her mother had avoided the summer house for over twenty years. And the last time she traveled this same road, she had been the same age as Clara.

Prescient. The word popped into her head, unbidden, and she recalled the phonetics of the word: *prĕsh'ŏnt.*

Outside—where all kids were meant to let their minds wander—the trees blurred a vibrant green panorama, cloaking skeletal branches and the layers of darkening shadows cast beneath. Clara began to lose focus, and her eyelids drew heavy and low. Her breath deepened. She verged on sleep, but remained aware of her surroundings, at least for the moment. Her parents carried on just above a whisper, sometimes glancing back to see if she were paying attention.

"There's nothing you could've done, Krista. You were twelve."

"Breann was my best friend."

Silence broken only by the steady purr of the engine carried them for another mile. Clara didn't know what had kept her mother from returning to the summer house. It was almost impossible for Clara to imagine her mom being a kid.

"Sometimes I wonder ..." her mom said, hesitating, "like in the grocery store checkout line, or when we're finding our seats at the movie theater ... I'll see a woman who'd be close enough in age and appearance that I can't help thinking—"

"Krista," her dad said, "you shouldn't do that to yourself—"

"But I do! Don't you get it? I *do*. And I can't tell you how many times I've made eye contact with those women, hoping to see some spark of recognition reflecting back at me."

"Krista ... there was a trial. Edgar Jenkins—"

"Don't speak his name ..."

"Fine. *He* is never going to see the light of day."

"No matter how many times I try to convince myself that that's enough ... I just can't. He might never see the light of day, but damn it, I can't bring myself to believe she's not out there somewhere ... and that she's somehow happy, somehow whole."

Her parents didn't speak for a long time after that.

Clara stared out the window, piecing together the details.

The sound of the engine changed as the Volvo slowed.

"This is beautiful," her dad said.

Her mom grumbled in agreement.

"Are we almost there?" Clara said, leaning forward between the seats.

"Just at the end of this road." The corners of her mom's mouth curved into the slightest smile, but the apprehension in her eyes betrayed any possible joy.

Clara looked from her mom's short auburn curls to the road ahead, searching for any sign of Poppa's house. She had never been here before, and neither had her dad for that matter. Even so, she had pored over so many grainy photos that she had a clear mental image.

They approached a stout white A-frame building, but Clara knew to look for a chocolate-colored house. A twinkle of silver sparkled in the distance. Little Whisper Lake. It had to be, which meant they were getting close. According to her mom, no more than ten homes lined the perimeter of the lake, Poppa's included.

After a half mile of seemingly untamable wilderness, they came across a nook carved into the beech and pinewood growth.

"This is it," her mom whispered. "Oh my God, this is it."

The car pulled into a crushed gravel driveway.

Nestled at the center of the clearing was the house from the fading Polaroids: a dark brown bungalow that nearly blended in with the surrounding shadows. Broad windows with forest green storm shutters were set on either side of the central mahogany doorway. An arching cobblestone path led to the front porch. And much to her delight, through the wide and open windows, bookshelves filled the front room from floor to ceiling, filled with books in every color, breadth, and dimension, like a library.

"Wow," Clara said.

"Definition, please?" her dad said, and they all laughed.

Maybe this summer vacation isn't going to be so horrible after all.

An old man struggled up from a porch swing. Once on his feet, even from a distance, Clara could see his legs tremble and a slight tremor in his hands.

Oh, Poppa.

Clara was filled with both longing and a queasy trepidation.

"I thought he'd be in bed," her mom said, "or at least resting inside."

Her dad nodded. "Me, too."

The Forresters left the Volvo, all stiff-limbed after the four-hour drive. The spattering of nearby pine trees suffused the air with their lush scent. Clara could have just woken from a dream of wintertime splendor to discover it's still the beginning of summer vacation. The breeze was cooler than back home. *Clean.* The simple word could find no better physical representation.

Poppa came shuffling down the narrow cobblestone path, arms outstretched, a broad but tired smile on his face. He wore a red polo shirt tucked into gray sweat pants that hung on his stick-figure frame. It was shocking how much he'd wasted away. His skin was loose, gray and liver-spotted. His hair was pure white, erupting in downy curls around his ears and the back of his head. His eyes were alert, crisp, like little shards of blue ice. Clara clearly noted underlying fatigue mixed with pain.

From the corner of her eye, Clara sensed movement from one of the windows, and glimpsed a tousle of dark hair before the person drew away.

Yay, Heidi is here!

She hadn't seen any of her cousins since the holidays.

"Poppa," her mom said, "what are you doing outside in the damp?" She hugged him hard before he could answer.

"Oh ... oh, you don't need to fuss. Really. I'm having a good day. The fresh air lubricates my weary bones."

"Pierce," her dad said when the old man was free from the hug.

"Neal, a pleasure."

"Likewise."

They shook hands, and it looked like her dad would embrace the old man as well, but Poppa turned away when he noticed Clara.

"Oh, my dear lord, is this Miss Clarabelle? Aren't you supposed to be knee-high?" He placed his quavering hand on her head, leaned in close to apprise her.

She felt a mad desire to curtsy, but remained unmoving, silent.

"Clara, don't be rude. Say hello to your great-grandpa."

"Hi ... Poppa."

Poppa pushed his wire-rimmed glasses higher up his nose. "You look like your momma when she was your age, like two peas in a pod."

"Poppa, let's get you inside," her mom said.

"Sure, sure." Poppa turned slowly toward the door. "The four of us can talk peacefully before all the others arrive."

"Others?" Clara said, confused.

"Yeah," her dad said. He placed a hand on her shoulder. "You know, your uncle and aunt, your cousins? Remember, this is a family vacation?"

"You Forresters are always on time," Poppa said and chuckled. "Your mom's brother and sister on the other hand ... not so much."

"But, I thought ...?" Clara glanced at the window again, saw only bookshelves in the background. The bountiful sunlight afforded no possibility of tricks of shadow.

No, she *had* seen someone. Perhaps not her cousin Heidi, but *someone*. Someone with long unruly dark hair.

Poppa and her dad filed inside.

"What is it, honey?" her mom asked.

Clara wanted to glance once more to the window, but she was too afraid of what she might see. "Never mind." She forced a smile, but seeing the apprehension in her mom's face, she asked, "Are you okay, Mom?"

"I am, honey." Her eyes betrayed the full extent of her unspoken feelings, but Clara thought there was some truth to her words.

CHAPTER 2

Poppa walked with a limp favoring his left leg, but he shuffled with surprising quickness. He didn't hesitate at the spacious den and its comfortable couch, preferring instead to head for the kitchen on the far side of the house.

"You sure you don't want to have a seat in the den?" her dad said.

"It's better for me to sit in the kitchen."

"Okay then," her dad said.

Poppa sat on one of the cushioned stools lining the kitchen island and squinted with a sly smile as he gazed through the sliding glass door leading to a two-story deck.

Clara felt disoriented.

How would everyone be able to stay under one roof?

All told—with her family of three, plus Aunt Leah and Uncle Curtis, their kids Robby and Heidi, and Uncle Jack and his son Trevor, as well as Poppa himself—ten people would be together under one roof. Yet the interior of the house seemed to sprawl beyond its exterior limitations. Perhaps it was the bright afternoon sunlight gleaming on the knotty wood flooring, or distant rooms with hidden nooks and passageways. Perhaps it was even the subtle way the home was built into the hill leading down to Little Whisper Lake. Whatever quirk of design explained the effect, Clara felt like she was walking through an optical illusion.

"See, the light's better in here," Poppa said when she reached his side, "and I can see the lake out the window."

"We have a lake out our window, too," Clara said. She absently ran her fingers along the pleats of her skirt, her apprehension beginning to ease.

The sunlight certainly was brighter here, though she saw only a thin ribbon of the lake through the rugged terrain of the wooded lot.

"Mighty Lake Michigan, right?"

"Yes, sir," she said and grinned. "It's like an inland ocean. We see it clear as day from our balcony, which is on the twenty-third floor."

"Do you know I've stood on that same balcony, with you in my arms?"

"No, sir, I didn't." Clara glanced at her dad for confirmation, and he nodded.

"You were a couple days old, still all wrinkles, and with the tiniest fingers and toes I've ever come across."

"Sounds like a hobbit!" Clara blushed and chided herself for blurting out the first thing to come to mind. She had been obsessed with everything Tolkien for over a year. His fictional characters and landscapes were everywhere, it seemed.

"Now that you mention it, there was the slightest resemblance. But you know what? You were even more magical than any old hobbit. Still are."

Poppa laughed and Clara wanted to leap into his arms but she resisted.

"And just so you know, there's no need to *sir* me, Clarabelle. I've never gotten used to that pretension, no matter the circumstance."

"Yes …" she said and paused, biting her tongue, "Poppa."

Clara felt an immediate kinship with Poppa. Since her mom announced they would be vacationing at the summer house, Clara had read a couple of his books about nature conservation. She'd heard his voice in her head, narrating his clear and impassioned prose. Even though they had rarely been in the same room, she felt like she knew him through his writings.

He patted her head, and he looked as handsome as in his author photo, though certainly more gaunt.

Her mom sighed. "She's just trying to be polite, Poppa."

"I know, dear. I just don't have the time left on this earth to get bogged down with it. Straight and to the point is my new motto. I should have it stamped on my forehead."

"Well, if that's the case …" Her mom rested a hand on the refrigerator door. "Do you want ham and Swiss, or turkey and provolone?"

"First, two questions," Poppa said.

"Yes?" She crossed her arms, impatient.

"First off, you know what's in my fridge?"

"Am I wrong?"

"No, I suppose not." Poppa chuckled. "And secondly, I'm having a sandwich?"

"Yes. You look hungry, but I didn't want to take the time to ask." Her face was a stony façade, but she couldn't hide the conflicting emotions in her eyes—lighthearted warmth mixing with raw sadness.

"Krista—" her dad cut in.

"Ham and Swiss," Poppa answered, "and I love you."

"I love you too, Poppa. Mustard and mayo?"

"Yes, dear."

She turned to her dad. "Neal?"

He gave a thumbs up. "Make that two of the same."

"Me, three!" Clara added before her mom could even ask.

"Ready in a jiffy." Though her mom was making light of the situation, it wasn't a light situation they were facing.

She watched her mom bustle about the kitchen, amazed she remembered where everything was kept after such a long absence. She found the plates on the first guess, the knife and bread on the second.

Poppa and her dad chatted about their shared interests in law and environmental conservation, their time apart now inconsequential, their voices jovial and familiar.

No matter the outcome of this visit, no matter the grim provenance behind her family's long absence, Clara could already declare this visit worthwhile. She inhaled deeply, easily, and when she exhaled she was surprised when her chest hitched with a sudden jolt of sadness.

Her dad, sensing something amiss, glanced her way.

By the time their eyes met, Clara managed to turn a potential onslaught of tears into a soft chuckle. Her dad smiled and she managed to mimic him. She hated losing control.

"I'm going to check out the library," she said, wandering from the room before anyone could be the wiser.

She let her family's voices wash over her, let their gathering laughter cocoon her from reality. She crossed her arms across her stomach, wanting nothing more than to capture this moment—*their* happiness, *not* her stupid silly emotions—and remember it for all her days. But she couldn't, not for the life of her.

tur-*muh*-nl.

in-op-er-uh-b*uh*l.

Two weeks ago, while she'd been peering out her cracked bedroom door, she heard her mom utter those two words. Clara had only gotten out of bed after hearing her parents' raised voices—such an alien sound in their home. And when she heard those two words, Clara immediately mouthed the phonetics of each, hearing every nuance and texture, every etymological wrinkle.

Sometimes her photographic memory was as much a curse as a blessing. It helped with spelling bees, but in real life it tended to complicate matters both big and small.

With those words still on her lips, she'd retreated from her hiding spot and jumped into bed, pulled the covers to her chin. She'd barely slept that night, and the nights after had been plagued by fitful, broken slumber.

Her ever-churning mind, even now upon recollection, wanted to blurt out the definitions for those two horrible words: tur-m*uh*-nl … in-op-er-uh-b*uh*l.

She squeezed her eyes closed until stars shot across her vision, until the words receded to the background. The sunlight warmed her eyelids, swaddling her in amber hues. She opened her eyes and breathed without torment, without the threat of unsettling emotions.

Her heels clicked along the hardwood floor, the voices becoming senseless enunciations she still found some small comfort upon hearing.

The initial glimpse of the library had only teased a small portion of the bibliophilic splendor she now entered. The heady smell of old leather engulfed her like a favorite blanket. Her eyes panned the hundreds of vertical spines, barely registering a single title as she marveled at the limitless possibilities within her reach. Her mind soared as she reached at random for a thick brown tome. She smiled; if judged by its heft alone, the book would be centuries old.

She read with some difficulty the thin cursive script of the title: *Terrenum Quidem Monstrum*

Her heart rollicked in her chest. The title was Latin, she had no doubt, but she didn't know what it meant. Something about *Terre* … terra … earth. And *monstrum* … monsters?

She had no idea what this book was about—nor most of the other books extending high to the ceiling—and that feeling was so exhilarating! She slid the hefty book back in its place, making sure the spine sat flush with the edge of the shelf.

She paced the length of the bookcase, letting her fingers brush the soft leather. At the corner of the room stood a low cabinet with a large open book atop it. The cabinet divided the room into halves; one half housed the antique books, the other modern books with a motley mixing of dust jackets. She glanced at the enormous book. A dictionary.

If Clara were to sketch her idea of heaven, it would be this very room.

"Clarabelle, your sandwich is ready."

She almost jumped at the sound of Poppa's voice. She turned quickly to see him leaning against the door frame, a bemused look on his face.

"Your books …" She was going to say *are beautiful*, but that wouldn't have completed the thought. To complete the thought, she'd also have to ask what would happen to them once he was gone. He no longer *existing* was something she didn't feel capable of understanding.

"Yes, I know exactly what you mean." Poppa placed a gentle hand on her shoulder, and together they walked back to the kitchen. "I'm so glad you decided to come visit me."

Poppa's hand gripped her shoulder, and by the time they reached the kitchen he was pretty much using Clara as a crutch. When he sat on his cushioned stool, he looked exhausted but still somehow at peace.

CHAPTER 3

After Neal insisted he and Clara could handle washing the lunch dishes, Krista retreated with her grandpa to the deck off the back of the kitchen. A light breeze carried the scent of the lake through the surrounding trees, hinting at what was hidden below.

She watched her husband and daughter working like a well-oiled machine. Their fluid movements surprised her, considering they rarely did much housework back home.

"You can't help yourself," Poppa said.

"What's that?" Krista said, reluctantly glancing his way.

"Being on the clock." He lifted his chin and squinted in contentment, the wrinkles deepening at the corners of his eyes.

"I know, it's just—"

"Krista," he said, "I didn't want you here just because of … well, *what's coming.*"

"I know, Poppa," she said absently.

"Even though there is more to your return than my ill-health, I don't think you would've come unless I was on death's door."

"Poppa, that's not true." Her gaze dropped to her hands resting in her lap.

"Yeah, you were never a good liar."

She glanced nervously inside, witnessing Clara pass a wet but clean plate to Neal. She looked back at Poppa. Although rail-thin, the gleam hadn't yet left his eyes.

"Besides this morbid ritualizing of my death, I wanted you and your siblings to experience this …" He extended a trembling hand, as if to indicate the entire world. "I want you to live, to *live* … to experience serenity. If I could give you anything more before my time is up, it would be that. I owe you at least that much."

"Poppa, please …" she said, her voice weakening, "don't talk like that."

"I have no other way to talk. I'll soon be dead and won't be able to tell you these things. Happiness, family … there is no more grand revelation. Money, power, heck, even a genius intellect … they all pale in comparison. By far."

Krista reached out and took hold of his terribly withered hand. His skin was so cool to the touch she could feel her heat radiating into him.

"Poppa …" She paused to gather her emotions. "Okay …" She bit her lower lip. "Okay."

They sat in silence, her hand still engulfing his. A warm breeze toyed with her short auburn curls. Songbirds sung their contentment, their unbridled joy. White, yellow, and blue feathers flashed among the greening deciduous leaves as they chased and cavorted.

Krista closed her eyes and remembered sitting here so long ago, on a day similar to so many others, but remarkable in one horrible respect. Her fingers tingled where they rested on Poppa's hand; the sensation traveled the length of her arm, across her neck, settling behind her closed eyelids. She felt a low buzzing, first in her ears, and then across her entire body. And then, as if a doorway had been opened within her mind, she suddenly recalled long-buried details so vivid and indelible they saturated her senses.

A peanut butter and jelly sandwich pasted her tongue. She swigged the last of her root beer as the scent of the dark woods swept over her in fragrant waves. The lake lured her down the dirt trail, winding through trees, calling to her in the unspoken language limited to children and nature. Without a second thought, she took off barefoot, skipping over roots and around blind bends in the path. When her dancing feet brought her from shadowy wood to golden sunlit beach, the coarse wet sand filled the gaps between her toes.

A chilling scream stripped Krista of her carefree thoughts.

This horrible yet familiar sound drew her closer to the shore, to where the midday waves lapped at the sandcastle she had built with Breann and Leah earlier that morning.

A screaming woman walked along the water's edge, tracking tiny footprints in the sand, footprints gamboling near the water's edge before veering toward the road. At the roadway, where a single lane dirt road had been carved through the forested valley, the footprints ended with a lone depression of the right forefoot. As if the person etching their path had stepped off the face of the earth.

"Breann! Where are you, baby!"

The woman looked shattered. Utterly destroyed.

"Breann!" she screamed until her voice cracked.

"Mrs. McCort?"

The woman turned at the sound of Krista's voice. She flinched hard, as if slapped.

"My baby. She's gone. My baby …"

A ruckus inside pulled her from her waking dream and Krista sat up with a start. She shook her head, feeling like she'd woken from a full-night's sleep.

"Are you okay, dear?" Poppa asked, his eyes glassy with concern.

Her fingertips tingled, and she clenched her hand into a fist. The sensation was gone, if it was ever there in the first place.

"Yeah … sure. A bit worn out, I guess. It was a long drive."

It took her a moment to focus.

Clara stood near the sink, the water drained, the dishes washed and put away. At first Krista thought something terrible had happened, but she saw no blood to indicate an injury, nor any broken glass stemming from an accident. Even so, Clara's eyes were scrunched closed, and her hands clamped over her ears.

Krista looked from Clara to Neal. He wasn't so much distraught as dismayed as he gaped at the front door and the source of her daughter's misery.

Of course. Trevor.

Krista's eleven-year-old nephew. Nearly blinding sunlight blazed behind him, as if flames trailed in his wake. His face was electric, with dark brown eyes that managed to reflect the slightest amount of light, a smile equal parts teeth and empty gums, and deep, incredibly cute dimples. He held his arms aloft with double rock 'n roll devil horns. He wore only swim trunks, two sizes too big for his skinny frame, and a beach blanket and Super Soaker water gun hung from his neck.

"Woohoo! Yeah!" Trevor cried.

Clara shrank from the noise.

Krista hadn't taken into account Trevor's outsized personality when she'd made plans for this trip, or how it might impact her sensitive daughter.

"We have *arrived!*"

My poor girl.

"Sounds like Jack and Trev are here," Poppa said, slowly gaining his feet. "If someone figured out how to plug him in, that boy could light the world."

"If only …" Krista said. She reached the sliding glass door first and pulled it open.

Clara looked relieved at her arrival and came over to huddle in Krista's shadow.

Krista's mind flashed with the image of a sandcastle slowly eroded by the Little Whisper's lapping waves. She shook her head until the image disappeared.

No matter her efforts, she seemed unable to tame her reawakened memories, or their possible implications for the rest of her visit.

CHAPTER 4

Wrestling with a trio of suitcases, Krista's younger brother, Jack, stepped inside and shoved the door closed with a foot. He wore a gaudy Hawaiian shirt, swim trunks, and flip-flops.

"There's my boy!" Poppa shuffled over to the new arrivals with his arms extended. He always doted on the youngest of the three siblings, and luckily it never bothered Krista or Leah.

"Hi, Poppa!" Jack said.

"Poppa!" Trev pushed past his dad and barreled into Poppa, his hug nearly toppling them both to the floor. Poppa clutched the boy lovingly, and to keep himself upright.

"Trevor, what did I say about being rough?" Jack sopped sweat from his forehead with the back of his hand.

"Jackson, your boy can hug me as hard as he likes."

Poppa kissed the top of the boy's head before he could escape, which he did a moment later, his Super Soaker jostling around on its nylon strap.

"You can't get away from me!" Poppa pretended to swipe at the boy to haul him into another hug.

"Poppa!" Trev said, and backed away, giggling. He raised his toy gun and made a sound like a jetting garden hose with his pursed lips.

Jack rolled his eyes and turned to shake Neal's hand. Though they didn't have much of anything in common, they both made an effort, which Krista appreciated. She hadn't seen her younger brother in some time, and he now looked a decade older than his thirty-one years. His hair was in Jack's typical just-rolled-out-of-bed style, but now graying at the temples. While Trevor had inherited his father's dark, brilliant eyes and deep dimples, Jack's unkempt beard hid his dimples, and though his eyes were still dark, their luster had diminished considerably.

"Woohoo, it's time to par-tay!" Trev held his water gun at firing height and charged commando-style into the kitchen, heading for the back door.

"Trev, I said to wait for your cousins!" Jack hurried after his son and gave Krista an imploring look.

Krista grinned, but it was fleeting. She normally enjoyed seeing Trevor tying her little brother into knots, but right now he seemed overmatched and unequipped for the challenge. He had raised his son as a single parent after Sheri, Trevor's mom, walked out on them when he was an infant. Krista had never seen her brother look so distressed to be parenting Trevor solo.

Trev stomped his foot. "Dad, come *on!*"

Instead of putting the boy in his place, Jack let out a long groan. "Oh, Poppa, you don't mind, do you?" He kept one eye on Trevor as he opened the sliding door leading to the deck. "He's been *dying* to hit the lake since I told him about the trip."

"No, go right ahead!" Poppa said, waving him away. "The Little Whisper is the reason I built on this very spot." Poppa cupped his hands around his mouth and shouted, "*Just wait for your father, Trevor!*"

"You got it, Poppa!"

"I'm not going to swim," Clara said with finality. She remained at Krista's side.

"How about you change into your suit and just hang out on the beach?" Neal added with an agreeable nod.

Krista's husband could be quite convincing. It was something about his eyes and the slightly gawky charm in his body language. It worked well at the law firm; it worked when they wanted the normally finicky Clara to try a new food; it worked on Krista the night they met, and many nights since. Even now, Krista felt a strange urge to comply, to head off and change into her own new one-piece.

"*Dad.*" Clara shot him a withering glance, but her defenses were already crumbling.

"Please, Clara." Neal paused a long three seconds. "Trev can't go down there alone."

"He's my age. What does it matter?"

"Safety in numbers." The power of Neal's kind reassurance forced Clara to look away.

Clara's gaze settled on Poppa, nodding in agreement with her dad. "Fine. Whatever," she grumbled before heading out to the car to retrieve her beach gear. She couldn't deny *both* her dad and her great-grandpa.

CHAPTER 5

It was too cold for swimming and would remain so until summer's heat took hold, at least for sensible adults like Krista. She eased into a low lounge chair, as did Neal, Poppa, and her brother Jack. She drew a circle in the damp sand with her big toe.

Decades ago, Poppa had built the fire pit, around which they now relaxed, from granite stones sourced from the surrounding hills. Charred remnants of previous fires lay dormant at the pit's center. As a child, Krista had spent countless summer nights in this very spot—her shoulders stinging from fresh sunburn—roasting marshmallows for s'mores. She recalled the chill coming off the lake at nightfall, the bone-weary exhaustion from playing in the water, but most of all, she remembered the laughter and the firelight and how one seemed to feed the other.

She'd forgotten about those fond memories until now, and they brought an easy smile to her lips.

Neal reached over and gave her forearm a reassuring squeeze. His concern for her softened around his eyes. For the duration of their marriage, Neal's worry was rarely ever his own, even with the stresses inherent to being a defense attorney. More often than not, his worry was merely a reflection of Krista's. For the umpteenth time, she reminded herself how lucky she was to have him in her life.

It was too cold to swim, true, but that didn't stop Trevor. He charged into the water, barely slowing as it reached mid-thighs. His water gun hung heavy and full around his neck, and his wet swim trunks sagged off his skinny butt.

After making a fuss of spreading her beach blanket near the shore, Clara sat ramrod straight and opened her worn copy of *The Hobbit*.

"That boy," Jack said with a groan, "will be the death of me."

Poppa tucked a blanket over his lap. "He's no different than you were at that age."

Jack leaned back in his chair and closed his eyes. "And is there any wonder why I'm going gray?"

"Want me to go hang out with him?" Krista said. She didn't want to go in the water. She'd already dipped a toe to test the temperature, and that had been enough for her. "At least until Leah shows up with the twins?"

"Nah," Jack said, not bothering to open his eyes, "he swims better than you and me combined."

The water reached as high as Trevor's waist.

"Oh, my frickin' *balls!*" Trevor play-acted a bone-jarring shiver, but pushed deeper still, heading for the anchored dock.

The adults all chuckled.

Clara turned around on her blanket until her back faced the water.

"Yep," Poppa said, "that could be Jack out there, twenty years ago."

The small anchored dock floated in about six feet of water, thirty feet from shore. The dock marked the edge of the safe swimming area. Any farther out and the lake's bottom fell away, lost in weedy shadows.

Krista remembered the dock's appeal. At different times it would double as a tropical island, a home base during games of splash tag, or a yacht adrift on the high seas. No matter the year or season, every child who came to Little Whisper Lake was drawn to that dock.

Trevor swam to the ladder bolted to the side of the dock as the adults watched in silence.

"See," Jack said, running fingers through his hair and sighing. "What did I tell you? He's part *fish*."

Krista so rarely saw her brother that she knew little about his daily life. Sure, he was a patrolman for the Rock Creek P.D., and he played center field for the department's softball team. But otherwise, they were practically strangers.

"So, how are things in Rock Creek?" she asked him. "Does Kemper still have you working those crazy swing shifts?"

"The shifts are what they are. I don't love it or hate it. It's just what it is, right? And no matter what shift I'm working, I wind up handing out ten or so citations per day to the out-of-towners who don't know enough to slow down when entering our little rural paradise."

"Sounds like an honest day's work, if you ask me," Neal said.

"True, but there's not much excitement. No crime. Husbands don't raise a hand in anger, even after tying one on. There's an occasional pot bust, but I haven't seen anything harder come through."

Krista arched an eyebrow and said, "You sound disappointed."

"What you're describing is a great place to raise a son," Poppa said.

"Sure, it's a nice town, but I sometimes wonder if they hired me for my qualifications, or for my name." Jack's eyes turned glassy, distant.

"You really think they'd hire you if you weren't qualified just because you played professional baseball?" Krista asked.

Jack laughed cynically and glared at his sister. "You don't know much about small-town life, do you? Rock Creek and Chicago are like different worlds."

Krista wasn't sure why he was so upset. Jack was normally level-headed. At least he used to be. She lowered her eyes and Neal squeezed her arm.

"Jack, be nice," Poppa said. "I don't want any arguing during this vacation."

"Well then," Jack said. He stood and clapped his hands together. "You know what?" He flashed a smile, but it was obvious anger was still a hair-trigger away. "This little get together needs some brews. I have a well-stocked cooler in the back of my truck." Jack nodded toward the trail before starting off in a jog. "I'll be back in two shakes."

"Do you need a hand?" Neal asked.

Jack looked back over his shoulder. "Naw, bro, I got it."

Before anyone else could say a word, Jack disappeared onto the dirt trail cutting through the woods leading to the back deck.

"What was that all about?" Krista asked.

"He's just tired," Poppa said.

"He has every right to be tired after raising Trevor by himself for a decade," Neal said. "I think it would be weird if he didn't show some wear and tear by now."

Krista didn't completely buy his answer. "Yeah, I guess you're probably right."

"It's a miracle!" Neal said. "Twice in one day she admits I'm right!"

"Even a broken clock is right twice a day, Neal," Poppa said.

"Well, Pierce, I see you're taking that whole straight-and-to-the-point bit seriously."

Poppa touched the tip of his nose with an index finger and gave Neal a knowing wink.

Krista laughed hard. She fully understood the reason behind this long-delayed return to the summer house. She had mentally prepared herself to make this trip, assuming every minute of every day would be a grim ordeal. Besides the dust-up with her brother, it had been anything but. Sure, her grandfather exhibited a wry cynicism regarding his failing health, but otherwise, he was simply ... *Poppa*.

Neal checked his watch. "Well, Leah's an hour late, which means she'll be here any minute."

Poppa chuckled. "She's just like her grandma. Always laughing, always empathetic ... always *late*."

"I think she does it on purpose," Krista added.

"I think she doesn't have a choice," Poppa said. "The universe has a path for each of us. For Leah, her path runs through a different time continuum."

Krista couldn't think of a better way to put it. She buried her feet to her ankles in the cool sand and watched a heron land in a grassy alcove. It dipped its beak into the water, chasing a fish, but came up empty. It waited motionless until the water again settled into glass.

Poppa kept his shoreline free of water plants to allow his family easy access to the lake. The next property over—*Breann's house, oh my God, poor Breann*—had become overgrown in the last several years. The lawn hadn't been mowed this year, as of yet, and cattails and lily pads curled out in small islands from the shore, blotting out the lake bottom. Krista couldn't see the light blue ranch, now lost among the encroaching trees. Soon it would be difficult to determine if anyone had ever lived on that land.

A twig snapped and everyone turned at the sound.

Jack cleared the dirt trail and stepped into the sand. A laden cooler bobbed against his thighs as he trudged toward the fire pit. "Look who I found strolling in?"

"Leah?" Poppa asked, hopeful.

Nine-year-old twins Robby and Heidi sprinted out from the trailhead behind their Uncle Jack. Robby stripped off his T-shirt as he ran, revealing a torso deeply tanned for so early in the summer. Heidi beamed a huge smile at the adults and waved. "Hi, family! I missed you!" she shouted without breaking stride. She kicked off her pink flip-flops and yanked an oversized shirt—most likely a hand-me-down from her dad—over her head and tossed it to the sand. Dark brown hair trailed past her shoulder blades, tied back in a single whip-like braid. The girl's floral two-piece suit looked adorable but would do little to keep her warm.

Krista braced for her to hit the water.

"Robby!" Trevor called out from the anchored dock. "You better get over here. The aliens are attacking! Where's your weapon, soldier!"

The twins dove into the water, oblivious of the temperature.

Trevor laughed and fired his water gun in their general direction. "I'll cover you!" he shouted.

Clara barely gave the new arrivals a glance before turning a page in her book.

"I knew I'd find you down by the fire pit!" said another voice from behind them.

Leah Whalen reached the sand and wiggled her toes and closed her eyes, as if indulging in something decadent. She wore a purple and red gypsy-style skirt and a formfitting white T-shirt. She balanced a picnic basket on her broad hip as she made her way over.

"Where else would we be!" Krista said and rushed to greet her younger sister.

Leah set down the picnic basket and embraced her.

Krista smelled a mixture of patchouli incense and spearmint gum; quintessential Leah. She never thought she would've missed such an incongruous combination, but now that her sister was here, she realized how much she needed Leah in her life.

"I halfway thought it would be just me and Jack," Leah whispered into her ear. "Thank you for not putting me through that."

Their embrace ended and they stared at one another, communicating without words.

Krista shrugged and Leah's eyes darkened. Her sister nodded, admitting a defeat long in the making, and then worked to affix a smile as she turned to embrace Poppa.

Curtis hadn't come along after all.

After Krista's recent phone conversations with Leah, she knew this time was coming. Leah, who was normally so sweet-natured, had never sounded so bitter and resentful.

Poppa patted her back. "You keep getting prettier by the day!"

"Oh, Poppa," Leah said. "I needed your hugs."

Jack set the cooler near the fire pit and opened the lid, revealing a couple cases of Budweiser chilled in ice. "Neal?"

"A little early in the day," Neal said, "especially for *that* nasty stuff ..." Neal trailed off, but when Jack looked honestly offended, he added, "Sure, I'll have one."

"My man!" Jack popped open a beer and handed it to Neal. Jack opened his own and chugged half the can.

Neal normally didn't drink, *especially* domestic beer, and especially not before sunset. He awkwardly blew the foam from the top of the can and took a sip.

"Cheers," Neal said, his smile no longer forced.

Jack held out his can and Neal clinked his against it.

"Cheers, bro." Jack finished off his can and grabbed another. "Krista? Leah? Poppa ...?"

"Not unless you want me to sleep the rest of the day," Poppa said.

Krista shook her head. "No, thanks."

Leah held out her hand. "Absolutely."

Jack opened the can and handed it to her. "So … Curtis?"

Leah sipped from her beer, eyes lowered. "Things are … complicated."

Krista didn't know how her sister had managed to have kids and cohabitate with someone she hadn't married. While Krista found comfort in the stability of a traditional family, Leah had never found the need. Krista had always been straight-laced, while Leah seemed born out of time and would have been more at home in the 1960s.

"Hasn't it always been complicated with him?" Jack said.

"I am *way* too sober to talk about this. Just suffice it to say … Curtis and I are on a sabbatical."

"Sabbatical?" Poppa asked

"Yeah, from each other," Leah said and took another sip of beer. "Please don't … you know, the twins don't know, so please don't mention it."

Poppa motioned her over to his side. "Come here, sweetie."

She leaned over to him and they embraced once again.

"You'll get through this," Poppa said. "Just like you always do. Strong. Resolute."

Leah kissed his cheek. "Thanks, Poppa."

Krista smiled and went over to the lean-to near the woods. The little building was starting to list. Moss covered the one plank-walled side as well as the shake roof. She grabbed a few split logs and quickly made her way back to the fire pit.

"Kind of early for a fire," Jack said. Joining her as he finished off his second beer.

"I know. Poppa looked chilled."

Jack stepped in front of her to block her path. "Can you believe that douchebag?" he said under his breath.

"Who, Curtis?"

"Hell yeah, Curtis." Jack checked to make sure no one else could hear them. "We always knew he'd do something fucked up."

She rolled her eyes.

"Come on, Krista, do you really think Leah would've done anything to force them to take—what did she call it—a 'sabbatical?'"

"No, of course not," she said. "But we don't know anything more than what she said. *Things are complicated.*"

"That's not all of it, and I'm sure you know what the hell's going on." Jack tipped his beer to his lips and furrowed his brow, and then remembered it was empty.

"What does it matter? It's not like they were married."

"No. But maybe they should've been. Maybe that would've made them work harder. There are kids involved, remember?"

"I think you're displacing your anger."

"What's *that* supposed to mean?"

Krista tilted her head. The logs were getting heavy and she wished her little brother would drop the whole subject.

"What, you think I'm still pissed about Sheri?"

He seemed shocked she would even imply such a conclusion.

"Maybe not pissed, but I do think it taints every relationship you see. And for the record, single women sense that pain a mile away."

Jack looked hurt, and Krista immediately wished she could take it back. But she couldn't. She'd spoken the words, had looked him in the eye even as they regretfully left her mouth.

Jack grunted and turned away. When he reached the fire pit, he crinkled the beer can in his fist and tossed it aside. He grabbed another and took a long swig. He glared at her over his shoulder then turned to answer a question Poppa asked him.

"What's wrong?" Neal asked when he saw her.

"Nothing. Just sibling stuff." Krista dumped the logs next to the fire pit and blew hair from her eyes.

Neal put his arm around her and rested his cheek against the top of her head. And in that small gesture, her tension vanished.

"Walk with me?" Neal asked.

The wind picked up, sending low waves to shore.

"Sure. Lead the way," Krista said.

Leah and Jack were at the fire pit. From their gestures, they were teasing each other good-naturedly. Some things never changed.

Poppa caught her eye. He nodded and she waved in return.

Neal steered her away from both the screaming cousins and Breann's old house tucked deep in a bend in the lake. Clara would be fine with her book, her blanket, and a brain that never seemed to ease to an idle.

"This has already been better than I expected," Neal said.

"Yeah, it has."

"Even with the 'sibling stuff?'"

"Comes with the territory. It's the same old Jack, but something is different. He's angry. He's ... I don't know. Different."

"He probably just needs to get laid."

"Neal!" She jabbed an elbow into his ribs.

"What? What did I say?" He grabbed his abdomen, feigning injury.

"Half a beer and your filter goes out the window." She rolled her eyes. "Yeah, sure, he probably needs to ... *find companionship*. But there's something else."

"People change, Krista. You barely see him. He could've taken up improvisational dance, or learned to speak Russian, and you would never know."

"I guess. I worry about him. And about Trevor, too."

"Yeah, me too."

They walked along the sandy shore of the lake for a while, which spread in a series of curling alcoves. Each home had its own little bay, making it feel like you were on your own private lake.

"Do you want me to talk to him?" Neal asked. "See if I can dig up any dirt?"

"Sure," Krista said. "I guess. Just don't interrogate him."

"Don't worry. I have ways to make people talk."

"Oh really?" she replied, cocking an eyebrow.

"Subtle, lawyerly ways—"

"Help!" a girl called out. "Help me, please!"

They turned toward the sound.

Just passed the anchored dock, Heidi's arms flailed above her head. She fell below the water, fingers grasping for nothing.

Leah bolted from her chair and ran for the water.

Jack was a second behind her in his reaction, but quickly sprinted past her.

Heidi's head broke the surface and she gulped for air before slipping below again.

Robby paced nervously across the width of the dock, while Trevor unslung his water gun and dove into the water, swimming dolphin-like toward his cousin.

Even though Krista, too, was running, Neal sped away from her and reached the water at the same time as Jack. Both men jumped into the water in what in other circumstances would've looked like choreographed dives. Jack surfaced first, and he quickly pulled ahead.

When Krista's feet touched the water, she became paralyzed. A presence stood next to her: *Breann*, hair pulled back in pigtails, sunny smile, sad eyes.

Disorientation returned, as it had earlier while sitting with Poppa. *My baby*, Mrs. McCort had wailed. *She's gone. My baby. My baby ...*

And then Clara was at her side. "What happened?" she asked, unaware of Krista's momentary confusion.

Krista's voice stalled in her throat. "I ..." She shook her head, looked intently at the girl standing next to her.

Clara placed her hand above her eyes to shield the glare from the lake. She looked so pale and skinny, so unaccustomed to being exposed to nature.

How did I ever see Breann? They look nothing alike.

"I don't know, sweetie."

Trevor surfaced near where Heidi had gone under. They were so far out, now easily twenty feet past the anchored dock and the safety of the shallow water.

Krista jumped up and down and pointed adamantly. "She went down over there!"

"I ... I don't see her." Trevor dove under.

Jack reached the same general area, dove under as well.

A plume of splashing erupted from below as Trevor surfaced with Heidi in his grasp. Her head lolled, and then her eyes fluttered open. Trevor kicked and fought with his free arm to keep his head above water as he supported them both.

"That a boy, Trevor!" Poppa said, joining Krista and Clara at the water's edge. He had stripped off his leather house shoes and had rolled his pant cuffs. If Trevor hadn't found Heidi, Poppa would've taken to the water within seconds.

Jack reached his son. "Here ... okay." He reached out to him as he treaded water. "I got her ... I got her."

Trevor shifted Heidi into his dad's arms.

Jack eased onto his back and started swimming while she rested against his chest. He carried Heidi ashore and set her down.

Everyone closed in to form a circle around them.

Clara rolled up her beach blanket and handed it to her dad. "Here, for under her head."

Neal placed the roll under Heidi's head, and she coughed hard, tilted her head to the side and spit out a mouthful of lake water. Her eyes panned across the familiar faces gathered around her, momentarily confused about all the attention.

Leah kneeled in the sand next to her daughter and took hold of her hand. "Are you all right? What happened?" To the rest of the group: "She's so cold!"

"My leg!" Heidi winced and writhed in pain as she reached for her right calf. The muscles were clenched so tightly the girl couldn't bend her foot at the ankle.

"It's a cramp," Jack said, pushing next to Leah. He took hold of Heidi's leg near the ankle, forced the foot to bend as he massaged the calf muscle.

Heidi cried out.

"Jack, you're hurting her!" Leah said.

He seemed unfazed and continued to massage the muscle. Second by second, the muscle began to release, and the pain lifted from Heidi's face.

"Shh ... it's okay," Jack whispered. "See, nothing but a cramp."

"That's one hell of a cramp," Poppa said.

Jack lowered Heidi's foot to the sand and slowly backed away, as if her calf muscles were a bomb that might go off at any minute. "The water's pretty cold for swimming," he said. "Especially after a long car ride."

"Are you sure?" Leah asked. She looked scared and lost. If there was one positive trait Curtis brought to their relationship, it was decisiveness, and since he wasn't here, Leah seemed rudderless. "Should we take her to the hospital? What if it's a muscle tear? Or a blood clot?"

Jack shook his head. "It's fine, Leah. Let's get her some water, and maybe aspirin. She'll be running around in no time."

Heidi looked up, offering a slight smile. "Mom, he's right."

"Are you sure, honey-bean?"

The girl flexed her foot. "The water got cold, like ice cold."

"That happens when you get farther out," Poppa said. "Pockets of cold water sit and wait for you to come across them."

Krista remembered coming across such pockets of cold when she was younger. Though an unsettling sensation, she couldn't recall it causing muscle cramps.

"Well, suddenly, it felt like something, *someone*, grabbed me." Heidi looked down at the sand. "That's why I was so scared. And then after it cramped up on me, I felt something glide across my feet. Something slick. And then my feet got tangled and I went under."

"Seaweed," Poppa said. "It grows like, well, a weed out past the dock."

"I think we should make a rule there's no swimming out past the dock," Leah said.

Trevor kicked the sand. "Oh, man!"

"Turn it down a notch, Trev." Jack placed a hand on his son's shoulder. "There's plenty of water on this side of the dock."

"How about we take Miss Heidi-belle up to the house and get her something to drink?" Poppa said.

Krista nodded. "Sounds good. We can plan dinner."

"What's to plan?" Jack gave her a crooked grin. "You and Leah can whip something up while the men retire to the den for cigars and a scotch."

"I might be older than dirt," Poppa said, "but that talk would get someone in trouble even back in my smoking days."

While everyone playfully chatted about the night's festivities, Krista noticed that Clara had dropped to her knees, staring at Heidi's

44

troublesome leg. Krista leaned closer, and though Heidi didn't seem to notice the added scrutiny, darkening bruises circled her legs.

A handprint?

Other plausible explanations came to mind, but Krista couldn't look at the bruises without thinking that she'd been grabbed, quite forcefully, while swimming in the Little Whisper.

CHAPTER 6

Lights were turned low in the main floor of the summer house. The windows at the front and back of the house were wide open, allowing cool air to circulate. Krista could picture a dozen similar nights from her childhood, but she didn't want to get lost in her strengthening memories. Instead, she focused on wiping down the kitchen island while Leah leaned against the stove. Together, they shared a comfortable silence.

The men had indeed relocated to the den, but they at least waited until everyone's dinner plates had been cleared. The talk at the dinner table had been so lively and full of laughter that Krista could barely imagine being back at their sleek yet sterile Chicago apartment. Whereas the city sounds back home seeped obliviously into her subconscious, she was now quite aware of the lake sounds coming from outside: the swish of the night wind battering the pine boughs, the crackle of logs in the fireplace, the intermittent call and response of songbirds.

Krista hung the towel from the stove handle and stood nearly hip to hip with her sister. Leah refilled her wineglass from the bottle of Merlot on the counter before offering it to her.

Neal's voice mingled with Poppa's in the other room while Jack periodically interrupted them with his inebriated comments.

"So … is it over between you two?" Krista said in a level tone, taking the bottle by the neck. She was well past her usual cutoff point. She topped off and brought the wineglass to her lips as she awaited her sister's answer.

"And the evening had been so peaceful …" Leah rolled her eyes. "I'm surprised you waited so long to ask."

Krista swirled her wine. "I debated asking at all."

Leah set her drink on the counter, untouched. "I wish I knew. When we left Champaign, there was no question it was over. You see, Curtis, he's never been as committed to our relationship as me. I feel like I've been chasing him for, God knows … a decade. Just little ol' me following him like a puppy, doing every little thing to please him, to get his attention. And sure, he's been with me the whole time, but lately, even as I'm chasing him, he's getting farther away. I finally realized I'm tired of our little game. So very tired."

"Oh, Leah." Krista extended her arms to her sister. She could only imagine what she was going through. "I'm so sorry."

Leah accepted Krista's hug and was soon embracing her just as fiercely. She didn't know from whom the trembling originated.

At long last, Leah pulled away. "Thanks, sis." She had tears in her eyes, but a smile on her lips. "And what is *your* big news?"

"What do you mean?" Krista said.

She didn't like Leah's knowing expression, one she had seen often. Since childhood, Leah had claimed the ability to see auras; she associated emotions with colors; she believed life's experience became etched into the soul's palette; and she alone could see, understand, and interpret these incomprehensible colorations. Leah somehow … *knew* things, and sometimes she knew them even before Krista did. Inexplicably, Leah would grasp Krista's guarded innermost thoughts like feathers floating on a breeze.

"Oh, crap," Krista said, and set her wineglass aside. "I'm not … I'm not *pregnant*, am I?"

Leah laughed before her face went blank. She stared intently at Krista for an unnerving twenty seconds. Then her smile returned.

"Nope, no bun in the oven for you."

"Oh, thank God." Krista picked up her wineglass and took a big swallow. Her face flushed. "It's not like it wouldn't be a pleasant surprise … it's not like we haven't talked about it. But …" She shrugged.

"Bad timing?" Leah offered.

"Yeah, it's just not good right now." Krista rinsed out her empty glass in the sink.

There. No more. I'm already going to have an awful headache tomorrow.

"But there's something right? Some big change?"

Leah nodded, but offered no more.

"But you can't tell me what it is—"

"Because I don't know. I wish it worked that way, Krista. You know it. But I *do* know something big is coming."

"Good? Bad?"

"If I were to guess …?" Leah looked out the back window, into the darkened trees, to the uncertainty beyond. "A little of both?"

Krista felt like shaking her sister until answers flowed from her lips, but Clara entered the kitchen. No, check that. She *stomped* into the kitchen with her arms crossed in front of her and her eyes closed to angered slits.

"Mom, can you tell Trevor he needs to—"

"Not now, Clara," Krista said.

"But Mom—"

"I said not now. Go work it out with your cousins."

Clara sucked in a breath.

Krista immediately regretted rebuffing her daughter so abruptly. She so often relied on Clara's innate maturity that she sometimes took it for granted. As she stormed away, Krista felt like the worst mother ever.

She waited for Leah to turn back to face her, but she didn't. It was like the darkness had entranced her. She stared unblinking into the roiling shadows.

"Is there anything … anything more you can tell me?" Krista asked.

"Just that I know you are strong." When Leah finally turned away from the window, she had that same blank stare. "And that's a good thing …" Leah paused before continuing, "because you're going to need it."

CHAPTER 7

In-dig-nā-shən. The word perfectly captured Clara's feelings after her mother's rebuke.

In-dig-na-tion. *Anger aroused by something unjust, unworthy, or mean.*

All Clara wanted was her book back, and her mom couldn't be bothered for even a second to help her. Her mind began to pinhole and was steeped in red. Her mom had completely dismissed her concerns, as if she were just a … a *child.* She paced the long hallway to the front door, stomping every step. She wanted to throw the heavy front door open wide … no, she wanted to rip it from its hinges. Oh, yes, she did! And then let loose and *scream.*

But doing so would reinforce the notion that she was merely a child with unimportant, childish problems. She took a deep breath, and then another. Her anger ebbed. Her thoughts less of an immature jumble. Until she heard Trevor's annoying giggle coming from Poppa's library.

It took all her willpower to hold her anger in check as she headed to the source of that nails-on-a-chalkboard sound.

Trevor's laughter died off when she entered the room.

Robby tried to hide a smile behind his hands.

Heidi sat on a recliner; a Tiffany lamp threw light across her lap, but it did little to illuminate her features.

"Can I help you?" Trevor offered her a slight but somehow arrogant bow.

"Give it back!" Clara held out her hand for her missing copy of *The Hobbit.*

Trev looked shocked. "Whatever you're talking about. I don't got it." His lips flashed with mischief, all the confirmation Clara needed.

In the dim twilight, Robby snickered next to Trevor.

"You took my book, and I want it back. *Now*." Her mind verged on snapping, and when Trevor's expression remained, when it overwhelmed his play-it-stupid *modus operandi*, she wanted to slap his face.

"Oh, you mean that ratty old thing you had down by the lake?" Trevor sneered. "I bet you've read it a million times."

"A gazillion!" Robby added. "I bet you've got it memorized!" Robby meant this last bit as an insult, but with her vault-like memory, it wasn't far from the truth.

"We want to play hide-and-seek," Trevor said, sounding like his statement justified any action.

"Then play. Just leave me out of it and give me back my book!"

"Heidi can't run around," Robby said. "It's just the two of us. We need a third."

"I'll show you where it is." Heidi stood from her chair. She winced with her first step, but her next stride was much more fluid.

Trevor balled his fists at his sides. "Don't you dare!"

Robby stepped in front of his sister. "Come on, Heidi."

"What?" Heidi cocked her hip. "Clara doesn't want to play with you, and bullying her isn't gonna change her mind."

"Whatever." Trevor shook his head. "We don't need you anyway."

"Yeah, we don't need you anyway!" Robby parroted.

Heidi thrust her palm into Robby's shoulder and he crumpled away. "Come on, Clara."

Clara's only complaint about the argument's outcome was having to leave the comfy confines of Poppa's library. If it were up to her, she would retrieve her book and read under the Tiffany lamp's warm glow until bedtime.

"Those two …" Heidi shook her head and looked over her shoulder as she led Clara down a hallway.

"Thanks," Clara said. She didn't want to talk about the boys anymore.

They turned a corner down an unexplored passageway. The

dark-paneled walls were covered in somber watercolor landscapes. For some reason, the rolling hills and darkly hued orchards, pasture-lands, and watermills gave Clara the impression they were sneaking through a museum after dark.

"I told them not to hide the book," Heidi said, drawing her away from the artwork, "and Robby wouldn't even think of something so mean—"

"But Trevor," Clara said.

"Yeah. Exactly."

"How is your leg?"

"It's fine." Heidi stopped and lifted the leg of her sweatpants. "See, it's just a bruise now. I forget about it until I have to move around."

"Ouch …" Clara stared at the purpling bruise a few inches above the ankle. "It looks like something … grabbed you."

"No, not some*thing*, some*one*."

"What do you mean?"

"Everyone thinks I'm crazy …" Heidi trailed off, as if waiting for Clara to refute the statement.

Even though Clara had been with Heidi at the lake, she couldn't deny how crazy it sounded. "Well, I'm glad you're okay."

"Thanks," Heidi said, then tried to lighten the mood by adding, "me too."

Heidi reached the end of the hallway where a low-backed chair upholstered in velvety gray fabric stood at the terminus. A window above spilled mellow moonlight across the hardwood floor. Two doors faced each other on either side of the chair. Heidi opened the door on the right and entered.

Clara followed her inside what turned out to be a bedroom laid out like a barracks. Four twin beds fanned out across the room, each with a footlocker. Suitcases sat open on two of them.

"Is this your room?" Clara asked.

Her own bedroom for their stay was at the other end of the zigzagging hallway. She had purposely requested the small room with its single bed.

"I was hoping we could share," Heidi said. She opened a footlocker, pushed aside folded blankets nested inside, and pulled out Clara's worn copy of *The Hobbit*

Clara nearly cried out in relief. "My book!"

Heidi handed her the thin volume. "What do you say?"

"Thank you! Thank you! Thank you!" Clara held the book to her nose. It smelled of dust and age and limitless possibility.

"No, not that. I meant, what do you say about sharing a room?"

"Sure … yes." Clara had never shared a room with anyone. What if Heidi snored? What if *she* snored? "I'll have to ask my mom."

"Yay!" Heidi took Clara into her willowy arms and hugged her. The girl was scrawny, even more so than Clara, but she was strong.

"But … what about the boys?" Clara said, pointing to their suitcases. "I don't want to share with them."

"I know! They are so gross, and smelly, and *ob*-noxious." Heidi went to the nearest suitcase. She made sure the clasps were secure and then hefted it off the bed with a grunt. "They'll just have to sleep somewhere else." She shuffled her way to the door and shoved the suitcase outside.

"You are incorrigible," Clara said and started to laugh.

Even though it didn't seem Heidi knew what the word meant, she soon joined in.

After they cleared the room of any evidence the boys had ever been there, Heidi asked if she could read Clara's palm.

"Sure." Clara held out her hand, certain there was no harm in humoring Heidi, who came by her quirkiness honestly—from Aunt Leah.

Heidi giggled and traced the lines in Clara's palm with an index finger. Clara couldn't help giggling as well, partially from nervousness, partially because it tickled.

And then Heidi's face turned to stone and any semblance of joy left the room like a swiftly extinguished flame.

"What is it?" Clara asked, trying to free her hand.

Heidi wouldn't let go. She tightened her grip and retraced Clara's palm.

"There's nothing. Your lifeline … it's *gone*."

CHAPTER 8

Jack loved having the kids around, but after a long day of their boundless energy, he was happy to have chased them all off to bed amid a mixture of protests and giggles. Late nights over the next week wouldn't be out of the question, not with everyone excited to see each other after months of separation, so whether or not the kids were asleep yet was anyone's best guess. Late nights and sleeping in? They were on vacation, after all.

"I'm going to check on Poppa," he said from the kitchen.

Leah was cleaning the already spotless island. She tossed the damp rag into the sink and said, "Look at you, Mr. Responsible Adult."

"Someone's gotta step up around here. Might as well be me."

Jack smiled, but with difficulty. He felt like such a fraud. In truth, he wanted to distance himself from his siblings. They only made him feel inadequate and like the world's biggest fuck-up whenever he was around them.

"I know we talked about taking the boat out at dawn," Neal said, "but I don't think tomorrow morning is going to work." Neal had his arms wrapped around Krista.

Always the happy couple.

"Yeah, what were we thinking?" Jack agreed.

"Another day?" Without waiting for an answer, Neal whispered something into Krista's ear. Her cheeks flushed and she elbowed him in the ribs.

"Definitely," Jack said and smirked. He stretched his arms over his head as a deep yawn snuck up on him. "After I check on Poppa, I'm gonna hit the hay."

Leah pretended to read a watch on her bare wrist. "Wow, it's barely midnight. Somebody's getting old."

"Not *somebody*, more like, the *all-of-us* are. Goodnight."

Krista shot him her middle finger, and Leah sucked in a breath in feigned shock. His sisters … God, he'd missed them. Jack laughed and left the kitchen, shaking his head.

They had not always gotten along, but they always seemed to pull together when they needed to. Jack never realized that until Sheri left him high and dry with colicky three-month-old Trevor wailing in the middle of the night.

During the first night alone, he had given Krista a call, asking her advice. She drove all the way from Chicago to Rock Creek in a little over two ours, which normally took close to three. She cared for Trevor so Jack could catch up on some sleep. And Leah drove in from Champaign, with a cloth bag filled with an assortment of homeopathic remedies. By the time he'd woken a couple hours later, Trevor was back to his normal, cheerful self. At first, he'd lashed out at Leah for administering whatever witch's brew she'd concocted, but after taking his son into his arms—him reaching out with his chubby little fist and boxing his nose—Jack had broken out into laughter and then tears.

His sisters had stayed with him for the next few days, until he felt like his feet were under him. When Leah packed up to leave, he tried to apologize for his initial anger. She explained that she'd brewed Trevor a simple tea of lavender and honey. The energy she'd brought to bear, she insisted, had helped tip Trevor in the right direction. *Positive energy. Positive, unquestioned love* … And while he'd had his arguments with both sisters since that tumultuous week, he always remembered that phrase. Sometimes it was difficult to manifest, but he tried to keep those words in mind whenever life turned bleak.

Jack paused outside Poppa's room. The door was ajar, as if Poppa had been too weak to get it to latch. Jack pushed the door open and gave it a couple light taps.

"There he is."

Poppa looked up from working the top button of his blue flannel pajamas.

"Come to tuck me in? Is it story time already?" Poppa said and winked, and even though he beamed with his familiar Poppa smile, he looked so incredibly drained, the skin of his face drawn and gray-tinged.

Jack chuckled and grabbed a book from the bedside table, a Neil Gaiman with an unbroken spine. "I will read to you any time you ask. Let's see," he said and paused to consider the title, "how about a little from *American Gods*?"

"Really, I'm not quite to that point in my descent, but I'll remember for future reference."

"Poppa—"

"But honestly, I just want to crawl into this nice warm bed. I'll probably be asleep in about ninety seconds. I love you all, and I want to know about everything going on in your lives … but I'm tired."

"Well, let's make this happen then."

Jack helped lift Poppa's matchstick legs onto the mattress. His limbs felt so painfully light. Once situated, Jack covered his grandpa with a heavy down comforter.

Poppa's eyes were glassy. "Thank you, son. Glad you made it."

They both understood the statement's subtext; Poppa didn't have long. Once Poppa had wrapped his mind around his diagnosis, he had forgone further treatment. The way he was facing his own mortality had only deepened Jack's belief that his grandfather was the most courageous man he'd ever met.

"You can't get away from me that easily, old man."

Jack blinked with watery eyes.

Poppa chuckled, closed his eyes. "See you in the morning. We'll have breakfast in the bright sunshine."

"Sounds good, Poppa."

Jack leaned over and kissed Poppa's temple. The tear finally broke across his cheek, and he quickly wiped it away. He didn't need to fear his grandfather witnessing his sadness; he was already in a deep sleep.

Poppa cast a long shadow, which would linger after he was gone.

All things considered, Jack thought he was handling his return to the summer house as well as could be expected. Sure, it was rough to see Poppa's decline, but he would've gladly visited him in a hospital night and day to avoid this place. He hadn't been here since his grandmother's funeral almost two years ago. And no matter how bad that day had been, it paled in comparison to the day of her death.

Jack pulled the door partially closed behind him and watched Poppa's chest rise and fall. "I miss you, Nan," he whispered, choking up with emotion. "We all do. Nothing's been the same ... I just don't know why ... Why did you have to do it?"

Poppa shifted in his bed, but remained asleep, albeit fitfully.

Jack sniffed and wiped tears from his eyes. He listened to Poppa's raspy breaths as his frail body continued to fight.

A light caress against his ear, then a whisper, "*Come here, son ...*"

Stark still, Jack's eyes widened in fright. He felt a presence next to him, an invasion of his personal space. Even though he'd nearly pissed himself hearing those disembodied words, he somehow managed to turn toward the sound.

The hallway was empty. Layers of shadows upon shadows.

It had been *her* voice—*Nan's* voice—so clear, so full of life.

He backed away from Poppa's bedroom, nearly stumbling over his own feet, before turning on his heel and hurrying down the darkened hallway. He reached the living room, immediately relieved upon seeing the moonlight streaming in through the wide windows.

Better yet, comforting voices came from down the opposing hallway—his nieces, up way too late, giggling at some shared secret.

He wanted to forget he'd ever heard the woman's voice in Poppa's room, but he couldn't. And he could no longer deny whose voice ushered from the lightless void—it could've only been his grandmother. He'd recognize her low lilting tone anywhere.

Jack considered heading off to his own bed, but he would never be able to sleep. He needed to get out of the house. After making a beeline for the front door, he flipped the deadbolt and stepped outside. The air was refreshingly cool, and he could breathe.

Nighttime sounds swept over him: crickets and cicadas, a lone owl's call.

After ripping open the Velcro on the pocket of his shorts, he removed the pint. He broke the seal and took a long pull, which burned like fire. Poisonous, purifying fire. He sucked in deep droughts of cool, humid air as he drifted from the house toward his truck. He took a shorter pull off the bottle and pocketed it.

Jack glanced back at the house and opened the passenger side door. With the tip of his car key, he removed the speaker cover from the door panel, then let the speaker dangle on its wire like an eyeball forced from its socket. From inside the gaping hole, he removed a cough drop tin. He sniffed but couldn't smell anything. The wrapped foil tucked inside the plastic baggie wouldn't stop a K9 dog from popping him, but he felt some amount of reassurance that at least his son wouldn't accidentally discover his stash.

A loon called from the lake, low and mournful. It sounded heartbreaking, so entirely alone. When a second loon replied, Jack felt an odd sense of relief.

He replaced the speaker and closed the truck's door. The bottle sloshed in his pocket, his head fuzzy. He'd already had three major buzzes today. He was getting to be an expert riding the waves, riding them from peak to shore without going over the edge. He could turn up the driveway and simply walk wherever his feet took him. While it sounded like an excellent idea, he wasn't nearly so drunk as to explore that particular whim.

Jack tapped his fingers against the metal box in his pocket, liking the reassuring ping. He gazed at the front of the house for a long time, daring his mind to empty, to erase from his memory what he had heard inside Poppa's room. Not only that, but what he had witnessed almost two years ago, the day Nan died. He again considered simply ambling away down the road, but he couldn't. Trevor was asleep inside the house. How could he be so foolish to have brought him back here? Why couldn't he have just stayed away?

Was his life in such ruin that this place represented a respite from what he had become?

Jack stared at the darkened windows, at the porch swing swaying almost imperceptibly in the breeze.

CHAPTER 9

The nearly full moon idled so low it appeared to sit atop the upraised branches of the surrounding trees. Angled moonlight cut through the wooden blinds, filling the bedroom with the brightness of dusk. It was after two in the morning, and Krista and Neal's tangled bodies caught the warm yellow light as they moved with a nearly painfully intense rhythm. At first, Krista had wanted to keep things quiet, but when Neal knocked the headboard one too many times against the bedroom wall, she pushed him over onto his back and took charge. Now they were drenched in sweat, even though the bed hardly moved beneath them.

Their muscles were taut and pressed against each other, and from the look in Neal's eyes Krista knew he was close. She rocked her pelvis against his, their sweat and heat mingling. When he groaned, she clamped a hand over his mouth.

"*Shhh* ..." she whispered, and then giggled as he grunted in frustration.

He panted against her palm and bit the meat below her pinky finger.

"*Ow!*" She gasped, but only for a moment.

Neal took hold of her hips and guided her, still ever so slowly; the intensity was euphoric.

Krista ran her fingers through his sweaty hair, massaging his scalp, before pressing her palms against his chest. He began to buck beneath her. She soon joined him, her senses funneling into waves of riotous but glorious physical sensation.

When it was over, she remained on top, her hands resting on his shoulders for balance. Eyes closed, her head swam with the warmth, with unguarded love.

She opened her eyes and found him staring up at her.

"What was *that* about?" He ran his fingers lightly over her smooth belly, to the curves of her hips.

She took hold of his hands and kissed them. "I just … needed you."

"Well, you can need me anytime you like."

She leaned over until her head came to rest on his shoulder. She could smell him—*them both*—and it made her smile.

Neal brushed her hair back from her face and said, "Are you okay?"

"I am now. I don't think I could've come here without you. I know it's difficult taking time away from the firm—"

He shook his head to waylay her guilt. "This is a hard thing to do—seeing someone you love drift away—for anyone it's hard, but for you, especially under the circumstances … having avoided this place for so long, and the bad memories it must hold for you … I couldn't let you do this alone."

She kissed his cheek. "Well, I'm grateful."

"And a little drunk still, I believe."

"A little? More like a lot."

"You haven't been like this since our first New Years together in Chicago."

"Oh, don't remind me. I think I'm still partially hungover from that night."

She ran her fingers across his chest. Neal had never been muscle-bound. He was lanky, but strong, and she liked how their bodies fit so perfectly together. She wanted this moment to last, for the outside world to recede to the horizon.

They were both verging on sleep when Neal mumbled something she didn't quite hear.

"Hmm …?"

"Do you think anyone heard us? God, that would be embarrassing."

"I don't think so. At least once I decided to take control of things. You and that silly headboard ..."

"Good."

"You know, I better pee before I fall asleep."

"Good idea. Go for me too." He chuckled, his hand stroking her back. His eyes at half-mast and fading.

"Sure, I'll get right on it."

She reluctantly pushed away from him and stood, too fast for her present condition, and the walls began to spin. She almost had to sit down on the bed, but the walls started to behave.

"Take some aspirin ... for your head."

"Do you want any?" she replied.

"No, I'm stone-cold sober."

"You don't sound like it." She grabbed her robe from the rocking chair next to the bed.

"Trust me, I am. Didn't have even a sip of beer after, like, nine o'clock. I'm groggy because you just screwed any sense out of me."

"I did, didn't I?"

She normally wasn't so demonstrative in their lovemaking. She had to admit that it gave her sometimes flagging self-confidence a goose in the right direction.

With his eyes fully closed, he raised his hand. She slapped him a high five and then slipped into her robe. By the time she had it cinched around her waist, Neal let out a soft snore.

Krista opened the door a crack and listened. All she heard was Neal's snoring. She padded out into the hallway, feeling like a kid getting one over on her parents. She remembered exactly where to place her feet to avoid creaky floorboards. It wasn't exactly a direct path down the hallway, but she was still so buzzed she probably couldn't negotiate a straight line anyway.

After being immersed in the bedroom's moonlight, the hallway's darkness was so absolute the air seemed flooded in sooty shadows. The surrounding cityscape always suffused their Chicago apartment with a liminal brightness, which made it difficult to pinpoint time. It would take a few days to get reacquainted with the western Michigan dead of night.

She heard giggling from next door. She reached for the door-knob, ready to reprimand Heidi and Clara for being up so late. When she opened the door, moonlight revealed a tent in the center of the room made from one of her grandmother's handmade quilts. After a couple of seconds, the girls stopped giggling, and a heavy stillness filled the room.

Krista grinned as she closed the door as quietly as possible and hurried across the hall to the bathroom. After finishing up, she flicked off the bathroom light, ready for her warm bed. All she wanted to do was curl up next to Neal and sleep.

She again heard the girls' voices. Yes, they were using hushed tones, but from the rush of syllables, they were nowhere close to falling asleep.

Her daughter was so serious sometimes that Krista hated ruining any amount of fun she was willingly engaging in, especially with her sweet cousin. She pictured both girls crabby and irritable all day tomorrow from lack of sleep. Against her better judgment, she again opened the door. Again, the voices quieted.

"Girls, it's almost 3 A.M. You're going to have to get some sleep or you can't share a room."

The room remained silent, unnervingly so.

"Got it?"

The quilt tent collapsed on itself, the four corners pulling taut in opposite directions until it lay flat on the bedroom floor. Cold air gushed from beneath the flattened fabric, buffeting her brow and billowing the sheer white curtains at the window.

Krista gasped and flicked the light switch near the door.

No one was there.

"Girls?"

Her palms became clammy. Thick pain throbbed at her temples as she took a step inside the room. The room looked unremarkable and obviously unoccupied; there was an antique bed with a white painted metal frame, a wardrobe cabinet. She checked beneath the bed, saw stars in her eyes from the sudden blood rushing to her head. Nothing. The wardrobe contained a few vinyl garment bags, a hatbox, and the pungent odor of mothballs.

"Girls?"

Desperation tinged her voice. She was alone, *knew* she was alone. But then again, she had seen what she had seen. *Right?* The quilt remained where it had fallen, appearing ready for a picnic or a child's pretend tea party.

There was no other place for the girls to hide.

Krista hurried from the room, not caring if anyone heard her footsteps. She went past her and Neal's room and turned the corner.

They have to be ... somewhere. Please, let them be—

She pushed open the door to her left. The hinge squealed, but no one called out in response. Two shapes in the deep of night. Two blanketed shapes snuggled together on two twin beds pushed together. One of the shapes moved.

Krista exhaled a pent-up breath. She inhaled deeply and the room started to spin. She leaned against the door frame until she regained her equilibrium and her eyes adjusted.

Clara and Heidi slept nearly nose to nose, as if they had fallen asleep while sharing conspiratorial whispers. She wanted to sweep them both into her arms, to hold them and feel their warmth. They looked so at peace, like angels. She smiled, happy Clara had allowed herself to bond with her cousin.

Krista eased the door shut and let out a ragged sigh. Her hands were shaky and a thin sheen of cold sweat swathed her skin. When she reached her own bedroom door, she kept going. She would never fall asleep now, not after what she'd seen.

At the threshold of the spare bedroom where she'd heard the voices, her fingers trembled a bare inch from the knob. She pressed her ear to the oaken door, heard nothing but her own reverberating heartbeat. Her breathing slowed with the chill of her cooling sweat.

Before she could have second thoughts, she turned the knob and hurried inside, throwing the light switch as she moved.

The room was empty, at least as far as she could tell. Moonlight illuminated the tidy bed. But the wardrobe's door was now closed. And quite disquietingly, her grandmother's handmade quilt was no longer on the floor, and now folded and neatly appointed to the end of the bed.

Krista almost screamed, but some fragment of her sober brain held it at bay.

Nothing is out of place, she thought. *There is no reason to freak out over absolutely nothing. Because nothing had been out of place just minutes ago. I'm drunk. The walls are still spinning, goofy woman.*

She embraced her inebriation, for only that could logically explain everything.

Krista retraced her steps, making sure to avoid the squeaky patches in the floor. She tried her best to ignore the image of the quilt hanging in the air, perfectly shaped like a tent any child with any modicum of boredom would take upon themselves to build. She tried to squeeze the stress from her hands, clenching and unclenching her fingers.

Looking back over her shoulder, to the room, was out of the question; she couldn't possibly look back while holding her senses together.

Neal's snore was reassuring and grounding as she climbed into bed. She placed her head on his chest and he wrapped his arms around her, muttering about aspirin. She'd forgotten the aspirin but wasn't about to leave her bed till morning.

Coiled into her husband's warmth, she doubted she could possibly fall asleep before dawn. Just as she completed the thought, she did just that.

CHAPTER 10

When Jack ventured back inside, he remembered to throw the dead-bolt. *Guess I'm not that far gone.* He couldn't face his bed. Not alone. Not without the fear knowing he wasn't alone.

Come here, son. Let me get a look at you!

A chill ran down his spine, and he dug his fingers into his palms to keep his fear at bay. He had challenged his memory of hearing that haunting voice enough times that he had begun to doubt its veracity. He had been drinking all day—pretty much the last six months—so everything got muddled after a while, both the good and the bad.

Someone had turned on the kitchen light while he was out at his truck. A half-empty glass of water sat on the kitchen island.

He found Leah on the deck, leaning with her elbows against the railing.

She turned around, as if sensing his closeness. Leah had always had the subtle ability to know things just ... *because*, as if her sensory antennae were more attuned to underlying stimuli. She smiled and he held up his cough drop tin and shrugged. She rolled her eyes and waved for him to join her.

He stepped outside to the haunting call and response of the loons.

"You chatting to your people?" Jack said. He stood next to her, mimicking her pose with his elbows braced against the railing, his body leaning out over the edge into the darkness.

"Who's that?"

"The loons, silly."

She laughed her throaty laugh and slugged him in the shoulder.

One loon's call quieted as it flew away, while the other sounded almost desperate.

"I'd forgotten about them," Leah said. "There's wilderness in downstate Illinois, but nothing like this."

"I never liked hearing them when I was a kid, but I kinda like it now."

Neither said anything for a minute or more. A breeze rushed through the surrounding woods; height-of-summer foliage rattled like uprooted beasts prowling the lakeside hills.

Leah pointed to the cough drop tin. "I see nothing's changed."

"This?" He shook the tin, then popped it open. He opened the baggie and unwrapped the foil bundle. He removed a joint, twisted one imperfect end and stashed it behind his ear.

"Yeah, I remember you used to hide your weed in a Sucrets tin just like that."

"Until Nan found it."

"Oh, she was so mad at you!"

"The only time she ever laid a hand on me. Any of us really. And it was a single hard smack on the ass. Just that one, and I knew it would take a long time for her to forgive me. I'd just gotten my driver's license, but the look she'd given me? I wilted like a four-year-old."

"Oh, that woman. Did she have to be so perfect? She kept us all fed and clothed. Kept the house spotless. Not just on cleaning day, but *every* single day. And I don't think she ever swore her entire life."

"One time she stubbed her toe on the kitchen table and I heard her mumble, 'Oh, dump truck!' under her breath."

"Close enough."

They both laughed.

"She made it look so easy," she said.

Jack pulled out his pint, uncapped it and took a swig. "Yeah, but it isn't."

"No, it's not. Raising kids. Keeping up on things. Being an *adult*." Leah grabbed the bottle and took a drink. She winced and waved a hand over her mouth. "This stuff is nasty."

He retrieved the bottle. "It does the job."

"I always tried to be like Nan, always held myself up to her standards. But with everything, you know, with Curtis? I realized I'm not Nan. No one could be her, but *her*."

"Preach it, sister," Jack said and laughed.

Leah's eyes were clear and unwavering. "Trying to be like her? It was a trap. It's what kept me with Curtis, long after I should've left."

"So what made you leave?"

Jack sipped from the bottle, then realized he didn't want any more. He recapped the whiskey and returned it to his pocket.

"You," she whispered.

"Me? What the heck did *I* do? I haven't even seen you guys in months!"

"You didn't do anything wrong, trust me. You and Trev ... I've always envied how you've taken care of him. You showed me it was possible to raise a child on your own, as a single parent."

"That was never the plan. I never wanted to be alone, but Sheri never wanted a family."

"But you made the most of it. You've made it work."

"Then how come it feels like the walls are always tumbling in on me?"

"That's the thing; that's how parenting feels even when you have a spouse."

"Really?" He paused to consider. "But Trev, he's so ..."

"Uninhibited? Energetic? Yeah, so? He's also a leader, and he's sharp as a tack. Trust me, Trev is going to turn out just fine, and that's all because of you."

Jack felt both raw and emotionally drained. He removed the joint tucked behind his ear and perched it on his lip, his hands shaking. He fished out his lighter and lit the joint, drawing the pungent smoke into his lungs. He held it for several seconds before slowly exhaling.

"So ... why did you leave? Did he hit you?"

He offered her the joint, but she waved him off.

"No, it was nothing like that. Curtis is the most nonviolent person I know. And, while I've always had my suspicions, I don't know for certain if he ever cheated on me." She blinked several times, as if deciding whether or not to continue.

"So … what was it?" Jack said and took another toke, his hands not so shaky.

"Don't tell anyone, especially Krista because she doesn't know the whole story."

"Scouts' honor."

"Curtis turned into someone I didn't recognize. We've never been wealthy people—"

"You don't say!"

"Hey, asshole, I'm trying to bare my soul," she said.

"Yeah, sorry, carry on, carry on."

"Anyway, last year I started working at an artisanal bakery. It's run by my two friends, Reece and Parker."

"Sounds expensive."

"It is, but it's so worth it. So I started working behind the counter, taking orders, keeping everything stocked. It wasn't much money, but it added up, and I got a nice discount."

Jack felt a deepening mellow. "Sounds like a good deal."

"It was … until Parker noticed checks and credit card slips went missing from the cash register whenever Curtis came to pick me up."

"No way!"

"Yeah, my hippie dippy partner got involved in an identity theft ring, and he's facing jail time. I wanted to let the courts sort it out, you know? If he went to jail, then our relationship would be pretty much kaput. But I decided I couldn't do it. Sticking by him through that? That would mean I supported his bullshit behavior."

"Yeah, that doesn't sound like you. You're all about the karma."

"I know! So, while trying to figure everything out, I thought about you and how well you do as a single parent."

"And, hell, if *I* could do it, why not you?"

"Take the *dang* compliment, will you?"

"If I must. But just because Trev isn't a felon yet, doesn't mean I've got life figured out."

Leah laughed softly and reached for the joint. She brought it to her lips and took a drag. She coughed most of it out, but smiled as she handed it back to him.

"I thought weed messed with your vibrations?" Jack said.

His sister was the only hippie he'd ever met who didn't partake in the occasional joint.

"Yeah, that's my first hit since before the twins." She looked like she was holding back, like she wanted to talk more. The corner of her mouth creased into a smirk. "Maybe I need some dulling." She turned toward the sliding door. "You might want to distance yourself from the house. Poppa would lose his mind if he found you smoking the wacky tobacky."

"Will do," he said and nodded.

Leah reached for the door handle.

"Leah?" Jack called before she could open the door. "I'm glad we all decided to come back, even just for shooting the shit like this."

"Me, too, little brother. Don't stay up too late."

"Can you do me a favor? Make sure Trevor isn't tearing down the house or setting fires?"

"I'm sure he's fine ... but I will."

"Thanks, Leah."

After slipping inside, she turned off the light and drifted through the darkened interior of the kitchen.

Jack was alone with the impenetrable woods, the glimmering stars overhead, the loons and their forlorn cries. He drew on the joint, held it in, and ambled away from the deck, the smoke seeping slowly from his lungs.

The wooden stairs creaked beneath his feet, but by the time he reached the sandy dirt trail winding through the woods, he moved unseen, like a subtle intruder in a foreign land.

The weed turned down the noise of his thoughts. The sand was cold under his bare feet. There were other houses nestled around the lake, but he couldn't see them. The black water stretched out to the horizon, to the curve of the earth. Pinpricks of starlight sprawled above, making him feel both incredibly small and incredibly lucky to be alive.

"*Come here, son ...*" the voice called out behind him.

Her voice. *Nan.*

He jerked around, his steady buzz descending to paranoia.

"Hello?" he called out, his voice cracking on the last syllable. His heart ached in his chest, a slow lurch of adrenaline fighting through the languor of a daylong drinking binge topped off with grade-A weed. He blinked, starting to doubt his ears.

He saw nothing beyond the dark blue of the midnight sand, and the grassy eddies of encroaching wilderness unfurling from the hillside. Even still, he felt a presence, an insistent pressure issuing from the night. It caressed him, and his skin coursed with cold sweat.

And then a slight human shape materialized from the gloom, a gauzy white shimmer among the dark and darker backdrop. It flickered on the breeze like an ephemeral white flame.

"I've been waiting to see you ..."

Graceful strides broke up the singular column of flowing white. Stick-thin arms reached out for him, and even though the person—*Yes, person! Not a ghost. Not some fucking ghost*—was still thirty feet away, he felt its icy touch against his face, tracing cold trails that held him rooted to the spot. He couldn't move a step; his left eye twitched spastically.

He wanted to believe he was hallucinating. Surely this had to be Krista. The steely eyes, the lush curly hair, the note-for-note mannerisms. But his mind wouldn't allow him this self-deception. This wasn't Krista, no matter how much he wanted to believe.

"What are you doing here?" He was speaking to something, some*one*, who could not possibly be standing before him. He cleared his throat. "You're not real. I saw you. You died. We had a funeral."

"Yes, you saw me ... you saw me die, and you did nothing to help me. Your face was the last thing I saw. Your fear. Your guilt."

Her lips didn't move, but he clearly heard every syllable.

"You fucking died," he said through wet sobs. "What ... what do you want from me?"

Finally able to move, he stepped backward, nearly catching his heel in the sand.

She said nothing.

A loon called nearby, the sound of utter despair.

He sensed movement in the periphery but saw nothing lurking in the woods. No one to save him. When he returned his gaze to

Nan—*Jesus, lord, it really is his Nan*—she was inches away. She no longer appeared as he last remembered her, stooped, pained, but with laugh lines drawn deeply across her mouth.

Layers of her cycled to the surface in glimpses before ceding to the next. Her image flashed through every stage of her life, until the images blurred, until they became one.

"You always were a wicked boy," she said, again her lips not moving.

She extended a hand veiled in white mist, reaching for him, and it drew in his heat, fed off him like a vampire gorging on blood.

Without thinking, he shoved both hands against her shoulders. Bitter cold greeted his skin and raced up his arms. She didn't move.

"And you still haven't learned."

He stumbled away, not wanting to ever again feel her wretched cold touch. His stomach roiled, ready to spew Jim Beam soaked vomit.

And then he saw movement through the woods as a half dozen or more gauzy white apparitions drifted out onto the sand as one. They formed a dome around him, pinning him to the shore. He backed away until his feet met water, and still they advanced.

"You wretched little boy. Wretched little thing ..."

The spirits had vacant shadows for eyes, as if their vision had been hacked out by a dull blade. They wore simple nightgowns, or play clothes once made of rugged material. Waifish girls, no older than Clara. They all advanced, arms outstretched. Every one of them but Nan.

A weak wave lapped at his ankles.

Jack backed away, farther still, away from them, away from the consideration that any of this was really happening.

"We fucking buried you!"

"You would never listen to your Nan. Would never open your eyes and see anything besides your own interests. You wicked little—"

Jack turned and dove wildly into the water. He kicked hard below the surface. Even with his eyes open, he saw nothing more than a hint of air bubbles leaving his lungs. As he thrashed, trying to force his drunken limbs into something resembling a rhythm, he lost his bearings. His chest burned. Hot bile and whiskey bubbled at the back of his throat.

His heartbeat throbbed in his ears as the pressure mounted. He couldn't do it. If he could only swim across the entirety of the Little Whisper, he would sprint away with some semblance of his sanity. But he was too slow, definitely too drunk, and in the depths of his soul, he was too weak. Weak of spirit.

Instead of fighting to reach the surface, he let his body go slack. He drifted in the darkness, his thoughts just as aimless, his body nearly passed out from exertion.

Vomit scorched up his throat and plumed around him as he surfaced.

He fanned his arms around him to keep his head above water. A loon's call greeted him; that, and nothing more. He was alone, a mere ten feet from the floating dock.

So much closer than the empty shore.

"What was all that?" he whispered aloud. "Seriously. What the fuck?"

Jack dog-paddled to the anchored dock, and since the ladder was on the opposite side, he took hold of the deck's edge to pull himself up. His feet kicked under the dock and encountered the slimy chain tethering it to the anchor. A sickening feeling, but he didn't care. He sputtered, short of breath. His hands slipped and his arms quavered. He finally hoisted himself onto the deck, like something rotten washed up on shore.

He panted as he caught his breath, his eyes fixed on the beach. *Nothing.* He began to question the weed, wondering if it had been laced with something. LSD maybe. He shivered, feeling foolish being stuck out here on the dock. He wanted to be in his bed, covered in quilts stitched from Nan's own hands. He wanted to put not only this night behind him, but the one from earlier, the night of Nan's death.

Shoving the thought away, Jack removed the pint of Beam from his pocket. It was still over half full. He sat and wrapped his arms around his knees, unscrewed the bottle, and took a warming gulp. The alcohol burned, fighting his vomit-coated throat. Not the first time he fought fire with gasoline, and most certainly not the last. He took another pull.

A loon called once, then the night air was still.

No, not just still, but *empty*. Void of life.

And as he strained to hear the second loon's reply, he noticed a number of shimmering white shapes, glowing as if lit up from within, lurking just beneath the surface of the water, closing on the floating dock.

"No …" he whispered. "No-no-no, this can't be happening. It has to be tainted weed. Has to be."

The shapes glided through the dark water, illuminating ringlets of sluggish seaweed as they passed. All at once the faces of eyeless children broke the surface, surrounding the dock on all sides. Arms rose from the water, reaching for him, imploring him.

The dock tipped to one side, drawing his frantic gaze from the water. Ascending the ladder—one hand after another pulling higher—climbed Nan. Every layer of Nan's life cycled through her visage like shifting photographs: from youthful beauty to withered old woman, with pain straining her every movement.

Jack stepped as far away as he could and the dock bobbed under his feet. The children, in their soaked play clothes and nightgowns, rose from the water, grasping for the dock. A dozen or more eyeless faces leered at him. The children hissed, as if their lungs were once again expelling their final breaths. Jack sank to his knees and tipped the bottle of whiskey to his lips. He drained it, fuck all, not caring what happened to him. He sobbed as the world beneath him began to sway.

He closed his eyes as one dead child after another stepped onto the deck.

"You were always such a wicked thing …"

He could feel Nan reaching for him.

Jack leaned over, pulled his knees to his chest. He plugged his ears with his fingers and started chanting, quietly at first, then louder and louder still, until he no longer feared ever having to hear Nan's undead words ringing through his head.

"Not going to hear no more … no more, no more. No, I'm not

going to hear no more, oh no ..."

He rocked himself, still chanting, still plugging his ears, waiting for the whiskey to take him in its murky embrace. Unconsciousness made more sense than what he found before him, where the barrier between the living and dead was no longer black and white.

His mind teetered, on the brink.

CHAPTER 11

Krista woke just after dawn but didn't know why. She hadn't gotten nearly enough sleep, didn't have to pee, didn't hear a noise, or have any pressing need to drive her from the comfortable warmth of the covers, but even so, as she lay in Neal's arms, she realized she wouldn't be able to fall back to sleep.

She listened to Neal's breathing, considered leaning in to kiss him, but from his inhalations she could tell he was in a deep sleep. His cheeks bristled with beard stubble. He normally shaved like clockwork every morning, but since they were on vacation he'd let the habit lapse. She only now noticed the beginnings of gray creeping into the growth, and she brushed her fingers ever-so-lightly across his jawline. His breathing remained steady, but his lips formed a slight smile. She wondered what he was dreaming about, and if her gentle touch had changed the course of his subconscious events.

The longer she remained awake, the more alert she became, and that alertness made her lament forgetting to down some aspirin. Her head throbbed with a dull ache.

Neal slept with his hand draped over her hip. She shifted away, rolling until her feet dangled off the edge. She stood slowly, carefully, trying to minimize the jostling of both the bed and her head.

She looked back at Neal, but he hadn't even stirred. After slipping into her robe, she slinked out into the hallway. A weighted silence filled the house, as if she had caught nature drowsily curled in on itself against the chill. She closed the door behind her as quietly as possible and made her way to the kitchen.

The view out the back windows made her nearly forget her mounting headache. Dense fog drifted off the lake, sweeping up the hillside, filling in the empty spaces between trees like quicksand finding its level. It reached the back deck, heavy clouds trapped by gravity.

As she stared into the white blanket, she filled a glass from the tap and drank down the water's rusty coldness. Poppa hadn't changed much since she had last visited, so it wasn't surprising when she found a bottle of Excedrin in the first cabinet.

It's like I never left the place.

She shook two pills into her palm and downed them with another glass of water. Though it was likely wishful thinking, the tension was already easing from her temples.

It crossed her mind to return to bed. Sure, she would most likely not fall back to sleep, but maybe she didn't need to. Maybe she could rouse Neal to rekindle their fun from last night. Remembering the intensity, heat rushed across the length of her neck.

She knew she should let him sleep, so she wandered the ground floor, hoping to hear someone else stirring. The house withheld any auditory reply; the walls themselves seemed to hold their breaths.

Krista stopped in her tracks when her mind flashed with the crystal-clear image of Nan's quilt suspended in midair, looking every bit a secret clubhouse fashioned by children. And the giggles; those sounds were so real in her memory. But she had been mistaken. Certainly mistaken. She shook her head, trying to clear it. If anything, she had recalled memory from her own youth, of Leah and Breann and herself, willing away a rainy summer afternoon.

Satisfied enough to quell her thoughts, she entered Poppa's library. The writing desk tucked into the near corner drew her attention. A crescent shaped clutter of papers, folders, and research books. The bare center of the crescent was his writing surface, where he jotted his work longhand before typing it into his computer. The desk faced a shelf of his published work. He'd written fifteen or so nonfiction books dating back forty years.

Even though he'd kept producing quality books for decades, he was mostly known for his second book, the now classic of the environmental movement, *To Heal the Land*. That one title alone had allowed Poppa to decide his own path in life, to pursue whatever his desire. Other people would have given in to sloth or decadence, but Poppa's relative wealth had freed him to live his authentic self. He'd long supported the conservation movement with his time, money, and passion. In the 1980s he'd led protests against a logging company wanting to buy up the local forests for clear-cutting. He'd wound up buying parcels of land amounting to hundreds of acres when the owners felt like they couldn't pass up the logging company's offer. He'd then turned the land over to the local park district, and with the help of a hefty donation on his part, they'd become caretakers.

Besides *To Heal the Land*, Poppa had mostly written about predatory relationships in the wild. He'd written about coyotes and opossums, and the ever-opportunistic raccoon. He'd also written about deer and beavers changing the very geography of their habitats based on the ebb and flow of their populations.

Krista ran her fingers across the old battered desktop. How many hours had he spent in the room, refining his words to exact precision?

A simple brown bi-fold picture frame stood next to the reading light. One half of the frame was a headshot of Nan from her early twenties. Her cheeks were rosy, her smile broad with an underlying deviousness Krista had never noticed till now. Nan had been drop-dead gorgeous. The other frame showed Poppa in a tan tweed jacket over a beige turtleneck sweater. His arms were crossed, and he faced the camera at a haughty angle—an early author photo, judging by the posture. His bushy sideburns matched the dark shade of his hair. Poppa had been an unabashed geek. Krista made a mental note to ask him how such a dorky-looking young man had landed a head-turner like Nan.

She smiled, sifting layers of paper on the desk, until she uncovered a black vinyl binder. She freed the dark wedge from the rest of the pile. Thick as a phonebook. Curious, she opened a ream's worth of typed pages held together by three silver rings. She read the title of the manuscript, and had to read a second time, and third:

FALLEN: THE MIND AND MOTIVATIONS OF A SERIAL KILLER

"What the ..." she muttered and turned the page. The writing was imperfect: words had been slashed through, notes jotted at the margins in pen, arcane editing symbols littering the page. She flipped through what looked to be a draft of a new work she had never encountered.

A word caught her attention as the pages whirled past: *Edgar.*

She desperately tried to find the page again, but couldn't. Frustrated, she returned to the introductory pages and began to read:

> The concept for this book had a long gestation period before I finally decided to explore its sometimes-gruesome subject matter. Over the years, I have often explored how the natural world tends to balance itself for the sake of the continued health of the entire ecosystem. Predator animals prune away the sick and weak. The remaining prey animals—the ones with inherent strength, smarts, agility and speed—reproduce. Their offspring are stronger for the pressure exacted by the predators in their midst.
>
> It is a basic concept, yet one that has left me utterly fascinated, even as I reach my twilight years. I am an old man. I have reproduced, and I have witnessed the birth and life of three generations following me. If it were up to nature, I would have long ago fed the predators stalking my pack. But humans have overcome the balancing force of nature, so I get to live long after my biological usefulness.
>
> As I have explored the predator/prey dichotomy, and how it applies to human interaction, I have been drawn to the concept

of the human predator, the humans who embody the exacting force existing in nature. Humanity's desire to kill has been explored at great length in other well-researched books, for many years, so I won't get into a long psychological exploration of that general topic. But one particular killer has made me interested, perhaps obsessively so, in the subject matter. Edgar Jenkins is a man, who, as of this writing, is spending his life in a maximum-security prison. He is still relatively young, not yet fifty, so he is facing possible decades of isolation for his crimes. He can no longer act as his basic nature dictates. He can no longer kill. He can no longer act as he sees himself, as a predator pruning away the weak.

Edgar Jenkins lived in relative anonymity for the first quarter century of his life in an unincorporated area outside of Green Bay, Wisconsin. He killed for the first time the year he became a teenager. For over a decade, no suspicion ever fell on him. It was only when he crossed Lake Michigan and abducted and killed eleven-year-old Tanya Williamson that he was finally cornered, and finally brought to justice.

The page fell from her fingertips as she backed away from Poppa's writing desk. She couldn't believe he would write about such a horrid subject. Why would he spend his final days writing about a monster like Edgar Jenkins?

The view through the front windows was steeped in fog. The vibrant colors of early summer were gone, draped now in banks of misty white. Goosebumps traveled from her wrists to her shoulders. She rubbed her palms against her arms, but she couldn't shake the unsettling feeling.

Someone was walking down the hallway, dragging slippered feet along the hardwood. Krista left the library, glad to put it behind her.

"Hello?" she called out as she neared the kitchen.

She found Leah opening cabinets.

"It's just me." Leah rubbed her eye with the knuckle of her index finger. "Couldn't sleep, so I thought I'd start on breakfast."

"Waffles?"

Krista guessed the meal by the ingredients her sister had already gathered.

"Is that okay?"

"Sure, as long as I can help."

Leah smiled and hesitated, as if she had something important to bring up. "Sounds like an offer I can't refuse." She hauled out two waffle irons from a cabinet under the island. "You're up early."

"Yeah, no idea why. I should still be dead to the world."

"Especially with how drunk you were."

"I was not drunk!"

Leah placed her hand on her hip and pursed her lips.

"Well," Krista said, "maybe I was a little drunk." She remembered the walls spinning, how they still hadn't fully regained their stability. "Okay, I was *a lot* drunk. So, you see my predicament. I should be asleep, but I'm not."

"Must be all this fresh country air," Leah offered with a smirk.

"Could be." Krista grabbed a couple large mixing bowls. Since she and her sister were little, they had always doubled up on the waffle makers, otherwise it would take all morning to make enough to feed the family.

"What do you think?" Leah said, eyeing a big bag of flour, a measuring cup in her hand. "A triple batch?"

"At least." Krista figured the basic math in her head. "Might want to make it a quadruple. We can always serve scoops of ice cream over the leftovers."

Leah grinned. "Yeah, *definitely* a quadruple batch."

Baking with her sister while the rest of the family remained asleep would bring normalcy to her otherwise unsettling morning.

"Okay, let's do this."

The sisters went to work, and the years fell away. They worked as a team, not needing to say much as they passed ingredients. They readied the waffle irons, warmed the maple syrup, set the table. They were nearly finished when Clara entered the kitchen.

"Good morning," Krista said.

Clara yawned. "Good morning."

"Sleep well?" Leah asked.

"Heidi snores, but I don't mind. The only problem I had were the boys."

"Robby and Trev?"

"Yeah, they kept sneaking up to our door and giggling and tapping on the walls. I'd see the shadows of their feet passing by. When I'd get up to chase them away, they were already gone. Happened, like, three times, each time after I'd fallen asleep." Clara yawned again, as if to emphasize her misery.

Leah nodded and ladled a dollop of batter onto the sizzling waffle iron. "Boys sure can be a pain sometimes."

"It's a big house, but there are a lot of us under one roof," Krista added. She couldn't help but wonder about the laughter, if that's what she'd also heard.

What you thought *you heard, which wasn't anything but your drunken mind playing tricks on you.*

"Breakfast is almost ready," Krista said. "Can you go wake Poppa?"

"Sure, I guess." Clara hesitated before slowly turning away, not entirely up to the task.

Treading into unfamiliar territory usually created anxiety for her daughter, but Clara would forever remain within her tiny comfort zone without a gentle push.

"Clara ..." Krista called. "Thanks. He appreciates every moment he can share with you."

"Okay." Clara's frown turned into a straight, tight line. It wasn't even close to a smile, but it was an improvement. Her quiet strides padded down the hallway.

"That girl of yours ..." Leah shook her head. "I swear she's more mature than anyone else here."

Krista rolled her eyes. "I have to admit, she does worry me sometimes."

"She's been that way since before she could walk. She's always had a dour, serious expression, even in diapers! Not that she was angry ... more like she was examining the world around her. And, however much she doesn't like it, she does interact socially, so I don't think it's anything to worry about."

"Are you sure? I see how she is around other kids, adults even, and I can't imagine her grown up and in the real world."

"Trust me. She's just a kid. The only thing you need to worry about with that girl is helping her figure out which college will have the honor of paying for her scholarship."

Krista sighed but still took solace in her sister's words.

She carried a platter laden with golden waffles to the dining room table. The fog must have been breaking up; a wedge of sunlight splashed across the polished maple wood table. Seeing the place settings laid out, and the delectable waffles wafting at the center of the table, brought a surprising surge of emotions to the surface. She had long avoided this place, and in all that time she had missed out on sharing innumerable memories, both good and bad, with her family. Instead of memories, she had a gnawing void, an absence of memories.

Leah paused at her side. Neither said anything, but they shared something in the silence.

"When we were kids," Krista said, "do you remember making blanket forts in the spare room?"

"Nan's extra room? Yeah, that was a blast. We'd dress up in her old clothes, the polyester suits with the garish patterns. Oh, and her ridiculous hats."

"I'd forgotten about those! Remember, we used to call them Jackie-O hats?"

Krista smiled at the memory. "I don't think we even knew who she was at the time."

"Right! Just that it was a glamorous way to spend a rainy day." Leah's face lit up. "Just you, me, and ..."

"And Breann," Krista said softly.

"You know … I always liked her." Leah fidgeted, straightening a fork that wasn't out of place to begin with. "I still think about her sometimes. Her smile with the crooked eye tooth. The freckles on her nose. Her spirit … so free."

"Yeah, me too."

"And sometimes I wonder … why her? Why not me? Why not some kid down the beach?"

"Leah, you shouldn't do that to yourself," Krista said, hearing Neal's words coming from her mouth.

"I just know." Leah paused to steady her nerves. "I know that she was just about the sweetest girl ever."

Again, silence filled the room, but its tone had changed and was no longer welcome.

Krista spoke, if only to say something, *anything*. "That's how we should remember her then, don't you think? Like she's still that sweet girl and nothing bad ever happened to her."

"Easier said than done."

Krista embraced her sister. Neither cried. They'd had years of misery, many decades worth between them, and while they shed no tears, they both still needed the embrace. Krista breathed deeply, knowing that if for no other reason, waking at such an ungodly hour was worth it for this very moment. This was a memory she would cherish for years.

Finally, Leah pulled away. "Thanks, Krista."

"So much about coming back here sucks." Krista crossed her arms. "It really does. But I'm also glad we're here."

"That's twisted, but I think I know what you mean."

They went back to the kitchen island and sat on stools as they let the morning unfurl around them.

"Shouldn't we wake everyone?" Krista asked.

"Let's have a minute without any chaos."

Krista asked, "Did you know Poppa is still working?"

"What, on a book?"

"Yeah, it's …" Krista hesitated, "it's about Breann."

Leah's face twisted, as if she'd eaten something sour. "No … really?"

"Not her exactly, but about *him*." Krista refused to speak his name aloud, and just recalling Edgar Jenkins in her head made her lose her appetite. "Poppa's making some connection to predators, like some of his other books about nature."

Leah furrowed her brow. "But, why … *him?*"

"Her disappearance has bothered him as much as the rest of us. Just imagine, this has always been his refuge. He built this house from nothing. He's been a leader in the community. The McCorts lived next door. I didn't read much of the manuscript, but it seems like he's exploring the psychological profile of someone who could do such horrible things."

"I guess I understand." Leah's expression didn't match her words. "He's tying up loose ends. He called us all to stay at the summer house. He's trying to say goodbye."

"On the one hand, it makes perfect sense. But, really, who wants to dredge up the details of a monster like *him?*"

"I say, whatever brings him peace. Whatever it is, we should support it."

"I'm not going to bring it up with him. He might be okay dwelling on what happened, but that doesn't mean I am."

"Agreed," Leah said.

Clara entered the kitchen, and both women looked at each other, wondering if she had heard any of their conversation.

"Poppa's awake, but tired. He asked me if I'd bring him his breakfast in bed."

"Is he okay?" Leah asked.

"Yes, he said he's not used to such a full house. He's happy, really happy, but he's tired."

"Okay, I'll make him up a plate," Krista said. She piled up a plate and placed a fork and knife next to the waffles. Leah poured orange juice into a glass and handed it to Clara.

"I'm going to drop this off," Clara said. "Would it be okay if I sat with him?"

"Sure, that sounds like a great idea," Krista said.

Clara nodded, took the plate from her mom, and went back out down the hall.

"See what I mean?" Leah whispered. "You don't need to worry about her."

The door off the deck slid open and Jack stepped inside, his clothes dripping wet, his eyes bloodshot.

"What happened to *you?*" Krista asked.

"I, um …" Jack looked down at himself. "I went for an early swim. Best time of day for it." He hurried across the kitchen, peeling his sodden shirt from his skin.

"Didn't you wear that yesterday?" Leah asked.

"Yes, *Mom*, thanks for noticing," he said, leaving sandy footprints and a trail of droplets along the floor.

"Breakfast is ready," Krista said. She found some levity in his pained expression; if she felt hungover this morning, she could only imagine how horrible her brother was feeling.

Jack grunted. "Not now. Not for me."

"We'll keep an eye on Trev for you," Leah called out before he got out of earshot.

"Thank you, Leah. I owe you."

Krista wondered if she'd missed something, considering Leah looked deeply concerned as she stared off in the direction Jack had gone.

CHAPTER 12

While sitting on the wooden rocker at Poppa's bedside, Clara balanced her plate on her lap and methodically cut into a waffle. A handmaid quilt hung from the back of the chair, and swayed as she rolled her feet from heel to toe and back again.

Poppa swallowed some of his breakfast, cleared his throat, and said, "Thank you for sitting with me."

"I don't mind," Clara replied. She brought a forkful of syrupy waffle into her mouth and had to turn her mouth sideways to wedge it in between her teeth. Poppa's eyes went wide as she struggled to chew and she couldn't help laughing.

A shout came from down the hallway—Trev declaring his intention of stringing a zip line from the back deck all the way down to the lake—and Clara's eyes went as wide as Poppa's.

"I'm guessing you like the quiet solitude of our dining experience."

"Yes, Poppa," she said with a nod.

"I like raucousness every once in a while, but with everyone's arrival … well, I'm not used to so much excitement at this point in my life."

"Raucousness," Clara whispered. She took a sip of orange juice to clear her throat, and then mouthed the letters, barely audible. "R-a-u-c …o-u-s-n-e-s-s. Raucousness."

"Nicely spelled. You're going to do quite well at the next National Bee."

She rocked faster, appreciating the compliment. "Dad doesn't want me to practice while we're on vacation. He thinks I need to let my mind wander."

"I think minds do what they want to do. If yours wants to spell, let it spell." Poppa leaned forward, lowering his voice as he said, "Don't tell your father I said that." He gave her a conspiring wink.

Clara took in the room as they ate in amenable quiet, the only sounds coming from their cutlery scratching against their plates.

Large framed black and white photos filled nearly all the available wall space in Poppa's bedroom. It didn't look cluttered by any means, but the intimate, intricate detail of the landscapes was awe-inspiring. One photo captured a dense stand of trees in a wooded hillside, the bark like wrinkles in ancient human skin. Another showed craggy mountaintops ringed in cloud cover. From her Earth Sciences class, she knew that even though the mountains looked incredibly old, as if they existed as long as the earth itself, they were relatively young, as far as mountains were concerned. The earth's geology followed an opposite trajectory to human beings; mountains, born rough and sharp, were old when wind and rain battered their surfaces smooth.

"Those are all by Adams," Poppa said, drawing her away from the stunning photos.

Clara swallowed a mouthful of food. "I'm sorry?"

"Ansel Adams. He's the photographer of all these prints. Nan introduced me to his work shortly after we began our courtship. That was all the way back in 1959."

Even though she tried, she couldn't help saying, "Whoa."

"I know, I know, I'm almost as old as the subjects in those photos." He pointed to the wall with his fork. "When I first saw his work, I knew my own life's aspirations had a purpose. Adams captured the essence of nature, its spirit. He put us—*humanity*—in context with the greater world. He wanted his work to not only expose people to the wonders of the natural world, he also wanted us to understand our role and our obligation to protect it."

"I can't stop looking at the depth of these photos."

"I met Nan at a café in Chicago. She was looking at a book of prints. When I walked by her table, I noticed one photo in partic-ular—the one on the wall with the clouded mountaintop—and I hovered over her shoulder much too long for politeness. She thought I was being rude, that I was ogling her." Poppa laughed and started to cough, hard enough to shorten his breath and bring a rosy splash to his pallid cheeks. He regained control and then continued, "And when she looked up to confront me, I didn't immediately notice her. I was still taken by the Adams print. And then she cleared her throat, and I looked at her. And that's when I fell in love with her. That very instant."

Clara wrinkled her nose at the mushy talk.

"If you live as long as me, you'll be lucky to experience a single instance that will literally weaken your legs. When you become light-headed, and dizzy ... dizzy with the notion your life has not only changed instantly, but for the better."

Poppa made falling in love sound not only possible, but something she might actually look forward to. Although she didn't like it. Falling in love sounded like a loss of control, like completely ceding your life over to someone else.

"Did she ... did Nan feel the same way?"

Poppa chuckled. "Not one bit! It took weeks before she let me pay for her coffee. But on the day she did, something changed. After she let me buy her coffee, she agreed to have dinner with me that night. The rest is history."

Clara bunched her brows "I think you have it wrong."

Poppa sat up higher in his bed. "Excuse me?"

"I don't believe she didn't like you right away. I think she might've fallen in love with you the day you met."

"Why ... why do you think so?" he asked, puzzled.

"You saw her regularly, right? And she probably sat in the same chair, ordered the same coffee?"

"Well, yes."

"If she didn't like you, she wouldn't have continued her pattern. If you were a pest, she would have gone to the café down the street. She would've stayed home and brewed her own."

Poppa nodded as she spoke and long after she finished, parsing her explanation. The fatigue lifted from his eyes, and he smiled. He no longer looked tired, or sick.

GLEN KRISCH

"You, Miss Clarabelle, are far too wise for your years."

"So you think it's true?" she asked, forking the last of her breakfast into her mouth.

"I think you just rewrote the history of my life." Poppa set his plate on his side table and held his arms wide. He waved her to him with both hands. "And for the better."

Clara released a relieved breath.

She got up, set her empty plate on the rocker and practically leapt into his arms, not realizing how much she needed his hug. His hair smelled dry and unwashed, but she didn't mind.

"Can you do me a favor?" he whispered into her ear.

"Of course," she said.

She pulled away as he wiped wetness from the corner of his eye.

He opened the drawer in his side table and removed a small leather-bound book. He placed the book on his lap and ran his fingers over the smooth brown surface.

"What is it?" she asked.

He opened the slim volume and turned a few pages: handwritten paragraphs, sketches of plants and animals, charts of data.

"This is a book of memories." He flipped through until he found what he was searching for. Carefully, almost reverently, he creased the page near the spine, first one way, then the other. He leveraged the paper until it tore, then he tore along the crease until he freed the page.

Clara leaned in close to get a better look.

"Is that ... is that a map?"

"It is indeed."

"What does it show?"

"Like I said, a memory." He traced a finger over the paper. It looked like the crude drawing detailed a path through foliage. "I would like to give you an adventure."

"A ... what?" She was totally thrown by the change of subject. They had been talking about nature photos, then the nature of love, and now he wanted to send her on an adventure?

"An adventure. Oh, it's nothing too harrowing for someone young and able-bodied."

92

Her apprehension eased, but barely.

"There's a clearing not too far into the woods, just west of the house. It's a low flat plane without a tree to obscure the sky, and the only thing growing there, for the most part, is a little purple flower. There's a whole field. I want you to pick a bundle and bring them back to me."

"What kind of flower are they?" she asked, already eager to find a thick botanical book in Poppa's library.

"I don't really know, but they were Nan's favorite. Sometimes it's better not knowing the names of things."

"Really?" Clara couldn't imagine not wanting to learn the name and history behind Nan's favorite flower.

"Sure, the name doesn't particularly matter. What matters is that they were Nan's favorite, and every time I see them, I smile. I'd like for you to bring me some so I can have them at my bedside. It would make it feel like she's in the room with me."

"I …" She hesitated, not wanting to disappoint him, but knowing she wasn't the right person to ask to fulfill this task. "I don't think Mom would want me to."

His face sagged, as if his cheek bones had retreated into his skull. His eyes dulled, the gleam draining away.

Clara's fingers absently toyed with the edge of her blouse. She didn't want to go on an adventure. She was the least likely person to intentionally pursue an activity that would be considered an adventure. But seeing the longing in Poppa's eyes, and seeing him perk up at the mention of Nan and his memories of her, she couldn't bear to deny his simple wish.

"Okay. I'll do it."

"Outstanding!" Poppa punched the air in his excitement

Clara couldn't help feeling his energy.

CHAPTER 13

The morning fog had lifted but had yet to burn away; it remained condensed and low in the sky like a lumbering gray curtain. Krista had changed into a light windbreaker, lime green board shorts, and slipped on some strappy sandals before heading down to the lakeside.

Heidi appeared well on her way to full strength after the leg cramp. She and Trevor laughed hysterically as they kept a beach ball away from Robby, kicking it back and forth. Robby didn't seem too angered; evidently, he found the whole situation just as fun as the others. As they played, they approached the water's edge, not quite venturing into the depths, even though they all wore swimwear. The sun would have to come out to heat the lake for a good while before even this adventurous trio could be tempted to swim.

Jack sat in a low-slung canvas beach chair, his bare feet submerged in the water. The other adults remained at the summer house; her brother was supposed to keep an eye on the children, but his gaze never strayed from the gentle waves spurred by the still cool breeze.

"Hey, how's it going, little brother?" Krista said for no other reason than she didn't want to startle him.

He looked up at her, gave her a grunt. His bloodshot eyes made her wince. "They always have to screech like banshees, huh?" he said, his voice as rough as sandpaper.

"Yeah, afraid so."

Krista had seen Jack hungover before, but something else troubled him.

She glanced at the children. Robby had managed to steal the beach ball, and Trev and Heidi were in hot pursuit as he sprinted across the sand.

Jack picked up a flat stone, dipped his arm to the side and spun the stone off his index finger. The stone seemed to come to life, hopping frantically across the dark water. He grinned, and then his lips curled into a grimace when the stone sunk for good. He stared out at the anchored dock, wind-milling his surgically repaired shoulder counter clockwise.

Krista heard an audible pop, and then some of the pain left his face.

"Are you going to tell me what's wrong, or am I going to have to dunk you in the lake like when we were kids?" Krista kneeled in the sand next to him.

He didn't even react to her presence, so she looked out at the water, watched as the tiny ripples disappeared.

He sucked on his lower lip, shook his head, but didn't say anything. He raked his fingers through the wet sand until he found another flat stone. He raised his hand above his head to loosen the joint and pain again creased his face. The stone dropped from his fingers. His balky shoulder wouldn't even allow him to skip stones; that simple pastime was the essence of Jack. When they were kids, he'd skip them across the lake for hours. He now looked aged, no longer like the youngest sibling, perhaps even the oldest. The fine lines at the corners of his eyes had deepened; she could picture him frail and old, as old as Poppa and just as feeble.

Finally, he said, "Something happened at work. Something bad."

"Something bad happened in Rock Creek?" she said, trying to make light of the situation. "What, a serial cow-tipper on the loose?"

His expression didn't waver.

"It was nothing to do with anyone but me. About a year ago, shortly after Nan died, I hit a rough patch. I started drinking heavy. Well, heavier than normal. I got sloppy. Waking up drunk. Needing to chase away the hangover with a shot and a beer. All before work."

"Jesus, Jack," she scoffed. "You can't do that."

"You don't think I know that? A few weeks ago, the chief

smelled it on me and called me out. I tried to brush it off as the stink from a late night. He was sympathetic, but wanted me to take a breathalyzer ..." He turned back to the water. "I refused."

The sky grumbled as a storm neared. The sun dipped behind a bank of clouds; it now appeared near to dusk, even though it was just past lunchtime.

She shifted in the sand to face him, but he wouldn't look at her. "You did *what?*"

"He caught me. I knew it. He knew it. I told him I couldn't do it. So I left. Just like that, I walked out."

Krista shook her head in disgust. "You've always had it easy growing up." She seethed. "You know that? *Everything* came easy for you. Looks, charm, sports. One by one, you're pissing those away. What are you going to do now?"

"I ... I don't know. I got a sixty-day severance. It'll run out soon enough."

"Before you refused the breathalyzer, you could've called Neal." She couldn't look at him anymore. She stood and brushed the sand from her knees. "I don't get it, Jack. You're smart. You knew what would happen. Why would you do something so ... so stupid?"

"I know, I fucked up." He fought back tears. "Let's just say ... I saw something I didn't want to see, that no one should have to see."

He looked over his shoulder at the summer house.

She felt like a heel. Jack, no matter his outward bravado, was a sensitive soul. He was a patrolman, sure, but the job was more than handing out speeding tickets. Gruesome car crashes happened all the time, and patrolmen were often first on the scene.

"Jack ..."

Something in her voice made him finally return her gaze.

"I'm here for you," she said. "There are other jobs, other professions."

He smiled cynically. "Sure, and I've already pissed away two. I'm sure I'm lucky enough to find a third."

A thunderclap rumbled through the woods. The gray clouds opened, all at once, and sheets of rain fell, the droplets fat and cold, splattering against their skin in thick splotches.

The kids broke into laughter as they rushed for the path leading back to the house.

"You know …" Jack said. "I hate the look in your eyes. The disappointment. That's the last thing I wanted."

She wanted to hug him. She wanted to slug him. All she could do was glare, but he again wouldn't even deign to look in her direction.

"I know I made a mistake … many mistakes." His eyes drifted from the raindrops dancing on the lake to the disappearing speck of his son's shirt as he scampered up the trail. "But I'll do whatever it takes … for Trev. For my family."

Krista patted his shoulder. "You're shivering. Let's go. We'll make some hot chocolate."

Jack nodded, looking down at his feet. "Okay …"

"You're going to figure things out. I know you will. You always bounce back. You thought you'd be a Major League Baseball player. That didn't happen, so you moved on. You thought you'd be a cop. That didn't happen, either. You'll find what's right for you. For Trev."

Jack squeezed his shoulder as they cut across the sand to the path.

Lightning crashed, and a peal of thunder a second later. Krista practically jumped at the sound. A gust of wind sent the beach ball the kids had been playing with toward the water; Krista felt an odd compulsion to chase after it, to make sure it was secure during the storm, and broke away from Jack, hoping to catch the ball before it touched the water.

"What the heck are you doing?" Jack called out, his voice nearly lost in the storm.

Lightning flashed across the sky.

Krista snagged the ball, inches before it reached the water's edge. She stared out at Little Whisper. For a disconcerting moment, the surface appeared to be a mat of human skin, raindrops stippling the surface like goosebumps.

"Are you coming, or what?" Jack said.

He looked pathetic with his clothes now clinging to him, his wavy hair like a wet mop.

"Go on ahead," she said. "I'll be right there."

"Suit yourself." He pulled his shirt over his head to block the rain and ran away, cutting across the sparse dune grass jutting from a narrow peninsula at the edge of the woods.

Krista turned back toward the water, letting the rain soak through her clothes, letting its chill invade her core. She closed her eyes and listened to the vibration of the storm dancing on the lake. After a minute or more, a crash of thunder forced her eyes open. She was alone, the sky the color of charcoal and day-old bruises.

The pelting rain erased all evidence of footprints; even her own had been wiped clean. A new-formed trail of child-sized prints wended through the sand near the shore and suddenly came to a halt, inches from her own feet, the tiny toe impressions pointed toward her. She searched the beach for an explanation but was left wanting.

A warm glow filtered through the trees on the sloping hill; by now, Jack would be inside the house, supervising the kids getting dry and warm.

The remaining footprints indeed led right to her very spot, but the fresh prints continued down the beach, no more than seconds old. She sucked in a ragged breath. Through the storm's gray gloom, she followed their path, picking up speed, not wanting to lose them to the sheeting rainfall.

"Please …" she muttered. "Please, wait …"

The trail curled toward the shore, then skirted higher, as if to avoid the waves churned by the sudden turn in weather.

A voice came to her on the breeze, along with a light laughter of sheer joy—a child's voice, a *girl's* voice, she was nearly certain—but dispersed like a fragment of dream losing coherence upon waking.

In a panic, she ran as fast as her sandals would allow. She focused on the prints as they neared the single-lane blacktop road, which carved through the flat plane of forested valley.

The trail suddenly disappeared, and the finely articulated prints ended with a lone depression of a right forefoot, as if the person had taken one last stride and had stepped off the face of the earth.

CHAPTER 14

After her breakfast with Poppa, Clara returned to her bedroom to get dressed. The sky threatened rain, so she pulled on her hooded poncho just in case. She checked the mirror on the back of the door and straightened the wisps of hair coming free from her ponytail. The twin beds they'd pushed together reflected back at her in the mirror. Her own bed had been made minutes after her waking. Heidi's looked more like debris left behind by some natural disaster. In some ways, she envied her cousin for her ability to relax, to not feel compelled to keep her surroundings tidy, or using the proper words for their proper usages.

Clara wore sneakers her mother had insisted on purchasing for her before this trip. They were uncomfortable and stiff, but she supposed they would suit the purpose of tromping through the woods. Her red vinyl poncho was her own selection. The fact that it reminded her of Little Red Riding Hood barely steered her decision-making process, a foolish little secret she would never admit aloud.

Before she left the room, she went back to her bed and flattened a wrinkle in the blanket. She fluffed the pillow, replacing it perfectly center on the bed. Heidi's bed drew her attention like a car wreck on the highway. She picked up the scattered pajamas on the floor, where her cousin had left them when getting dressed for a day at the beach. The urge to fold them was nearly overwhelming, but she resisted. After placing the pajamas on the unfluffed pillow, where it sat askew and nearly falling off the bed, she headed for the door without looking back.

She nearly collided with her father at the front of the house.

"Whoa, where are you going in such a rush?" he asked.

"Just trying to escape Hurricane Heidi."

"She's a bit less organized than some people I know." He grinned from the corner of his mouth. "It's not that bad, is it? I mean, sharing a room? You've always had your own space, so I know it can be an adjustment."

"It's fine," she said impatiently, wanting to get outside. "We get along great."

"Are you heading down to the beach? All the cousins went down after breakfast. I didn't know if you'd heard, since you ate with Poppa."

"I heard. But no, I'm not heading to the beach right now. I'm going for a walk."

"A walk, really?" He looked at her from head to toe. "I don't see a book. Do you have one hidden under your poncho?"

"I'm doing what you asked." She rolled her eyes. "I'm going to let my mind wander. You know, because I'm a kid, and that's what we're meant to do?"

"Yeah, I do remember saying something along those lines." He scratched his head, confused. The expression made him look a decade younger.

She smiled, leaving him to his puzzlement, and opened the door. "Goodbye, Daddy."

"Buh-bye." He shook his head as she closed the door.

She passed the porch swing, crossed into the grass, and veered off toward the garage. She hadn't seen the tiny shed built next to it until now. It was close in size to her closet back in Chicago. The door opened on rickety hinges. Even though she was still pretty short, her head nearly brushed the ceiling. She could grab something off the shelving without taking a step inside. A narrow workbench sat on the far wall, littered with plastic planting cells, a torn sack of potting soil, trowels, and a variety of seed packets. The closed-in air smelled of stale earth, as if no one had been in here since ... well, since Nan died.

A chill ran through her. *Nan.*

She had never known her great-grandmother. Sure, she had received cards from her great-grandparents on birthdays and holidays, but those brief correspondences didn't reveal anything about the people who had pretty much raised her mom and her siblings after the death of their parents. She knew even less about her grandparents. They had been good to their kids, at least that's what everyone always mentioned on the rare occasions they ever came up. It was like that whole generation of her family tree had disappeared with little trace left behind.

And now she stood in Nan's potting shed, looking for a basket, one in particular Poppa thought would serve the purpose for collecting flowers—purple nameless flowers from a narrow plateau marked out on a map crudely drawn by Poppa's tremulous hand.

"Okay, Clara, let's be ..." she whispered, "*childlike.*"

As she searched the darkened shelves for the basket, her mind flittered about from one thing to another—her odd family tree, how incongruous she was to her cousins, the ill-defined reason for her mother's hesitance over returning to the summer house.

She'd nearly given up when she spotted the straw mesh basket tucked on the bottom shelf near the door. It was well-used, the straw material frayed. Squatting low, she removed the basket from the shelf and held it up to the sunlight. Powdery dust floated in the shed's enclosed air, swirling from an invading wind gust. The basket was frayed, sure, but lightweight and collapsible. She agreed with Poppa that it was perfectly suited for the task at hand.

A powerful yet peculiar feeling overwhelmed her. A dull ache in her sternum bloomed across her ribcage and deep into her gut— momentary fright—as if sensing someone was secretly watching her from inside the tiny shed. She slammed the door closed. The shed's uneven boards revealed glimpses of interior darkness. She felt watched, and even though it was a childish flight of fancy, she hurried away, determined to not look back even when she reached the woods.

"Stop being silly," she told herself, hearing a quiver in her voice as she removed the hand-drawn map from her front pocket.

The path into the woods was directly across from the front corner of the house. She soon found a narrow trailhead between two trees, similar to the ones on the map. Heading off into the woods, she was surprised how willingly she was venturing into the unknown.

Poppa's map wasn't to scale, but when she found a geographical detail highlighted on the map—a unique copse of trees, a distinctive rock formation, a deep seam through the undulating hillside—she could easily determine her next direction. An unsteady pencil stroke indicated the path, and as she went from mark to mark, she found it easier to relax. She spotted a huge rock, taller than her, and matched it to its counterpart on the map.

The overwhelming feeling from the shed was something akin to guilt, maybe closer to regret, but it was unmistakably built whole-cloth out of a greater feeling of loss. A loss for someone she had never really known. And it frightened her.

Poppa had spent decades married to Nan. She couldn't imagine being alone so long after being a part of something greater. She wanted to know not only more about Nan, but the singular 'Nan and Poppa.'

Poppa would recount stories about their time together, if Clara felt brave enough to ask. She decided she wanted to be brave enough to ask, that she *would* be brave enough.

The sky looked anguished with motley shades of dark gray and purple clouds fighting for supremacy. Even so, as she stepped away from the surrounding trees—eyes on the map and the next cautious stride in front of her—the atmosphere around her changed. Despite threatening cloud cover, the sky brightened. The canopies retreated as the trees thinned, revealing an unfettered view of the sky.

She'd arrived at her destination.

Thunder rumbled in the distance and the air seemed to thicken. Within seconds, the ambient birdsong accompanying her tromp had silenced.

"What the?" she whispered as breath escaped her lungs.

She stood in a plateau of unquestionable beauty. Purple flowers with vibrant blossoms no bigger than her thumbnail stretched from one edge of the woods to the next. The flowers reached her knees and tickled her as she slowly walked among them, not wanting to damage a single stem or stamen. She couldn't help smiling, so full of joy that she wanted to share it with someone.

After setting the basket among the flowers, she began to pick, choosing only those at the height of their beauty. With long stems she could later trim, the basket quickly filled. She purposely spread out her harvest across the carpet of blossoms, lest she create a barren area where an invasive plant could get a foothold. After twenty minutes, she'd gathered more than enough to overflow the basket.

"Poppa's going to love these."

She grinned as she hefted the basket, before backtracking to the tree line toward the trail leading to the summer house. Disoriented, she pulled the map from her pocket.

Another peal of thunder rumbled the sky, closer. She'd have to hurry home to beat the rain. She matched the maple tree bordering the flower field with the one on the map, and then noticed someone had carved into its thick trunk: a heart the size of her palm, the carving relatively fresh. She read the inscription:

PIERCE

+

FRANCIE

"Poppa ... Nan," she whispered.

Her heart ached as she touched the rough bark.

"Isn't that silly?" a voice called out from over her shoulder.

Clara dropped the basket of flowers and nearly tripped as she whirled on her heel. A girl approached from the other side of the field. She picked a flower and pushed the purple blossom behind her ear. Untamed golden locks bobbed as she walked, her skin as pale as cream, eyes a luminous blue. They were around the same age, but that's where their similarities ended.

Clara subconsciously stepped away from the girl. "Excuse me?"

The girl bent down for the basket and opened the straw flaps. "The heart." She looked up at Clara as she carefully placed the blossoms in the basket. "I heard you giggle."

"No, I didn't laugh." Clara paused, thrown off by not just the girl's sudden appearance, but the *appearance* of her. Her fingernails were cracked and caked with dirt. She wore cuffed jean shorts and a white short-sleeved shirt over a dark green bikini. Sweat dampened the shirt's collar. Grass stains and mud streaked her clothes and legs. Clara became aware of how sore her own feet were getting from her new stiff sneakers, and then realized the girl was barefoot. "Well, I did laugh, but not like that. I ... I think it's sweet."

The girl placed a final flower and then handed the basket over to Clara.

Clara wanted to grab the basket and run back to the summer house. "Thanks."

The girl put her hands on her hips. "Do I know you? You look so familiar."

"I'm not from around here. My family is visiting ... from Chicago."

"Oh, okay."

"You're from around here?" Clara asked.

More thunder rumbled, and the sky darkened even more.

"I'm from the other side of the lake."

Leaves fluttered as it started to rain. The wind kicked up, but the branches above sheltered them.

"Are those," the girl said, pointing at the basket of flowers, "for Nan?"

"Well ... kind of." The basket felt heavy in her hands, even though its contents weighed next to nothing. "How did you—?"

"I heard you mention Nan. Nan and ... Poppa, right?"

"Yes. My great-grandparents. Nan is ... well, she died."

"Sorry to hear that."

"It was a while ago. I hardly knew her. Poppa asked me to pick some of Nan's favorite flowers."

"That's nice. Real nice." The girl's eyes dimmed, and then she looked away. "Everyone dies. Isn't that awful? My dad died. And my mom ... she ... um ..." She shook her head in frustration, as if she was having trouble remembering. Her hands, with her fingers splayed, began to palsy at her sides.

"Are you okay?" Clara rolled forward on the balls of her feet but hesitated to step closer.

Rainfall breached the protective canopies, splattering icy cold against her skin.

"My mom …" Suddenly, the girl clapped her hands together and her eyes flashed wide as the rain pelted down, flattening her untamed curls. Her skin seemed to glow, becoming translucent with the wetness streaming across its pale surface. "She's an evil bitch."

Lightning flashed, and as Clara gasped at the girl's coarseness, thunder tumbled through the woods. Clara could never speak so ill of her own mother.

"I'm sorry," Clara said, her voice swallowed by the storm.

"What?" The girl stepped close, clearly inside Clara's personal space, inches away. She leaned in, offering Clara her ear. An earthy scent drifted off the girl. Dirt and grime and sour sweat.

"I said I'm sorry!" Clara nearly shouted. "You know, about your mom."

"It's okay," the girl said and shrugged. "I'm used to it. She leaves me alone. I just wish her boyfriends would do the same." The girl pulled away, her mad grin tilted up to the rain. An unnerving energy flowed from her; the arms' width of air between them practically crackled. "Let's get out of this rain."

"The house where I'm staying is close," Clara said. She couldn't imagine what her family would think about this girl.

"Not close enough." The girl looked around, as if deciding on a direction. She surprised Clara by taking her hand in her own. "Come on, let's go!"

Clara didn't know why she went so willingly, but as they crossed the field and entered a path on the opposite side, they were both running, and as lightning illuminated their footfalls, the girl's energy trip-hammered into her own body. Clara felt alive, intensely so, as if she had only now taken her first breath, her first step, her first waking thought.

The girl tugged her up a muddy hill, and then down into a gully of sopping wet ferns and hanging vines like writhing snakes in the drenching rainfall.

A stabbing cramp formed in Clara's side.

"Where are you taking me?"

"Down there!" The girl beamed a toothy smile. Soaked hair draped her brow, nearly touching her eyes. "Just a little farther!"

They nearly ran right into a swollen creek at the gulley. The girl dug her bare heels into the mossy forest floor, sliding to a stop. Clara, still holding the girl's hand, whipped around almost a whole circle before finally arresting her momentum. The creek rushed a foot away, a torrent of muddy water, floating leaves, and torn up vegetation.

"There it is!" The girl released Clara's hand and scampered away.

A centuries-old tree had recently fallen over, creating a concavity at its base. Tangled roots, stripped tree bark, and a thick mat of underbrush formed the walls and roof of a natural cave Clara would've easily overlooked under different circumstances. The girl climbed inside, disappearing from view, save her mud-caked feet dangling from the opening.

Clara felt a paralyzing moment of indecision. Her anxiety, already roused by the adrenaline-infused run through the woods, was now a raging fire.

"Come on!" the girl called out.

Clara stepped closer, the cold rain running in runnels beneath her shirt. She saw beyond the girl's muddy feet—clear up to the knobs of her knees and the cuffed shorts—from where she sat in the gloomy shelter. The storm was nearly as chaotic as her thoughts. She reached the tumbled-over tree and its enormous girth became evident; it was at least twice as thick as her own height.

"What are you afraid of?" the girl yelled.

"Everything," Clara whispered.

In truth, she wasn't afraid of everything. Just mud and spider webs, and muddy spider webs, and burrowing animals—*and what burrowing animals lived in the Western Michigan forest? Foxes? Wolverines? Werewolves?* Not to mention the wild barefoot girl.

Is she feral? Clara wondered.

She took a deep breath, leaned over, and pushed aside the curtain of roots and underbrush.

"See? It's dry …" the girl said, "well, drier than out there."

Clara shivered, her arms coursing with gooseflesh. She climbed into the opening. A small log ran the width of the covered space, and the girl sat on it like it was a park bench. Clara couldn't stand with the low ceiling, so she sat next to her.

The sound of the storm retreated, even though it was raining just as hard.

"By the way, my name's Melody."

Both girls stared out into the downpour. It was hypnotic, like staring at the white noise of an empty TV channel.

"I'm Clara."

She didn't spot any spider webs, and the space was so small that she would've readily seen a burrowing animal.

"I should've asked you before I showed you this place … can you keep it secret?"

"I, well, sure. I won't tell anyone."

"Good."

They were quiet for some time, watching the rain and lightning, counting the seconds before the accompanying thunderclap. The time between lengthened. The storm was passing.

"I come here sometimes when I need to be alone. I've never showed it to anybody. I figure, sometimes you need to be left alone. Sometimes that's the only way to confront the noise in your head. Know what I mean?"

Clara didn't have a clue. If she ever had the desire to be on her own, she would merely retreat to her bedroom and her growing library of books. She couldn't fathom the state of Melody's home life if she felt the need to escape to a fallen over tree in the middle of the woods.

"It's weird being in here, right? But there's something, I don't know … comforting, enclosing yourself in a tight space, almost like the dirt walls are embracing us. This is the only place I can let everything go. When my head can be clear and empty."

Clara smelled dirt and moldering decay in the humid air as she shivered. Melody scooted closer until their arms touched. The girl tilted her head, resting it on Clara's shoulder. The intimate contact made Clara's muscles tense. She waited for Melody to say something, but all she heard was her steady breathing. It soothed her, in a way, how the girl's breathing sounded so normal, so human, especially against the chaos of the passing storm. Clara didn't mind the silence.

CHAPTER 15

Krista stood under the hot shower spray, as she had for going on twenty minutes, trying to forget the solitary trail of footprints on the beach. Though she'd chased away the chill from being caught in the storm, she couldn't help the goosebumps still prickling her arms. She nudged the dial hotter and steam billowed around her like fog. It condensed on the glass door, obscuring the rest of the bathroom. She closed her eyes and angled her head down as far as it would go, luxuriating in the near-scalding water rolling off her shoulders.

She was desperate for her mind to meander aimlessly through mundane matters, but her thoughts kept returning to the one particular morning that had so indelibly marked her more than twenty years earlier. There was so much about that day she couldn't remember, *refused* to remember. The memories only brought unbearable pain.

It's all my fault. Exhaled breath caught in her throat. *If I hadn't been so stupid ...*

The shower was nearly hot enough to blister her skin, but she was no longer present to feel it. Her memories strengthened, almost painfully so, gaining depth and constitution.

The trail of footprints was so clear in her mind that she could lean over to see their sharp edges and distinctive patterns in the sand. Swirls and curlicues. *Flowergirlz* ... an off-brand shoe, cute, but cheaply made, white with pink flourishes on the sides, the tongue a solid palette of pink flowers. She knew this because she had always known this, at least since that long-ago summer.

Breann had loved those shoes.

Krista squatted, her knees popping, the shower spray drumming into her back. She reached out through the heated steam and the fog of time and ran her fingers over the nearest shoe print, crumbling the sharp edge, the sand cold to the touch and with the just-after-rainfall consistency of brown sugar.

Her brow furrowed as she tried to draw in the details. She wanted to see more, but couldn't. The harder she tried, the more the past receded, leaving her a red and wrinkled mess on the shower floor.

"We had a fight ..." she whispered, pushing wet hair from her eyes, remembering.

Of course! We had a fight!

For the life of her, she couldn't recall why she had argued with Breann, but their one and only fight had taken place after breakfast on the morning of her disappearance.

It wouldn't change anything, but Krista wanted to know what they had fought about, needed to know what had sent them on diverging paths.

She clenched her eyelids tighter, wallowing in the misery of that morning, of that afternoon and the subsequent days, letting the pain fuel her recollection.

A flash of memory: Breann's smile, a close-up of Breann's crooked teeth, and how she would absently run the tip of her tongue across the eye tooth whenever nervous; and the freckles on her nose, how they were imperceptible at the start of summer and seemed to darken until she went back to Indianapolis, where her family spent the majority of the year.

Krista wanted to recall her laughter, but it eluded her. Instead, she got those August-dark freckles, clear as day, and the crooked smile sagging until it became a twisted snarl. Brown eyes boring into her, darkening, like two specks of coal pressed into her flesh.

"Say something!" Krista said, crossing her arms and glaring at her friend.

Breann stomped her barefoot into the beach sand.

"I can't believe you would do that to me!"

The sun baked down on them. Over the weeks, Krista's skin had transformed from a scalded red to an even caramel. Even though she had been at Little Whisper for just as long, Breann's skin peeled raw in places, patchy tan in others.

"What? What did I do?" Krista felt like her world was crumbling.

"That's the thing—you don't even know!" Breann's lip curled. Crimson spread across her cheeks, equal parts sunburn and escalating anger.

Krista thought long and hard. "You're mad because I went to see *The Nutty Professor* with Sandy Armstrong?" She took a stab at the reason behind her friend's anger, and from Breann's nasty scowl, she'd hit her mark. "You said you didn't want to go. You said it looked stupid. Guess what? It *was* stupid!"

"You don't even know how lucky you are!"

Breann kicked the sand.

"I invited you. I invited you *first!* Before Sandy. You said you didn't want to go. What's the big deal?"

Breann turned away, absently running her fingers over the heart charm hanging by a chain around her neck. Her head bobbed and she was obviously crying, but she didn't emit a sound. Krista had given her the charm for her birthday at the beginning of the summer, and had never seen her without it.

Krista reached for Breann's shoulder, but drew away before touching her.

"Bree, I ... I don't understand. You're my best friend. Nothing's going to change that."

"Movies cost money. Going to the Shop 'N Gas for candy costs money. Going to the outlets costs money. You have it. I don't." Her friend turned to face her with bloodshot eyes.

"That doesn't matter! Don't you get it? I would've paid for you."

"That's the problem. I *do* get it. You're the one who doesn't." Breann shrugged, wiped at her falling tears.

Krista watched as her best friend stormed across the beach, all the way across her grandparents' lakefront and the adjacent properties. Breann slowed to a stop but didn't turn around. Krista could call out to her, but that would be giving in, and she felt like she was *always* giving in. While she'd wanted to go to the movie with Breann, she could be *so* moody sometimes!

Breann started off again, her arms crossed in front of her, the sand kicking up from her strides like a snow plow clearing the streets after a blizzard.

Krista couldn't remember ever being so mad. Breann had basically called her a snob and stormed off before she could defend herself.

And then Krista had …?

She couldn't remember anything more. She could've gone up to the summer house and lounged on the back deck. She could've retreated to the den to watch TV. It didn't matter what she had done after Breann had stormed away. The only thing that mattered was that she had let her friend leave in the first place.

It's all my fault.

She stood and wiped tears and shower spray from her eyes.

She'd assumed they'd have a chance to make up, to put the stupid fight behind them. At that age, how could you not assume there would be time for apologies?

Someone knocked on the door.

"Yes?" The tremor in her voice surprised her.

The door opened and someone stepped inside.

"It's just me," Neal said. "You okay?"

"Yeah, just caught a chill out in the rain, so I'm trying to warm up. I'm almost done."

The shower door slid open a few inches and he peeked inside. He raised an eyebrow as he stared at her naked body. "Good." He held up a fresh towel. "I'm your personal drying service."

Krista rolled her eyes and shut off the water.

"Okay, but no funny business."

"No funny business," he agreed with a frown, "but just so you know, I work for tips."

She wanted to be angry at him for interrupting her shower, for ruining her reminiscing … but she wasn't angry. If anything, his timing couldn't have been more perfect.

"You're without shame."

"You wouldn't have it any other way."

Krista couldn't help cracking a smile. He *was* shameless. Neal would often conveniently find an excuse to see her in the shower, and then insist on drying her off. These coincidences sometimes led to immediate heated encounters. Other times they planted seeds for later on that night. Whatever the case, her husband adored her, and she felt lucky to have found someone she clicked with, on so many levels.

Krista stepped out onto the floor mat and turned her back to him. He dried her hair until it was merely damp, and then ran the towel over her back, down to her buttocks. He lingered longer than needed, and right when she was going to call him out, he said, "Arms."

She raised her arms as Neal continued to pat her dry.

"We had a fight."

"Excuse me?" he said, and handed her the towel. "I don't remember any fight."

She wrapped the towel around her head.

"No, not *us*. Me and … Breann. The morning she disappeared. I just remembered. I wanted her to come with me to see *The Nutty Professor*, and she said she didn't want to. I wound up going with another girl from around the lake, Sandy Armstrong. I just realized … she *did* want to go. But she couldn't afford a day at the movies, and I'd gone without her. And I didn't understand how I was rubbing it in her face."

"Krista, don't. You can't—"

"And, yeah, I remembered the fight, I guess, over the years, but I never really understood it until now. It was a stupid fight, but back then it felt like the world would end. It hurt so bad to have my best friend turn her back on me. For a long time, I blamed her. I thought she was being controlling since she didn't want me to go to the movies without her, with someone else. But it was my fault."

"Krista …" Neal said. Instead of continuing, he wrapped his arms around her and drew her close. He held her for several minutes, until her limbs had no choice but to relax.

They swayed together, enjoying the closeness.

Krista exhaled a long breath and pulled away from him. "We

need to get going, or people are going to wonder what's going on in here."

"It's vacation! Wild rumpuses are supposed to be had!"

He was trying so hard to lift her from her malaise. She chuckled, feeling so much better than before he entered the bathroom.

"We've already had a wild rumpus, remember?"

"There can never be too many wild rumpuses!" His eyes widened expectantly, but when she didn't react, he handed her the bra from the pile of clean clothes stacked on the toilet seat. "Okay, but I'm going to watch you get dressed so I can imagine it in reverse."

"Shameless!" She took the bra and quickly covered up. She turned her back to him and he worked the clasp for her. She stepped into Capri pants and buttoned the top button, completing the reverse striptease.

"Leah asked me for legal advice," Neal said.

"Oh, yeah?"

"She's thinking about leaving Curtis. For good. She wants to move here. Her and the kids. And she wants sole custody."

"What? She can't stay here. What did you tell her?"

"Well, first of all, to talk to you. I also mentioned I'd look into it, if that's what she really wants. Sid Lowrey, he's in my pick-up basketball league at the club, one of the best family law attorneys in Chicago. I told her I'd give him a call."

"I know it's over between them … she explained a lot of it to me already. It's just, moving here with the kids?"

"Think how much more we could see them."

"I don't know. I always assumed after … you know, when the time comes, we'd sell the place. It has too many memories."

"I know you're sensitive about it, but if it's the best solution for Leah and the kids, then you should keep an open mind about it."

"Well … I guess." It was hard to argue with his reasoning.

"Good. How about a bite to eat?"

She nodded and Neal kissed her forehead and opened the bathroom door. Steam escaped the enclosed space as they entered the hallway. Her mood brightened, not just from the shower, but also Neal's presence, his persistence, his care. She twined her fingers in his and squeezed, hoping her contentment would last.

She attempted to see the summer house differently, through the lens of an adult, through the lens of someone who might come out to visit her sister and kids in the not-so-distant future. It had been such a wonderful place to spend her childhood summers—at least those summers before Breann's disappearance—but it had also been the place of her darkest nightmare. She didn't know if she could reconcile the two differing memories.

When they reached the entryway, the door opened wide and Clara stepped inside. She was sodden from the peak of her head to the tips of her toes. Water dripped from the edges of her soaked rain poncho, forming a circle of wetness around her.

"Hello, parents!" Clara beamed with exuberance.

Krista stood stunned, unsure what was happening. Clara's eyes sparkled, almost disconcertingly.

"What is it, Clara?" Neal said. "What happened?"

"I let my mind wander. I let myself be a kid."

"Where were you?" Krista asked. "I thought you were some-where inside, with a book?"

"She went for a walk," Neal said and cleared his throat.

Krista glared at him. "You knew she was out in this mess?"

"Well ..."

"It's okay, Mom. I was just off in the woods." She held up a full basket of purple flowers. "I got these for Poppa. They're Nan's favorite!"

The mesh basket dripped rainwater.

Krista wanted to be angry at her daughter, but she didn't know what the official reason would be. Going for a walk? Picking flowers for her ailing great-grandfather? Letting herself relax and enjoy the day?

"Okay ..." Krista reached for the basket. "Let's get these in a vase. Aren't you freezing?"

"No, not at all!" Clara spun in a circle, sending the water beads on her poncho flying in every direction. When she finished two revolutions, she pulled the poncho up over her head. "I better hang this up!" She stopped long enough to give her father a peck on the cheek, and then spirited away, down the hallway.

"What in the world just happened?" Krista asked.

"Our daughter decided to be a kid for once?"

"Why do I feel like I should be worried?"

"Lack of experience?" Neal wrapped his arm around her. "It's not like you've ever raised a child before."

CHAPTER 16

The bedside chair creaked as Breann climbed onto it. She squatted on her haunches and rested her elbows on scabbed knees. As she settled, her toes curled over the edge of the chair, the nails long, cracked, and caked with drying mud and blood.

The woman slept, curled on her side, unaware of Breann's observation. She inhaled cleanly, deeply. Her exhaled breath rumbled, her lips fluttering and wet.

Leah.

Breann snared the word from the flotsam floating through the house. Words, emotions, desires, and still more, hovered among the house's overburdened bookshelves, the forgotten knickknacks, the dusty quilts; every square inch of its extremity. The air the family breathed seethed with energy they emitted—now trapped—among the spirits, among the memories of this place. They inhaled the debris of time, added to its burden, released it back out into the world, soiled further.

Leah Whalen … Could this woman be …? She's just a girl … a girl just like me.

Breann toyed with the name, rolling it over her tongue as if a solid object. She extended a hand across the short divide between the chair and the bed, between the long chasm between the dead and the living. Her fingers hovered over Leah's cheek, trembling. She remembered her, vaguely, beyond her name, but there was more depth to the elusive memory. There had to be.

The corner of the woman's mouth twisted in a familiar way,

making it quite obvious this was the same person as the little girl she once knew. *Leah Whalen, it really is her!*—stirred, shivered as she slumbered and snugged the quilt over her shoulder. Her brow tensed as her lips formed muted words. She stirred, ready to rise from sleep.

Breann would rouse her, she decided, would demand an explanation, one that would reconcile the little tomboy girl captured in her fading memory with the woman before her now.

Before she could do anything, Breann sensed another presence. One like her, but … void and vile. It was here, now, inches away, a shadow of a shadow. Breann felt a sudden depth of cold unlike any she'd ever experienced descend over her like a shroud.

She tightened her trembling fingers into a fist and pulled her hand away. Just as quickly, Leah's facial muscles relaxed, and her lips ceased their silent susurrations.

Breann jumped down from the chair, snared blindly into the void, lashed out with her muddy-nail stubs. She hunched over defensively, ready for whatever might beset her.

"Leave me alone!" She screamed herself hoarse as Leah shifted onto her back, discerning some vague reverberation of Breann's disembodied voice. "You can't have me!"

The shroud darkened around her, taking her away from this place, this time. A pinprick violet iris formed at the center of her vision and swirled, growing vast as it picked up speed, subtly lightening the surrounding deadscape. Breann tried to shut her eyes from the awakening sight, from the memory being forcefully recalled for her, but she was unable to discard it from her senses.

Cloying motor oil and cheap aftershave. Rank body odor and blood.

She couldn't move. Sweat drenched her skin. In the brightening gloom, she saw a porthole window with brighter light beyond, light so vivid it brought stabbing pain to her temples. As she tried to steady her breathing in her confined space, a chemical odor swept in, making her eyelids heavy. She shifted again and the plastic pulled taut across her body, her knees tightening against her chest, the sweat gathering on her shoulders painful from her sunburn.

"You don't even know how lucky you are!" a man said in a fake falsetto.

She wanted to speak but was unable to form words. Her head lolled, and it took all her will to keep her eyes open.

"That's what you said," the voice said, no longer falsetto. "I heard you plain as day. And you know what? You're right, Breann. She doesn't have a clue about her luck. Her privilege."

Her narrow vision filled with beauty—stunning blue eyes in a handsome face. His eyes carried laughter, a trace of madness, even though it never reached his lips.

"I wasn't sure about you," the man said. "Not until I heard you tell off that rich little cunt. No, you're tough as nails. And I want to know more about *that*. All of it. I want to know what made you so. We have much to learn."

He brushed a lock of hair from her eyes, tucking it behind her ear.

"Please," Breann said, or thought she said. Her mind was so foggy that her voice could've been trapped shy of her teeth.

"I'm sorry I was so rough with you. I couldn't risk being seen."

Pain throbbed at the back of her skull.

The man moved around the enclosed space, momentarily blotting out the light from the porthole window. Pain lanced her scalp from where …

From where he hit me. With one of those tire-changing thingamajigs.

She remembered fireworks sparking across her vision. But before that …

Sand. Running in the sand. Running and so mad at the world. So mad at Krista Whalen … Krista and her snobby friend, Sandy.

It wasn't stupid. Krista shouldn't have gone to the movies without her. Shouldn't have switched her out for that snob Sandy like she was changing into a clean pair of socks. Not when I'm now trapped in this … this …

Van.

The dark blue van had pulled up alongside her, stopping her just shy of the road. And the sliding door opened to the lakeside beach like a hungry mouth. And his gaze rooted her in place. There was something mesmerizing, and she stared back at him, trying to figure it out. And in those violent few seconds, he'd taken her. His strength a monster strength. Her feeble attempts to defend herself subdued with a backhand to the face, followed by the blow to her head.

And now, he wants to learn from me. About me.

"You're so strong, Breann," the man said. "And beautiful. So incredibly beautiful." He caressed her cheek with the back of his fingers, his touch gentle across the patches of sunburn and freckles. He shushed her and wiped a tear from the corner of her eye. "I bet no one ever tells you that, but you are. Seeing you now, in this very moment, your beauty makes my heart ache, and I want to know everything …"

She thrashed about, but it was no use. She'd been bound in pliable plastic wrap. All she accomplished was to stoke a heat that had nowhere to go. It gathered across her skin, making her feel feverish and ready to pass out.

Please, God, save me …

She had never prayed in her life.

Not honestly. Not with full hope and devotion. Not until now.

I will give myself over to You. I will spend my life doing good things for others, and I won't ever get jealous or angry again. Please, God, get me out of here. Please, God, oh, please, I don't want to … I … I don't know what causes that glint in his eyes.

Breann learned about the glint in his eyes, but not until long after the man learned what made her tick.

Breann sobbed incoherently as she cradled her knees to her chest. Her spirit could no longer move, not while trapped in the nightmare of her death, not so long as the new presence—the presence like her but void and vile—held her in its grip.

She relived her time with the man, an endless stream of horrors stretching across three incomprehensible and agonizing days ending only with the mercy of her final heartbeat. The longer she obsessed over her final torturous days, the more darkness swept into her spirit. And the darkness gave her strength.

~

Leah sat up, drenched in sweat, certain she'd heard a child's cry.

"Heidi?" she whispered.

She listened, growing uncertain about what she thought she'd heard.

"Clara?" she called out to a night trapped in the stillness just shy of dawn.

She wiped sweat from her forehead with the back of her hand, peeled the fabric from where it clung to her chest. A sudden chill rolled across her skin. After turning her pillow over to a fresh side, she settled back in, now cooled off enough to pull the quilt back over her shoulder.

Her eyes started to flicker closed when a sudden thought crossed her mind.

"Breann?" she asked the empty room. She waited for a reply long into dawn's advance, never trusting the silence.

CHAPTER 17

The purest form of madness thrived during the ambiguous hours after nightfall. Jack had long known this truth and tonight was certainly no exception. Sure, not all things mad happened at night, but the absence of light left no room for equivocating or self-deception. The darkness revealed all.

He leaned against the den's leather couch, staring at the dying embers in the fireplace. Children's voices surrounded him, disembodied pleas he had no sane reason to hear, let alone acknowledge as real.

Jackssson ... Why did you let it happen? they said in a collective hiss.

They heckled and berated him one moment, innocently cajoled him the next. Nothing would please him more than to lash out, to shout for them to leave him to the silence, to the aloneness he so deserved. No matter his inner turmoil, they continued unabated.

You could have stopped it, Jackson, the little whispers repeated. *We're so lonely. Won't you come see us?*

He patted his pockets, only to remember he'd left his flask on the sideboard next to his bed. *Probably for the best,* he thought.

Booze and weed had done nothing to numb him from the unravelling around him. *Inside* him. It had started long before his return to the summer house, had plagued him since Nan's death. To pinpoint the moment of his decline, the initial tugging at the assorted loosening threads of his sanity, he would have to admit it had begun right damn here, in this very room.

Trying to ignore the voices, he pushed away from the couch,

took hold of the poker and rattled it in aggravation against the ashy logs. A shower of sparks flitted high toward the flue before shedding their heat and light and settling back to the hearth. Almost desperately, he tried to enliven the spent logs, but they had nothing left to give. He sighed and dropped the poker in its stand.

To his astonishment, even though it was the middle of the night, pure light illuminated the kitchen. The brightness nearly staggered him. Pain throbbed behind his eyes until they adjusted. He braced a hand against the couch until he regained his bearings. Not only did sunlight stream through the windows, he also heard voices in the kitchen, but not those of the tormented children, which had retreated to the periphery.

He stepped toward the sweet, frail voice he'd nearly forgotten.

"I remember packing sandwiches like the ones I'm making. I'd make enough for your grandfather and me, but he'd be so nervous watching you play he'd never eat his share. Every. Single. Time."

Laughter; the sound magical, soothing.

Nan ...

Adrenaline seared his heart, left his limbs sluggish. His feet grew heavy, so impossibly heavy, but he pressed on, stumbling through the doorway and into the impossibly lit kitchen.

Pain exploded across his temple when he saw her, a bone-deep ache that nearly blinded him. He rubbed at watering eyes, blinking until his vision cleared and the pain began to ebb. She stood with her back to him, oblivious, busy making something on the prepping counter. His legs became unsteady as an anguished groan escaped his lips.

"No, no, this can't be happening," he whispered.

She didn't react.

"This can't be happening!" he shouted.

Nan remained unmoved by his intrusion. She lifted a bottle of yellow mustard, shook its contents toward the spout and sprayed some on the sandwich she was making.

"Why did you make the food for Poppa if you knew he wouldn't eat it?" The voice sounded familiar, but tinny, as if heard through a failing stereo speaker.

A younger version of himself sat on a stool at the island, waiting for his lunch.

He didn't realize how much he'd changed in such a short amount of time.

"Because he didn't want you to know he was nervous!" Jack shouted, suddenly remembering Nan's reply verbatim from this very conversation.

"Because he didn't want you to know he was nervous," Nan said. She turned from the counter with a smile and a plate of food for her grandson. "If you knew he was nervous, then you might not focus on the game."

"Nan, that's silly," the Jack sitting at the island said. He bit into the sandwich and mustard gushed across his lips.

Jack's mouth began to water as it filled with something tangy. *Mustard.* He ran his tongue across his lips, tasting it. His mouth began to fill, even as he instinctively started to chew: ham, lettuce, tomato, delicious and cold against the roof of his mouth. He swallowed the guts of a nonexistent sandwich down a throat as dry as desert sand. He gagged, and closed his eyes, gasping for breath as a sliver of ham went down the wrong pipe. Mustard stung his nostrils. He coughed and spit, feeling helpless as his body resisted choking.

A hard slap hit him between the shoulder blades. And again. His windpipe opened and he took a gulp of air. The chair beneath him felt real. Solid. Familiar. The food slid down his throat. Air inflated and calmed his lungs.

"You always eat too fast. Ever since you were little." Nan stood at his side, still with her hand on his back, no longer slapping but rubbing in gentle circles. Like she always had. Like she had when she was alive. The pain at his temple flared and ached.

He wondered what was happening: a seizure, an embolism, something to disrupt his grounding in reality.

Jack blinked through watery eyes, looked back over his shoulder—from the island, now—only somewhat surprised not to no see a slightly older version of himself standing near the doorway observing this interaction. He was here. *Now.* In the daylight. It was once again November 3rd, a year and a half ago. He would always remember the date. Always.

He remembered feeling so happy in this moment during its first iteration. Nan, just as she had before, left his side to fetch him a glass of cold water. It was all playing out as it had. Why did it have to be this day of all days?

Nan brought the water to the island, set it next to his plate, placed a reassuring hand on his forearm. "You okay now?"

He stared at her, certainly longer than the first time he experienced this conversation, as if expecting to discover something amiss. Her eyes narrowed as she awaited his answer. He rested a hand on hers. Warm. Solid. Real.

"Yeah, I'm fine." Jack cleared his throat. "Just the wrong pipe is all."

"You're thirty years old, Jackson. I shouldn't have to tell you to slow down when you're eating."

He felt a sudden immeasurable anger. This couldn't be happening. Not again. Not when he could vary from the script of this memory at any moment. He could climb onto the island and back-flip to the floor. He could sing the theme song to Sesame Street at the top of his lungs.

Nan, she was here now.

Since her passing, he'd often thought he'd trade nearly anything to see her alive once again. And, somehow, it was happening. Instead of pushing back against the memory, he embraced it. He delved into his memory, found the appropriate response.

"I know. Funny, I find myself doing the same thing with Trevor."

Something niggled at the back of his brain, but he tried his best to ignore it.

"You're doing such a fine job with my great-grandson."

Nan sat on the stool next to him.

He'd forgotten the sparkle in her eyes, the mixture of wisdom and love. He wanted this moment to last, but just as any memory was merely a series of details and chain reactions, this recollection continued, as if propelled by some greater outside force.

"I never thought I'd live long enough," she said, "to see another generation born, let alone grow into a fine young man."

He felt an even stronger reaction to Nan's words than the first time around. Emotion tightened his throat. He'd come here to get away from Trevor, who was staying for the weekend with Leah, Curtis, and their kids. Jack had felt guilty for feeling overwhelmed by his own son, who only wanted to spend every waking minute with him, to strangle him with hugs and sit antsy-pants while Jack read aloud, yet again, *James and the Giant Peach*. He'd felt guilt then, more so now.

To defuse his emotions, he grabbed the one remaining plate from the counter. He'd bring it to Poppa's writing desk, where he was hard at work on his new book.

He would. Not Nan. No, not again.

"Oh, thank goodness you noticed." Nan took it from his grasp, even though he tried gripping the plate harder, tried to clench it so hard he imagined the ceramic shattering into a million pieces. "When he's in the middle of a book, he'd forget to eat if I didn't put food right under his nose."

"But …" Jack wanted to divert her from the task, to sway her from her destiny. His body wouldn't cooperate.

"Be right back." Nan left the kitchen, humming a light tune.

"Okay," he said, as if the choked whisper of a word had been forced out from his lungs by a giant fist.

The niggling at the back of his brain—a warning.

He tried to turn back in the direction Nan had gone, but his motions were not his own, or rather, at least not of this moment. As he strained to move counter to history, sweat traced his forehead, gathered at his temples. He tried to avoid sitting. His eyes widened as his hand lifted the sandwich to his mouth. He tried to avoid its advance, but he bit into it, chewed.

Nan returned to the kitchen, her face stark white, her gaze distant.

"Is something wrong, Nan?" he asked. The words came easily. It was no stretch to feel unease with how drastically her appearance had changed in that short time.

"Just … I'm just fine, dear." She walked zombie-like toward the sliding door leading to the deck. "I need to water my plants."

"I can do it."

Please let me do it! Please, just stop. Please don't do it! The words stuck at the back of his throat. Jack tried with all his might to spit them out, but couldn't.

"No need. You finish up your lunch."

She went out the sliding door, closing it behind her. She lifted the metal watering can from the corner of the deck and walked out of view. The spigot squealed when she cranked the dial. Water gushed into the metal can.

Jack smiled. Not that he wanted to. Not when he knew what was about to happen. He smiled because, in truth, in the time of its happening, he didn't really want to help Nan. He'd wanted to finish his sandwich, maybe peruse the fridge for iced tea. He'd only offered to help because he'd known she'd turn him down. The smile broadened as he took another bite from the sandwich. Sweat streaked his face, dampening his shirt collar.

Nan came back into view.

Jack watched, transfixed, as she touched a delicate yellow blossom. She pinched a weed from the soil, tossed it over the railing. After watering each and every plant, she returned the watering can to the corner of the deck.

Jack finished his lunch and placed his plate in the sink.

Nan stood at the threshold of the top stair. She crossed herself—something he'd found odd the first time, and doubly so now—and stretched her arms out wide. She shifted forward on the balls of her feet, as if bracing against a great gale blowing off the lake. She leaned farther still, and somehow he knew her eyes were closed.

Jack, still fighting the force holding him in place, felt the grip on his muscles loosen. He managed to take a step against the will of history, and a second step more easily, the third nearly normal. He reached the door and yanked it open, but he was too late.

Nan pitched forward until gravity took hold of her and she fell out of view.

Her body thudding down the twenty-odd steps came back to him in memory even as he relived them. By the time he reached the railing, she had come to rest in a twisted heap of broken bones.

Jack screamed—then and now—descending the steps two and three at a time. When he reached her side, he lifted her bloodied head onto his lap.

She was dead. Again, she was gone.

Madness roared through his head with the force of an approaching storm, a rush of screaming wind. The violence played a shrill song upon the surrounding trees. It was inside him, threatening to tear his mind apart.

Unable to witness her perpetual stare, Jack covered Nan's open eyes with his palm. The heat of her face drained away. The roaring in his ears dampened to a whisper.

He looked down at his lap, now empty.

Darkness pushed away the remnants of memory.

He sat on the sandy final step, alone, his head swaying. The sounds of laughing children filled the audible void; they jeered his weakness, his absence of light.

CHAPTER 18

Clara fought against rising from sleep, not wanting to ruin the nearly overwhelming sense of joy strumming through her. A smile creased her face. Low laughter filled her belly. Her eroding dream made her nerves tingle with excitement, yet she could no longer ignore the cool pillow against her cheek. As she struggled to maintain the elusive tether, she not only drifted toward waking, she felt impelled from sleep, thrust from its warmth.

Clara willed her eyes closed as she grasped in vain to the tenuous details funneling away from her. She had been running, all day and night and the day to follow, through brambles and tangled under-growth, a wilding crossing burgeoning creeks, through quiet prairies filled to brimming with whispering grasses. And still she ran, with enthusiasm, joy, and … *jubilation*.

She could no longer hold on to the final wisp of her dream; just realizing it made it so. She was left with its effervescent emotion. As she acknowledged the willowy cotton sheet covering her bare shoulders, as she sensed the enclosed air around her, she immediately fell into her impulse to sound out the word.

"*Joo'bə-lā'shən*," she whispered.

The act of rejoicing. A celebration or other expression of joy.

Yes, that sounded right.

Her smile remained as her eyes opened to bright sunlight. She didn't normally wake up so chipper, feeling so full of life. But she didn't mind, not one bit, even though she didn't know why she felt so … jubilant.

Heidi muttered in her sleep in the bed next to her. Hoping not to wake her, Clara carefully swung her feet to the floor and stood.

A white envelope with her name scribbled in pencil across the front leaned against the lamp on top of the dresser. Poppa's shaky script. Her smile wavered as she pried open the sealed envelope with shaky hands.

For some reason her smile widened, even before reading a single word of the densely packed letter. She skimmed his words, knowing she would read them again and again throughout her day, only slowing to a snail's pace when she reached the midpoint:

" ...so I need to ask your discretion. This is a secret adventure I'm sending you on. No one needs to know but you and me. The power of a secret is in its keeping. The fewer people in the know only increases its power.

"I'm assuming you've heard the name Charles Darwin. A long time ago, he sailed on a ship called the Beagle. His duties were to record his observations of the natural world. Darwin noticed something peculiar once they set anchor in the Galapagos. The birds, finches in particular, varied from one small island to the next. He hypothesized the slightly different environments shaped their evolution. With the passing of generations, they changed according to their surroundings. This is one of the most monumental scientific discoveries of the last few centuries. And you know what? Darwin didn't publish his findings for twenty years. He cherished this secret.

"And so, not nearly as haughty an aspiration as Darwin's discoveries in the Galapagos, I do hope you take it upon yourself to follow this map and resolve a question I've long harbored. I need to know the answer found at the end of the enclosed map before I can find peace. If you can do this for me ... if you can maintain our shared silence on the subject, the power of our secret will grow, will manifest in its preservation.

"I hope you take heed and collect the necessary supplies for this journey ..."

Clara stopped reading, her heart beating rapidly through waves of adrenaline.

Heidi rolled over in her sleep, destroying the letter's disembodying effect.

The list of supplies wasn't long, but it only sharpened her curiosity.

The last page in the envelope was—*joy-of-joys*—another one of Poppa's maps. Similar to the one she followed on her first adventure into the woods, this map was different in that it was considerably more extensive. Before Poppa's request for her to collect Nan's favorite flowers, Clara would've never given a second thought to go on this next challenge. Now she almost couldn't contain her excitement. A *secret*. A map leading to answers to a long-held question.

After hastily gathering a fresh set of clothes, Clara tiptoed to the bathroom to change into a lightweight blouse and tan denim shorts. She slipped on the sneakers her mother had bought her for vacation. The shoes were dingy with streaks of mud, but they felt so much more comfortable than when they first arrived at Little Whisper Lake.

Clara cracked open the bedroom door, saw with some relief that Heidi still slumbered, and tossed her pajamas near the bed. She eased the door closed and made her way to the kitchen.

Poppa, her parents, and her Aunt Leah were all sitting around the table on the deck. Poppa noticed her, raised his bushy gray eyebrows. He looked gaunt and exhausted, even though he'd just woken from a full night's sleep. No one else noticed this small gesture, and no one else noticed her appearance into the kitchen just feet away.

Clara held up the letter, now stashed inside its envelope.

Poppa nodded and smiled. He turned his back to her and gesticulated at a robin hopping along a branch in the nearby pinewoods. This sly gesture drew everyone's attention while Clara hustled to gather—in a plastic shopping bag—a bottle of water, a sleeve of saltine crackers, an apple, and a nearly brown banana.

She backed away from the kitchen, feeling a sense of pride in her subterfuge. After stashing the bag of food outside the entryway to the kitchen, she hurried back to the balcony doorway. Everyone turned her way when she opened the door. Everyone appeared surprised to see her, including Poppa.

"You're awake," her mom said, turning in her chair.

"Yeah, I woke up a little earlier. I wanted to let you know I'm going for a walk."

"You're *letting* us know?" Her mom crossed her arms and shifted to face Clara directly. "Shouldn't you *ask* first?"

Poppa held up a hand and everyone looked at him. "I think it was implied, Krista."

"I'm sorry," Clara said. She looked at her feet. "I figured it would be okay …"

"I think it's a great idea to get outside," her dad said.

"Thanks, Dad."

"Just don't be too long." Her mom's lips tightened. "And don't go far."

"I won't."

Clara hurried to close the door before her mom could say anything more.

Poppa caught her eye as the door closed. She gave him a thumbs-up. He did likewise. He looked happy, but also on the verge of tears … tears driven by sadness rather than joy.

The next step in Poppa's list called for her to retrieve a leather satchel from his office library. She removed the letter from the envelope, rereading the particular section, though she had already committed it to memory:

"This pouch accompanied me on plenty of
my own adventures. From the dense forests
of northwestern Canada, to the enormity of
Patagonia, and every backroad place in between. It's a trusty pouch. Good for taking
the weight of a day's supplies from your
shoulders."

She smiled at the thought, picturing Poppa as a daring
contemporary of Indiana Jones instead of a staid environmental
conservationist.

She found the satchel where Poppa's letter indicated she would,
tucked in the forgotten small space behind the door. The leather
was dusty, and when she brushed it with her palm, patches of dried
mud remained, varied colors, possibly from different countries, or
continents even. She touched the mud lightly with her fingertips, not
wanting to scrape it free.

The bag had a long strap that she slung vertically over her shoulder like a purse. It hung too low and felt awkward. She considered
for a moment, and then slung it so it hung diagonally across her
chest. Just perfect, like slipping on a worn pair of slippers.

She gathered her bag of food and opened the satchel's top flap
to slip it inside. The bag was a maze of spaces within spaces for every
need and happenstance. Among them she found a leather-bound
notebook, several pens, a sketchpad and pencils, a long-bladed
pocket knife, and a heavy-duty flashlight. She pressed the flashlight's
button and found that it worked. She almost jettisoned it to save
weight, but the bag was strong enough to hold all the supplies when
worn correctly.

After cinching the belt-like strap closed, she considered fetch-
ing her rain poncho, but she didn't want to risk anyone seeing her
departing with so many supplies on hand. She didn't want to answer
anyone's questions. Well, at least not anyone's questions but those
tormenting Poppa for so many years, the questions he needed
answered in order to find peace.

Clara stopped by the front door at the sound of someone

making a *shushing* noise behind the couch in the den. What sounded like a one-sided conversation piqued her curiosity.

"Please, just another second, okay?" a whispered voice called out from the den, followed by another *shush*.

"Trev, is that you?"

"No ..." the boy called out.

Clara heard the fleshy slap of Trev's palm against his forehead. His head bobbed up above the couch.

"What are you doing in there?" she asked.

"Nothing. I must'a ... I think I was sleepwalking."

"You look wide awake."

"You're not supposed to wake someone sleepwalking."

"I'm pretty sure that's just a myth," she said, wondering about his growing look of guilt.

His brows bunched and he stood to his full height, still in his pajamas. The buttons didn't align with the buttonholes and his hair stuck out in garish sleep-horns. He could've been sleepwalking, she supposed, but his eyes were fully alert.

She heard a scratching sound, almost frantic in its intensity.

Trevor looked down in surprise. He *shushed* again and rolled his eyes in frustration.

"So ..." Clara entered the den and walked around the couch.

Trevor shifted his feet, trying to hide a shoebox behind him. The box jutted away from him a couple inches. He placed a bare foot, streaked in fresh mud, on top of the box. He coughed, attempting to cover up the scratching.

Clara continued, "What do we have here?"

"Nothing." He sounded defeated. "Just a whole lotta nothing."

The shoe box shimmied under his foot, followed by a frog's throaty ribbit.

"Nothing? Okay. I figured you had a frog in that shoebox, and looking at your filthy feet, I'm guessing you just caught him."

"I met Mr. Wartly the first day here."

"Mr. Wartly?"

"Yeah, a frog needs a name, and he's ugly with warts, just stupid ugly with 'em."

"How did you two meet?"

She couldn't help grinning.

"I heard him out near the woods, all throaty-like. But when I tried to catch him, he hopped away, like big giant leaps."

He cracked open the box and peered inside. Mr. Wartly greeted him with another ribbit.

Clara hadn't seen Mr. Wartly, but he sounded big.

"I heard him again this morning," he said. "That's what woke me up. So I went out, and I don't know. Maybe he's slower in the morning. Kinda like my dad is slow and all headachy most mornings? But I caught him."

"Well, that sounds like a fitting name. What are you going to do with him?"

"With you knowing? I probably gotta put him back out in the grass by the woods."

"What would you have done if I didn't know about Mr. Wartly?"

Trevor looked confused, as if Clara was setting up a trap.

"No, seriously. What if I hadn't come into the den just now?"

"Well ... there's a window in the garage. Flies get caught between the two pieces of glass. I was going to catch them and feed them to Mr. Wartly."

Clara adjusted the satchel on her shoulder, ready to begin her own adventure.

"Okay, then do that."

"For real? You won't tell?"

"Mr. Wartly sounds hungry. Make sure you catch him the fattest flies you can find." She headed for the doorway before stopping in her tracks. "Once you feed him, you're not going to do anything stupid with him, are you?"

"What do you mean?"

"You wouldn't hurt him, would you?"

Trevor's eyes widened in shock. "No, no, no! I would never hurt Mr. Wartly. Or any animal. Swear to God!"

"Well, okay then. This will be our little secret. You know that secrets are important, right? And a secret has power as long as the secret isn't given away."

"Sure. Yeah." Trevor turned an imaginary key between his lips and threw it over his shoulder. "I like secrets."

Mr. Wartly chimed in with a throaty ribbit.

Clara smiled, feeling a trace of emotion left over from her dream; it felt like joy, but stronger, perhaps even jubilation.

She opened the door and stepped out into the already humid sunshine, a dense heat full of promise and expectation.

CHAPTER 19

Krista didn't like how the color had gone from Poppa's face, how his eyes bulged from their sockets as he wasted away.

Poppa leaned back in his deck chair. "I sure don't bounce back like I used to." He stretched his arms and gave off a groan.

"Are you tired?" Krista said. "Would you like to go lie down?"

"I hate to be rude—"

"Don't think anything of it, Pierce," Neal said and got up from his chair.

Poppa gave a wan smile, relieved. "Okay, I guess I can doze for a while."

"Doze as much as you want, Poppa," Leah said.

Neal went over to Poppa's side and helped him slide back his chair, then hooked a hand under his arm to help him gain his feet.

Krista opened the sliding door, waiting for him as he shuffled stiffly. She found herself nodding encouragement, making her recall the stressful moments of Clara's first steps. Poppa's foot caught on the threshold, and she gasped. Luckily, Neal was there to support him, otherwise he would've fallen over completely.

Poppa paused to steady his feet. "Children, do yourself a favor and never get old."

His skin looked pasty and gray, even though the sun gleamed in the cloudless sky. He chuckled dryly. It felt morbid to do so, Krista considered, but she and the others joined in. She followed on Leah's heels into the kitchen and she and her sister exchanged looks of concern.

Leah removed her cell phone from her pocket. "I'm going to call the doctor."

"No, you're not," Poppa said. "I'm fine."

"Are you sure, Poppa?" Leah wrung her hands together.

"How about some tea?" Poppa said, to give Leah something to do, to help her feel useful.

"Sure, but we're all out," Leah said, "but I'll go get some."

He continued to shuffle, leaning on Neal. "I don't want to be a bother."

"Nonsense." Leah followed like an obedient puppy, anxious to please. "I'll jet over to the Peterson's Corner Mart. They have the Earl Grey you like, right?"

"Sounds wonderful. And some of those mint candies. The hard disc ones?"

"You got it." Leah kissed his cheek and glanced at Krista. Her older sister looked as scared as Krista. "Anyone need anything else?"

"I don't think so," Neal said.

Krista shook her head in agreement.

Leah headed for the doorway. "I'll be back in a flash."

"Don't drive like a fool," Poppa said. "I'm not dying today."

Leah laughed on impulse, but it quickly morphed into an agonized wince.

"Real funny, Poppa," Krista said. She went to the side opposite Neal, and between them they helped Poppa to his room with no other stumbling incidents.

Poppa sat heavily on his bed and groaned as he rubbed his abdomen. "Where is that brother of yours? I worry about him."

Krista looked to Neal.

Jack had passed out in bed, still wearing his clothes from the day before. After Neal found him in such a state, he'd asked Krista if they should do anything—*something*—to help him with whatever he was going through. She'd told him to let time deal with his troubles, that time would help him get past his rough patch. Until then, they would support him however they could.

"He's ... I think he took the fishing boat out for a spin," Neal said, none-too-convincingly.

"By that, you mean he's sleeping off another late night?" Poppa said and rubbed his thumbs across his eyelids.

In a quiet voice, Neal said, "Or something like that."

"You know Jack," Krista said. "He's sensitive. Even when he's being an asshole, he feels deeply. And to tell you the truth, I think it's something of a chicken and egg thing."

Poppa chuckled. "You're probably right. I guess this is a little much to ask of all you kids. It's a bit selfish, isn't it?"

"Nonsense," Krista said.

Poppa tried to lift his legs onto the bed, but he didn't possess the strength. Before frustration settled in, Neal lifted Poppa's legs and helped him swing around to ease back on his pillows.

"Here you go, Pierce. And don't worry. We want to be here. All of us."

Poppa patted Neal's forearm. "From the moment Krista brought you home, I knew you were right for her, right for the family."

"Thanks, Pierce. It means a lot." Neal didn't look like he knew what to do with himself. "Can I get you anything? The newspaper? Some water?"

"This is good. Good and fine. I'll doze for a bit, have some lunch with you kids later on. When Leah gets back with the tea and candy, tell her there's no rush if I'm sleeping."

Neal nodded gravely. "I can do that."

Krista met her husband's eyes. She often didn't need to speak aloud for him to understand her. This was one of those times, so when she said, "I'll be right out," all he did was offer a slight lowering of his chin, then left the room.

"Well, my dear," Poppa said, "what do you have to lecture me about?"

"I wasn't going to lecture about anything—"

"But ...?" he cut in.

She paced the length of his bed, wringing her hands. Her eyes settled on his bedside table and the photo of Nan from her early twenties. She looked like her beauty could carry a Hollywood film.

"Honey, what is it?"

She picked up the photo, brushed away dust from the edge. "I always liked this photo." She returned the photo to its rightful spot.

"Me too." Emotion tightened his words.

"I expected to see a dozen pill bottles on your bedside table."

"You would've a few weeks ago. When I made my decision, I cleared them all away. Made me depressed, when that's the last thing I want right now."

"Yeah, but … are you in pain?"

"Every minute of every day."

"But …" She paused when his eyes steeled despite his fatigue. "I guess you've thought this through."

"I have. I'm dying, sure, but I'm dying under my own terms. I don't want to slip away doped to the gills."

"So … no doctors?"

"Not anymore. I have the non-emergency police number written down inside this drawer." He pointed to his bedside table. "There's also the number for the medical examiner. When the time comes, that's all I want from you kids. Just two phone calls. Everything is arranged. I'm going to be cremated at Piedmont Funeral Home. I want my ashes scattered over the lake."

Tears formed in her eyes, trailed down her cheeks.

"Leah explained her situation," he said, "about her and the kids needing a place to stay. I'm willing the lake house over to the three of you kids. I've bought up over a thousand surrounding acres. It's all yours."

"Poppa—"

"You could sell off the house, but I wish you wouldn't. The remaining land is set up in a conservation trust, so it's essentially off-limits to development, thank God—"

"Poppa?" Her voice caught in her throat.

"But I think Leah wants to set up here. At least until she gets her feet back under her. Which is fine by me."

"Poppa, please!"

He looked at her tear-streaked face, blinked several times, as if surprised to find her there.

"Do we have to talk about this right now?" she said.

"I guess not, but time—"

"Time is short. I get it." Krista climbed onto the bed and lay next to him, sharing his pillow. She took one of his hands in both of hers. Squeezed. His skin was so dry and smooth, his brittle bones just beneath the surface. "Can we just ... can we just do *this?* For a few minutes?"

Poppa chuckled, and carried no trace of cynicism, nor any dark underpinnings. It was a sound she wanted to remember always.

Krista stroked the back of his hand, marveled at the dark spots that weren't there the last time she was here. How could she have let so much time slip by without keeping this man within an arm's length at any given moment? She began to calm. Her tears dried and her chest no longer felt gripped in an angry fist.

"I don't blame you," Poppa murmured.

"Pardon me?" Krista's said.

"I don't blame you for not coming back here. In truth, it crossed my mind to sell the place after Breann disappeared. But I couldn't. It's stupid, when I look back on it. I like to think I'd worked so hard to preserve the wildness surrounding Little Whisper. And nothing would make me put that aside, even the loss of your friend. And I wanted to let you know, I don't blame you for feeling resentment toward me. I'm sorry."

"Poppa, you don't need to be sorry about anything."

"We all have something to be sorry about. Some people more than others. I'd like to bring some balance to the tally sheet before my time is done."

Krista shifted on the pillow, regarding her grandfather with a sidelong glance. "Consider your apology accepted," she said, "even though I don't think it was necessary in the first place."

Poppa smiled and the fatigue faded from his eyes.

"When we were kids, you told us we could be anything in the world. You told me I could become president. I could walk on the moon. I did nothing like that."

"You became a wife ... a mother."

"Yes, and I've dedicated all my time and energy into making sure Clara is loved, supported, and that her world is enriching ..."

"But ...?"

"Well, Clara, one day ... my God, one day she's going to grow up. And that time is soon, believe it or not."

"It's soon," Poppa agreed, "but, I'm afraid, not soon enough for me to see."

"That's not ... I didn't mean it that way. How stupid of me." She paused, suddenly out of breath. "I meant to say ... she's growing up so fast—she's always been like a little adult intellectually—and she's going to be a full-fledged adult. And I've realized, since we came here, that I've been doing her a disservice. I know I can be overbearing, controlling—"

"You? Never!" He chuckled.

"Poppa, I'm serious."

"I know, I know. It's just ... I saw Nan in your face, how your lips tighten up at the corners when you're passionate about something. So, please forgive me, and carry on with being serious."

"So, anyway, I've always taken pride in protecting my daughter. For obvious reasons, I haven't wanted her out of my sight."

"Understandable."

"But I've also seen, since you've been talking with her, maybe ... maybe I've taken it too far. I see Clara opening up, coming out of her shell. Just even her smiling with abandon, without hesitation. It's like my eyes are opening to how sheltered I've kept her."

"Don't stress about instinct. Don't worry about protecting your family *too* much."

"I'm not. Or I'm trying not to anyway."

Poppa squeezed her hand.

"You should get your rest," Krista said.

"Is there something else you wanted to ask me about?" Poppa asked, his gaze probing, knowing.

"I ... I don't think so."

"There is. I can see it on your face. You're hiding something."

"Poppa ... I saw ... *something.*"

His lips curled into a coy smile. "Something, really?"

"*Breann* ..." She whispered the name, felt a chill across the nape of her neck. "I saw her. Down by the lake. Either that, or I'm going mad." She laughed uneasily.

146

His expression changed from whimsy to something akin to understanding, which was the last thing she expected from him.

He licked his lips, ready to say something, but hesitated, as if to gather his thoughts. "This land is restless, untamable." He scooted higher on his pillow. "Sure, there are houses, roads, utilities stretching from here to Grand Rapids. But settled, it has never been. And never shall it be." He took a steadying breath. "I didn't know this until a couple of years after *To Heal the Land* was published, when it was wildly successful, but I still didn't know what tomorrow would bring. But when I was able to rest after an extensive book tour, to finally breathe for the first time since your grandmother and I got married, I became aware of the strange energy of this place." He paused to catch his breath, his face a grim mask of pain and fatigue.

"Have you seen her, too? Have you seen Breann?"

"No. Never once. But as I've tired, as this mutation in my cells turns one after another of my systems against me ... I've seen Francie. Just glimpses at the corner of my eye. The scent of her perfume floating like a keen memory on the air. And sometimes, when I'm feeling particularly low, vulnerable, near my end ... I hear her voice. Not words, just her voice in her throat. Her laughter. That alone would be enough reason for me to not want to linger. It's the reason I've decided to live out my time here, at the lake. For those irrational moments of clarity. When I can hear my wife, see a split second of her profile, the mischievous sparkle in her eye."

Krista said the first words to come to mind. "You loved her—"

"Without question, without fail. It's a cliché to say losing a spouse is like losing a limb, but there's always some truth to clichés, otherwise they wouldn't exist. Sure, it's like missing a limb, but it's something more ... more like losing substance, clarity, cohesion. And I just want to see her again, to be with her again, not in mere glimpses, but wholeheartedly, with my full affection."

"It's probably selfish for me to want you for myself," Krista said, "for the entire family, but ... I think I understand." She went to his side and ran her fingers over the cottony white hair at his temple.

"I'm glad."

"I better go before Leah gets back. She'd be so angry knowing

I've been talking your ear off."

"That's probably a good idea." He chuckled again, but this time the tiredness had returned in its full glory. He looked more drawn and feeble than he did on the back deck.

"So you believe me about Breann?"

"Yes, I do. Without question. And if I were to hazard a guess, it would mean she never went far from Little Whisper when she disappeared, even though Jenkins was eventually caught on the ferry getting off in Wisconsin."

"Have a good rest, Poppa."

She remained outside the doorway, watching him unobtrusively, her mind whirling.

His smile deflated; he no longer had to marshal his energy to put on a brave face. Agony twisted his features into something hideous and shattered. His fingers curled to claws as he brought them to his chest. He held them there—a morbid mimicry of someone in deep prayer—as his eyelids fluttered closed in exhaustion. As he drifted off, the pain never left his face; if anything, it intensified.

Krista closed the door, heart racing as she neared Poppa's writing desk. She unburied his unfinished manuscript, the one about Edgar Jenkins. The binder itself seemed to give off a low vibration as she opened it.

FALLEN: THE MIND AND MOTIVATIONS OF A SERIAL KILLER

The title alone made her queasy. She didn't want to know about the mind and motivations of the man who had kidnapped and killed her childhood friend. She didn't want to learn about Poppa's reasons for writing such a morbid book, either. But she also couldn't *not* turn the opening page and start from the very beginning, this time no longer skimming but ruminating over every word, searching for understanding.

> The concept for this book had a long gestation
> period before I finally decided to explore its
> gruesome subject matter …

148

CHAPTER 20

Words shaped Clara's first memories. She could remember, even now, the comforting emotions of them—soft and lulling, the gentle voices of her parents reading her a bedtime story, the individual syllables like incongruent building blocks of magic that would coalesce, break apart, then reform to a new meaning. Even before she understood their words were mere symbols given sound, Clara was drawn to their power. Words had power; she knew this before anything else but the love of her parents.

Now, short of breath, her leg muscles crying for her to *stop, stop, stop!* she charged down an almost-there trail, a slight riffle in the underbrush known only to ground squirrels and the owls lurking overhead.

Poppa's satchel jounced on her shoulder as she ran freely—her reins tossed aside—with only the occasional glance at his crude map to alter her path. Her *destiny*. Oh, yes, destiny! She felt compelled through the woods, hurtled down declining swales her feet barely clung to as she raced ahead. Onward!

Now undeniably doubling back through the woods, but still following Poppa's crooked scrawl across the crumpled page, she noticed the lake house through the trees, seeing it as untamed nature would see it: foreboding in the high sun of late morning. She put the sight out of mind, her heart pumping in her ears, the sound blotting out all others but the muted clump and fall of her strides striking the moist earth.

She ran, exhilarated beyond measure. For the first time since she

started forming memories, Clara's mind was clear of words, unclut-
tered, sated by her exertion alone.

Sunlight flickered through the myriad layers of leaves above. She
wound through a tunnel of wilderness, and at its end, thirty feet
ahead, the trail terminated in blinding white light. She charged into
its maw, as if chasing the sun itself, slowing when her feet met sand.

A low gray wave uncoiled across the beach, losing its energy like
a tired exhalation before receding to the dark depths of the lake.

She sucked in a deep breath, and a stabbing cramp blossomed
under her ribs. She bent at the waist, resting her hands on her knees.
Sweat dripped from the tip of her nose. Fresh air ripped through
her lungs. Her vision dimmed for a few seconds before she felt the
worst of it passing over her like a retreating storm. In its wake, an
easy smile found her lips.

Her mind hummed blissfully as her feet took her to the edge of
the dark water.

Again, Clara glanced at the evidence of Poppa's house: the
lean-to where they dried wood for bonfires, the anchored dock
bobbing with the eddying waves, Heidi, Robby, and Trev struggling
to get a box kite into the sky. The trio ran along the shore, Trev in
the lead and tugging on the string while the kite stuttered impotently
against the sand. Robby let out an excited whoop while Heidi halted
in her tracks. No amount of running and cajoling would set the kite
aloft; it was not windy enough for kite-flying.

"Heidi, we need your help," Robby called out.

His twin sister waved him away, turning back toward the lake
house. Robby waved a clenched fist in exasperation and picked up
his pace to catch back up to Trev and his kite.

Before anyone noticed her, Clara hurried off in the opposite
direction.

Poppa's map was damp with her sweat, but she could still see
where he had wanted her to go. She mirrored the shaky directional
arrows down another hundred feet of shoreline, and as the lake cut
back toward the woods, the lake house disappeared from view.

No matter her determination, a side stitch forced her to slow to
a brisk walk.

With Poppa's house now nowhere in sight, the lake seemed to extend in inky swells to the horizon. The woods on the far side of the lake had become a single mass of green vegetation.

A heron waded with its broomstick legs in the nearby shallows, hunting small fish. It stabbed its beak into the lake and came up short. Preparing to strike again, it took a couple sly strides through the water before it noticed her. The bird squawked and flew into the air with mighty wings. Its feet dangled low, at first, but as it picked up speed, they lifted higher, flattening. Clara stopped in her tracks, marveling at its prehistoric beauty, even after it was gone.

Laughter drew her attention away from the lake. At first, she thought her cousins had abandoned their box kite and decided to follow her. She felt a wicked stab of anger at them, and then, as she stepped toward the sound and into the cool shade of the woods, she realized it was indeed laughter, but not her cousins'. She tried to pinpoint the sound, but the voices quieted before she determined anything more than their general direction.

There was no trail to follow, and Poppa's map didn't zag back into the woods at quite the same spot. But still …

Clara left the beach, left the known parameters of her quest, straining for the sounds of laughter. She soon found herself snagged on any number of overgrown raspberry bushes. She tried to pull free, but the thorns held fast.

"Oh, come on," she muttered.

The thorny branches would only come free if she worked each one individually, carefully. A few berries had ripened, and before thinking twice, she popped them into her mouth. Her mouth watered almost painfully at the fruit's tart juiciness.

She removed a final thorn from the hem of her shorts, and again heard voices, no longer laughing, but in deep conversation. Girls' voices, two of them. They sounded close, just over the next wooded rise.

She felt like an intruder, yet somehow connected to the unseen strangers. Why else would she get so easily sidetracked from helping Poppa answer a question so long in waiting?

She kicked past the last of the raspberries and reached the top

GLEN KRISCH

of the rise, or so she thought. Instead of a rounded peak, the hill abruptly fell away, as if a sharp cleaver had separated that portion of land from the rest. She toppled over the edge, stumbling forward, too far forward to arrest her descent.

The weight of Poppa's satchel sent her cartwheeling, and the world became a chaotic jumble—the scrape and rustle of her body plowing down the ridge, flashes of stark blue sky, the flicker and flash of layers of green leaves. She tumbled a good twenty feet before the crown of her head hit something hard.

Granite.

The word popped into her head, then was gone. So simple a word, yet the blow had fogged her mind, and she began to drift through layers of ever-deepening darkness.

CHAPTER 21

Gritty sand gathered between Krista's sandaled toes as she cut across the beach and away from the lake. The road's weathered spine stretched from one edge of her vision to the other. Cool air billowed from the woods looming across the cracked blacktop. Few cars ever passed this way. Desolate, full of murk and ambiguity. The perfect location to snatch someone without any witnesses. Her breath caught in her throat. She felt it in her bones; this was the spot.

Krista held her place in Poppa's manuscript with her index finger. After reading at the summer house for an hour, she felt the need to move, to experience the words in the real world. She lifted the binder and opened it. She had already learned Poppa had become obsessed with Breann's disappearance, so much so that he'd dedicated his months of declining health in order to make sense of the tragedy.

As she picked up where she'd left off, the outside world drew away, became muted from her senses. In moments, she could have been a fly on the wall of the interview room at Two Rivers Correctional Facility.

> The man sitting across the table from me in the drab gray bunker of a room didn't look like a killer, but he'd already admitted as much under oath when he claimed seven victims as his own. He looked young at first glance, just as he did on TV when he was shown being ushered from a squad car into the Two Rivers

Courthouse for his first hearing. I'd felt vindi-
cated that day, but not anymore.

There were still unanswered questions,
bodies left unburied, unmourned.

"Oh, God, Breann." Krista looked up from the binder, blinking through tears. She didn't want to read anymore, but knew she
couldn't *not* read it, either. She sighed, took a deep breath, and
returned to the manuscript:

I soon noticed crow's feet at the corners of his
eyes, creases in his forehead. His eyes ... no
corruption stared back at me from those icy
blue eyes. If anything, his gaze was inviting,
at ease. His untroubled disposition was the
most unnerving aspect of my first visit with
Edgar Jenkins. Even though he was a killer,
even though he had been caught with traces
of his last victim's blood and skin under his
nails, even though he'd been caged and cut
off from the world, Edgar Jenkins seemed a
man at peace.

"How many times did you troll the beach
road?" I asked him. "Ten? More?"

"Oh at least," he replied with a haughty laugh. "You're a lucky man to live in such
natural beauty. I'd had no intention of staying as long as I did in your neck of the woods.
See, it's a funny thing ... my thing had always
been to take the ferry from Wisconsin. I used
to never stray from Cheeseland to pursue my
... entertainments ... but I got crafty, see. I'd
get caught if I kept the same pattern. I learned
that from those cop shows on TV, right? So I
started taking the ferry across Lake Michigan
to expand my ... reach, so to speak."

Edgar paused in his explanation, over-come with a sickening, manic laughter.

"What is it? What's so funny?" I asked.

"After a few of these trips, the ferry line had gone up for sale." He wiped his eyes and got himself under control. "For some reason, between owners there was a two to three week gap when it wasn't running at all. Something tugged at me—all the way from my balls to my brain—something wanted me to come back to Michigan, even though I had to drive through the armpits of Illinois and Indiana to get there."

"I want to know ... no, what I need to know, Edgar, is: why did you come to Little Whisper Lake? Of all the places for you to stalk your victims ... you came to my back-yard."

Edgar laughed again, but now more sub-dued. "This is for your book, right? This is the $64,000 question you need answered to sell your half-million copies?"

"Your lawyer explained my book, who I am. But if you tell me the truth, the honest to God's truth, and you don't want me to write about it ... I won't. Just tell me the truth."

"If you can't answer that question, it'd kill your book, right?" Edgar rubbed the stubble on his chin, contemplating. Teasing. Measuring my desperation.

"I suppose it might. But I don't care about any of that. I just ... I need to know."

"Okay ... okay ... fuck it. You want the truth?" Edgar leaned in until his manacled hands pulled taut against the metal ring in the table. His eyes flashed madness, for a second or two at most. In that flash, I saw his true nature, the vile beast that would awaken to destroy the lives of children. But then it was gone, and he once again regained his composure. He settled back against the metal chair, back to stasis. He shrugged. "I got lost."

He again started to laugh. His eyes teared up and he slapped the metal table separating us. A corrections officer peeked through the window in the door. I gave him a nod to let him know everything was fine.

"I got fucking lost. That's the whole and honest to God's truth. Bad luck all around, I suppose. That's how I landed here."

"And Breann?" I hoped he would take my hook and run with it.

Edgar stared at me, not blinking. I've never felt the chill of evil so close before, so resolute and alive as that moment. We stared at one another long enough for me to taste my own sour breath idling on my tongue.

"So the day I got lost, got all turned and twisted in circles after leaving the highway north of Muskegon, I come across your Little Whisper Lake. So quaint, so charming. And that's when something spoke to me."

"What does that mean? Like voices?"

"Yeah ... no, not really. It was more than voices. More like God, if you believe in that sort of thing. Just something ... something not-of-this world. Like a ... a dark presence, comforting even. It guided me, both deep inside me, but also from outside ... from nature. If that makes any sense. It's like the voices were in my ears and in my heart at the same time, like a church chorus. And the voices led me to the beach and the rutted little road. And that's when I first saw the three little girls building their sand castles, looking like pieces of sugar candy glistening in the sun."

"Bastard," I whispered, unable to hold my tongue.

Edgar shook his head, as if he understood something I would never be able to grasp. "This guiding hand, this dark presence, it gave me a choice. Pick one. But I could only have one. So I studied like I always did. The tall blonde girl—"

"Leah. My granddaughter." I felt ready to vomit, hearing him so flippantly mention her as if she were a ribeye at the grocery meat counter.

"Yeah, she didn't have certain qualities that tickle my fancy. She seemed like she'd smile all the goddamned time, even when she's in pain. That girl had a spirit, a *glow*."

I imagined Leah. The traits he'd used to eliminate her from being a potential victim were also what made her so special to me. To Francie. Her lively spirit had unknowingly saved her life.

"That left me with one of two choices, and my God, it was a tough one. I damn near took them both. But two at one time would be a hell of a lot more complicated than just doubling my efforts. One is controllable. Two … two is chaos. So, I had to choose."

"And that's why you stayed, why you remained near the lake?"

Edgar chuckled. "I was torn, mister. Just miserable about the whole thing. I even went as far as scanning the local want-ads to help extend my stay. If I could avoid making a decision, I couldn't make the wrong decision, right?"

He paused, as if I might answer his question, or understand his twisted mind.

"But you saw me one day." He gave me a knowing smirk, a little nod.

I swallowed against a lump in my throat. "Yeah. In the blue van."

"Let me ask you a question. Was that the first time you noticed me?"

I hesitated but saw no reason to lie.

"Yes."

"Unfuckingbelievable. That one time you see me ... it put me on your radar, right?"

I nodded.

"It was enough. In my gut, I knew."

"That's all it took? When I'd already been inside your house?" He waited for my reaction. I kept everything in check, everything but my eyes. He nodded, satisfied at my rising anger. "So all those times I crept into your house, every time I rifled your drawers, your personal belongings ... you never once suspected a damn thing?"

I glared at him, dug my nails into my palm until I risked bloodying them.

"So no one even noticed a missing pair of panties—"

I slammed my palm against the table and stood, the scraping of the metal chair amplified by our close confines.

"What? Did I say something ... did I offend you, Pierce?"

"I asked you about Breann. You don't need to see if you can make me squirm."

"But I do! I really do. You see, I'm just explaining things. I had to be thorough or I might make the wrong decision. In my eyes, you don't fuck around when life or death are at stake. And that's exactly what this was—life or death."

"Get on with it, or we're done here."

"You look a little green. Are you feeling okay?"

I grabbed my tape recorder and pad of paper. When I was halfway to the door, he called out for me to stop.

"Okay. No more bullshit." Edgar sounded a bit desperate. "You've been patient, more than patient, and I've been dragging this out. You wouldn't believe how few people want to chat behind bars." Edgar let out a long breath. His eyes steeled, narrowed. "Your girl, your Krista ... what it came down to is she didn't suit my needs. There was too much innocence there. Too much love. From you. From her to you. Breann, on the other hand, was a lonely soul. In many ways, she was like Krista, but love was lacking in her life. And it made her so incredibly ... seductive ... to my guiding hand, the dark presence.

"As I neared my decision, I started taking more risks, trying to figure out which would be my prize. It all made sense after I spent a night under Breann's bed. I'd crept in when her family was out on their back porch grilling burgers ..."

Edgar paused, as if re-experiencing the fateful night. He blinked, his eyes distant. "I've never told this to anyone. Not my lawyer, the shrinks. Nobody."

I wasn't about to thank him. I came close to getting up and leaving anyway, but there was still something I needed to know, something beyond why he had decided to take Breann. The police had never recovered her body. If I could get that information from Edgar, I could chuck the rest of my book. I would do anything to bring the McCorts some peace.

"Breann's parents got into some argument. I didn't know what about, but it sounded serious. Slammed doors. A glass shattered against the kitchen wall. That sort of thing. Soon enough, Breann came to her room, crawled into bed just a few inches above where I hid. And she began to cry. It was so fucking heartbreaking, yet beautiful. It's what sealed the deal. Her cry was the saddest sound imaginable. And you can put this in your book—I don't give a fuck—but it gave me the rock-solidest hard-on in my life. Just the utter *aloneness* of that girl ... it about broke me. I damn near took her right then and there. But I had to wait. Like a good boy."

Even though I felt sickened, I managed to say, "So, where did you take her? Where is she now?"

"She thanked me near the end."

"I don't need to know this."

"But it's important. She thanked me for showing her mercy, for ending her suffering."

"Where is Breann?" I pressed.

"I will describe how to find her."

"What do you mean?"

"Open your pad of paper. Take out a pencil. Draw what I tell you."

"Draw? What, like a map?"

"Exactly like a map! And at the end of it, you will find a treasure!"

My hands shook as I opened my notebook. I drew to the best of my limited ability what he told me: the beachfront, the surrounding woods, trails I was never privy to until described to me by Edgar Jenkins ...

The page quivered between Krista's thumb and index finger as she read a notation at the bottom of the page:

[Insert map following this page]

Krista turned the page but didn't see a map. The following pages described how the jailhouse interview ended. It was brief and didn't reveal anything of substance. She flipped through the subsequent pages, then to the bracketed notation about the map. She sighed in frustration; the truth was taunting her just outside her reach.

"Honey!" Neal called out.

Krista looked up to see her husband jogging across the sand.

"There you are!" he said, short of breath when he reached her. "Have you seen Clara?"

"No, I haven't. She's not back yet?"

Neal shook his head, his gaze scanning the beach and distant trees. "It's been almost four hours. Can you believe it, our daughter out there for four hours?"

"Should we go look for her?" she asked.

"I don't know. It's still early. I say we give her another hour or so," he said, but still looked worried. "Now I'm kind of wishing we'd given her a cell phone."

"Me too. I'm just not used to her being so adventurous."

Neal wrapped his arm around her and they started back for the summer house. "This is going to take getting used to. Is that Poppa's book?"

Krista nodded.

"Is it any good?"

"I … I don't know. It feels … salacious. Not the book, I guess. More that I'm reading it."

"That's just because he doesn't know you're reading it. Are you learning anything important?"

"Yes. I shouldn't have stayed away. If not for Breann, for Poppa."

"Well, why don't we see if he's up for company?"

She rested her head on his shoulder and squeezed his waist.

"Sounds good."

They cut across the sand as the sun dipped toward the trees. She glanced over her shoulder at the weedy gravel on the side of the road. She had no way of knowing, but she would bet good money that Edgar had snatched Breann from that very spot.

"There's one thing I need to do first," she said.

"What's that?"

"I need to speak to Nan."

"Okay …" Neal said, somewhat concerned.

"Can you make me some tea? I need a minute alone with her."

"Of course."

When they reached the back stairwell, Krista veered toward the secluded alcove where Nan was buried.

CHAPTER 22

After tumbling down the hill, Clara finally came to rest on her shoulder. The fingers of her left hand began to wiggle, pinned beneath her, and as she struggled to breathe, she flexed her arm until she rolled over to her back. She sucked in a deep breath, relieved she felt no acute pains.

The sky had darkened during her fall. The bruised air carried flecks of light—*no, not light, but dust, bits of dust caught in the tumult*—swirling and bobbing before jetting away. Her thoughts were muddled, and this scared her more than the fall itself. She didn't dare move, not with night falling. Not with what the darkened stretch of wilderness had in store for her, a stranger in its midst.

The world felt unsteady beneath her. She blinked heavily, her stomach stirring with nausea, her every limb battered and abused. The worst part: she was utterly alone. But not just that—she had totally failed. Poppa would never have his question answered. His faith in her had been misplaced.

After closing her eyes, she didn't bother to reopen them. Her lower lip quivered. Tears ran down her cheeks as she gave into both the emotion and the physical hurt she'd just endured.

She didn't know how much time had passed when the sounds of the two girls brought her to her senses. And they were near, so incredibly near.

Clara strained to open her eyes, but tears had crusted against her eyelids.

"See, she's not dead," one girl said.

"Yeah," a voice replied, and Clara felt a nudge to her ribs. "I guess you're right."

"Hey ..." Clara rubbed the heels of her palms against her eyes.

A redheaded girl stood closest to her. She had her foot raised to give Clara another nudge. Her canvas shoes were muddied, but patterned underneath with pink flowers.

"It's her," the other girl said. "You know, the kid I told you about?"

Clara blinked several times, her vision coming into focus. Warily, she sat up at the waist. At least her nausea had gone.

"Easy now, Clara. That was some tumble you took."

Clara pressed her hands into the dirt on either side of her.

She knows my name.

"A big stupid tumble, you ask me." The redhead wrinkled her nose. "You were so loud we thought you were a bear crashing through the woods."

"A bear?" Clara's thoughts were still a jumble.

She laughed and her vision again dimmed. When it solidified, the other girl, a dirty blonde with intense green eyes, kneeled down so they were nearly nose to nose. She stared at Clara expectantly. Though she felt an immediate recollection, her brain wouldn't process the information properly. She *knew* this girl. Heck, the girl knew her, having already mentioned her by name. And yet ... and yet she couldn't place her name or how she knew her.

The blonde girl gasped. "You have blood in your hair."

Clara froze, as if the girl had instead mentioned a spider.

The girl peered down at her scalp and probed near the wound with a light touch. "Don't worry. It's not so bad. A goose egg, all right, but the bleeding's pretty much stopped."

"You're the girl ..." Clara pulled together the threads of her memory. "You're from the other side of the lake, right?"

"Yeah." The girl's voice deflated on that single syllable. She looked away, toyed with the purple flowers braided into a bracelet around her wrist.

The redhead barked out a snarky laugh before something near Clara's feet drew her attention. "What's this?"

The girl picked up Poppa's map.

"A map. Kind of like a treasure hunt—oh, my God, you're *Melody*, right?"

The puzzle pieces came crashing together: Poppa's first adventure, picking Nan's favorite flowers, finding Melody in the field of purple blossoms, and then waiting out the storm with her under the tumbled-over tree. How could she not remember her until just now? Not once, not even in passing, had she thought about Melody since they'd split up that afternoon.

Melody's eyes softened. "Yes! So you do remember."

"Of course I do!" Clara tried covering up her faulty memory with enthusiasm. "I just ... you know, I hit my head. Those are the flowers from the field, aren't they?"

Melody nodded.

"They're beautiful."

The redhead scoffed and rolled her eyes. "Geez ..."

Melody ignored her friend and turned to Clara. "Thank you." She smiled and extended her hand to Clara and helped her to her feet. "Are you okay?"

"I ..." Clara's vision wobbled, but only briefly. "I think so."

"I can't believe you didn't break your neck." The redhead tipped her head to the side and made a cracking sound. "Seriously. You must have flip-flopped like a hundred times." The girl looked from Melody to Clara and then back again. She ran her tongue absently across one of her front teeth, which jutted out more than the rest.

"Guess I'm just lucky." Clara held out her hand. "Can I have that back, please?"

"Well ..." The girl clutched the map to her chest. "I suppose."

She looked unsure how she would respond to Clara's demand. After a few tense seconds, she handed it over to Clara, who smoothed it as best she could.

"I better get back," Clara said. She hefted Poppa's satchel until the strap sat on her shoulder properly before starting away from the girls. "My mom's probably wondering where I am. She worries a lot."

"So what did you find?" the redhead asked.

Clara looked back at the girl. "What do you mean?"

"At the end of the map. It shows a pile of rocks or something at the end of it. You said it's a treasure map, so what's the treasure?"

"I don't know. I fell before I could find out."

"And you're just going to go home?"

"Of course she's not!" Melody said. "We'll help you. I bet it's not far."

"Really, my head …" Clara just wanted a good excuse to go back to the summer house.

"Maps are only made to lead you to something important," Melody said. "You can't go back now."

Clara looked back up the way she had fallen, realizing how dangerous a fall it had been. She *could* have broken her neck. And the sky wasn't nearly as dark as she'd thought it was.

"What time is it?"

"No idea." the redhead said. "Daytime?"

"Neither of us has a watch," Melody added.

"So I wasn't lying here all alone for a long time before you guys showed up?"

"Nope. We heard the racket, then came running. Why?"

"It's weird. I could've sworn it was almost nightfall."

"Not by a long shot. So, are we going to help you, or what?"

"Yes. Sure. I could use the help."

"Yay!" the redhead squealed.

"Don't mind Breann," Melody said, patting Clara's shoulder as they started back up the hill. "She doesn't get out much."

"*Breann* …" Clara whispered the name. "*Breann* …"

"What is it?" Melody asked.

"My mom, her friend's name was Breann."

Neither girl said anything in reply, but they shared a glance. It was obvious the coincidence unnerved them both.

Starting up the hill, Clara alternated glancing at the map and the enormity of the wilderness surrounding them.

"I can't believe you two have this place as your backyard."

"It is pretty nice," Melody admitted.

The trio worked single-file from foothold to foothold, slowly regaining the ground that had blurred by Clara on her way down.

"I want to see more than these woods," Breann said. "I want to travel the world. You know, Paris and Tokyo and Chicago."

"I live in Chicago," Clara said and stopped at the top of the hill, letting the other two catch up before they started again.

"Chicago? Really? With your parents?" Breann sounded awed by the prospect of living in a big city.

"We have an apartment. It's on the twenty-third floor."

"I bet the view is incredible," Melody said.

"It is. But I hate getting anywhere near the balcony's railing. Vertigo makes it feel like you're going to fall right over the side."

"What are your parents like?" Breann asked.

Something in her tone made Clara look back over her shoulder. Breann's brown eyes were intense, probing. The freckles across her cheeks seemed to flare.

"They're nice." She could have said more. She could have rattled off a long litany of great qualities, but something about Breann made her hold back.

"What does your mom do?" Breann asked.

"What do you mean?"

"What does your mom do for a living?"

"She ... she takes care of me."

"Like all the time?" Melody asked.

"Well, yeah. She went to law school, but she met my dad and they got married."

"What does your dad do?" Breann asked.

"He's a lawyer."

"Well, isn't that nice?" Breann said with a snide curl of her lips. "Why isn't your mom a lawyer, too?"

"Like I said, she takes care of me." Clara felt guilty but didn't know why.

"Breann, lay off," Melody said.

"Geez, I didn't mean anything by it."

Clara turned her attention to the map. She held it high, trying to find where the trail met up with Poppa's directions. She didn't have a clue, other than knowing the lake was straight ahead and that she'd be able to pick up where she'd initially left the trail. She could hear the lake's soft lapping waves.

They pressed on, pushing the pace, as if spurred by the sound, until the woods thinned and the sky brightened.

"It's so beautiful here," Melody said. "Sometimes I walk the beach at night. It's so dark, especially if the clouds block out the stars. I close my eyes and wander across the sand. It makes me feel so free, so alive."

"And that's when I find her stumbling around like some blind bum, and I laugh and laugh," Breann said.

"You can be so cruel sometimes, you know that?" Melody crossed her arms and stomped her foot in the sand.

Breann gave her a cold smile. "Did you know you can be *too* sensitive?"

Melody looked on the verge of tears. "I don't know why I put up with you sometimes."

Clara felt like an interloper on a long-running tension between them.

Breann glared at Melody, then reached out and snatched the map from Clara's hands. The girl sprinted away, kicking up sand with every stride.

"Hey, wait a second!" Clara said.

"Breann!" Melody called out.

Clara took off after the girl, but she quickly lost ground. "That's not yours!"

"Come and get it!" Breann disappeared into a break in the woods.

Melody caught up to Clara and sprinted ahead.

"What is she doing?" Clara felt helpless as the chase left her farther behind with every passing second.

"She's just ... she's lost," Melody said. "She doesn't know what she's doing. Not anymore." She sprinted away, leaving Clara far behind. "I'm sorry, Clara."

Breann and Melody were nothing more than rustling underbrush and the snapping of twigs. They followed no discernible path, but Clara would do just about anything to not lose them, to not lose Poppa's map.

Soon the sounds of the sprinting girls died away, and Clara realized her utter aloneness at the bottom of a rocky gully carpeted in ferns. Lost and without a map, she held her tears at bay, even though they threatened to fall. She followed an almost imperceptible bending and disorder in the plants, as if they had witnessed the slightest touches only seconds earlier.

The trail led to a clear pond fed by a gurgle of water lacing down from the hills. There were depressions in the mud near the pond's edge, she noticed, outlines of tiny flowers in fresh footprints. A series of wide smooth stones spanned the water, each a couple of feet apart, each extending like links of chain.

Clara held fast to Poppa's satchel and leapt from one stone to the next. Silvery fish as long as her forearm darted between the stones. Startled, she pin-wheeled her arms and her heart lurched in her chest before she managed to steady herself.

Halfway across the pond, a brief and mournful cry interrupted the singular sound of the gurgling water. At once, her feet solidified beneath her as her ears pricked up to the sound. Again, she heard the sound, and before thinking twice, she leapt across the stones without rest. She reached the far side of the pond and sprinted toward the cries.

She burst through a mass of underbrush, and found Melody staring with great concern at Breann. The little redheaded girl with the angry freckles across her cheeks was on her hands and knees, heaving rocks from a manmade pile. She tossed them aside, scraping her knuckles and fingernails, drawing blood from her crazed efforts.

"What is it?" Clara asked. "What's going on?"

"It's the end of the map," Melody said, fear in her eyes. "This mound of rocks. What is it, Clara?"

"I have no idea."

"It's here. I know it's here. It's gotta be." Breann tore another heavy stone from where dirt and debris had conspired to consign it to history.

"Breann, wait a second. Let us help you." Clara approached the girl and set a hand on her shoulder. Her skin was hot, like the embers of a long-stoked bonfire.

Breann turned, glared at her with malevolence.

Clara stepped quickly away, nearly stumbling as she collided with Melody.

"Let's just ... let her be," Melody said.

"But her hands, she's bleeding."

Breann pried a slab of gray granite the size of a dinner plate from the mound. It tumbled to rest near Clara's feet. Breann didn't move, just gazed at the opening in the rock pile.

Melody inched closer. "What is it, Bree?"

Breann reached into the darkened opening and removed a small wooden box. With trembling hands, she handed it over to Clara. "I ... I can't open it," she said. "You do it." She sniffled and wiped the back of her hand across her nose.

"O ... kay," Clara said.

The box felt light enough to be empty. Barely bigger than her palm, its nearly black wood seemed to shine. It was only after Clara searched for a locking mechanism that she realized the effect was from Breann's blood. She tried avoiding the wetness as she used a fingernail to pry open the little hasp keeping it shut. The hinged seam gave off a cry of rust.

Inside, the box was lined with black velvet, and coiled at its center, a necklace with a heart-shaped charm. A held breath escaped Clara's lips—echoed by the other two girls—as she touched the charm's smooth surface. A tingle coursed through her finger and up her arm.

"It's beautiful," Melody said, looking not at the necklace but at Breann's reaction.

Even though she fervently needed to discover what was at the end of the map, Breann stood with her arms folded, staring off into the woods. She tried to act disinterested, but her trembling lower lip gave her away.

"What is this?" Clara said. She picked up the charm and its chain fell free from the box. "Whose is this?"

"Wait!" Breann turned on Clara, tears in her eyes.

"Breann, please don't!" Melody cried.

"It's not hers!" Breann lashed out for the charm, and as Clara stepped back, her foot caught on one of the many rocks tossed aside from the pile.

Clara fell backward, her vision scrolling from the forest floor to the dense canopies and to the shard of blue sky beyond. And she continued to fall—slipping between geography, through the liminal spaces dividing time and anguish—where true horror lived at the axis of those two elements.

CHAPTER 23

With Poppa's manuscript under her arm, Krista circled around to the front yard. Spread out across the lawn, Trev, Robby, and Leah were attempting to play croquet with a playset that might've been new midway through the last century. Even with splintered mallets and rusted wickets, they were all enjoying themselves, so much so that no one noticed Krista slinking through the yard.

Pastel chalk in hand, Heidi ignored their game in favor of her canvas—the broad cobblestones lining the walkway between the porch and driveway. As if sensing her presence, Heidi looked up in Krista's direction. Her serious expression softened into a smile and she offered a little wave. Krista waved back and the girl returned to her chalks.

Krista crossed the lawn to the far northern part of the property. As she neared the graveyard, nestled in the wooded wedge of land near the road, her irritation resurfaced.

How could he keep so much from us?

Her free hand trembled when she brushed the hair from her face. She needed distance and time before facing him, but she definitely needed to face him. It was unavoidable, but still, she seethed.

How could he?

She didn't want to hurt Poppa, but that would be almost unavoidable when she asked him about the map mentioned in his manuscript. She had so many questions. Did he follow through and search for Edgar's "treasure" hidden at the end of the map? Did he find anything? Why had he never mentioned it to her?

Krista couldn't help picturing mud-stained bones and child-sized clothing buried in a shallow grave.

She had so many questions, but Poppa was weak and only getting weaker. She needed answers, but she couldn't imagine tearing open that wound—one they both shared.

The short path into the dense woods provided enough seclusion to hide the graveyard from view at the house. Krista didn't realize someone was already at Nan's graveside until she entered the little alcove.

Jack didn't notice her right away. He pulled weeds from around Nan's marble stone, and carefully tugged on a dandelion until it gave up its root with a pop before he tossed it onto a growing pile.

"Hey there, little brother," she said.

His head jerked up, revealing bloodshot eyes with dark bags beneath. His unhinged gaze made Krista pause in her tracks.

He blinked a couple times, as if he didn't recognize her, before his senses seemed to crystallize. "Oh, hey, Krista." He got to his feet and brushed his hands on his thighs. "What are you doing out here?"

"I just needed …" Her shoulders slumped as she looked over at the headstone. She read the inscription: *In loving memory of Francine Whalen, who cast the light for many.* She glanced toward the summer house. The kids and Leah were laughing and carousing just out of sight. "I needed to step away for a minute."

"Yeah, I know what you mean." His voice was a strained wisp. He pointed to the binder under her arm. "What's that?"

She hesitated.

Jack looked so unmoored, as if he could snap at any moment and float away.

It was only out of concern for him, and for Trev by extension, that she said, "It's Poppa's new book. Oh, by the way, don't tell him I'm reading it. I found it at his writing desk."

"Really? I didn't know he was still working."

She nodded slowly. The question had never crossed her mind.

"Yeah, I guess a writer never quits."

Jack nodded too, satisfied. He brushed a palm over the arching top of Nan's headstone, smoothing away a thin layer of dust and pollen. Just as she expected, he didn't press her for more details about the book. Her brother, love him, wasn't much of a reader. It certainly pleased him that Poppa was a successful writer, but she doubted he'd read more than a paragraph or two from his vast output.

"I wish I could have helped her, you know?" he said, barely audible. "That I could've stopped her from doing what she did."

"She didn't *do* anything, Jack. She fell down the stairs. It was horrible, but there's nothing you could have done."

"I was here, Krista. I could've ... I don't know ..." He stopped when his chest began to hitch. "I could've brought Poppa his sandwich."

Krista almost laughed. She didn't understand what he was talking about, just that he was terribly upset and burdened with guilt. She stepped closer to him, close enough that her nose wrinkled at the mixture of booze, weed, and unwashed skin wafting from him. She placed a hand on his shoulder, her fingers no longer trembling. Somehow, she found a way to pull it together when someone close to her needed her help or support.

"Are you okay?"

He shot a look back at her. "Do I look okay to you?"

"I've seen you better, no doubt," she said, trying to make light of the situation, but it sounded hollow, even to her own ears.

She sat on a fallen log near the woods. It looked like it had fallen naturally, but from the worn bark, it also looked like it had served as a bench quite often. Krista pictured Poppa visiting Nan's grave, sitting in this very spot. The summer house was always a place of belonging, of sharing, of being with others. This sad little island felt distanced from the living world, even though it was surrounded by the abundance of nature.

"Jack, come here." She patted the log next to her. "Come on, I'm not going to bite."

He glanced at her and rolled his eyes.

"Fine, I'm not going to lecture you, either. Just ..." She again beckoned him over. "Sit with me before I start crying."

He complied with reluctance, looking up from the headstone.

As he sat next to her, his knees cracked, and he let out a heavy sigh.

After they hadn't spoken in a minute or more, Jack cleared his throat. "Do you think she can hear us?" He stared down at his feet. "Nan, I mean."

"I hope so, I really do," Krista said.

"If she can hear us, do you think that means we could, I don't know, hear her, you know, in some way?"

"It would only make sense, I guess. I know Poppa believes it. That's why he's staying here instead of at the home in Grand Rapids. Or in a hospice. He thinks he's seen glimpses of her from the corner of his eye, that he's smelled hints of her perfume."

"*Unforgettable*," Jack said. "That's what it was called, right?"

"How do you remember that?" Clara said and grinned. She wouldn't have remembered the name of Nan's perfume, even with a gun pointed at her head.

"It was the one fancy bottle on top of her dresser. She didn't wear a bunch of makeup or jewelry. But she always had that fancy pink bottle."

"Maybe Poppa's right," Clara said. "I can smell her perfume, now that you mention it." She closed her eyes, pictured Nan spraying a single spritz on her neck. Her warm smile. Her unbelievable patience. "Ah … the power of memories."

When she opened her eyes, Jack's expression had darkened.

"You know, Mom and Dad … I can't remember them. I mean, at all."

Krista didn't know what to say.

"We have that picture," he said. "I think it's the last one of all five of us together."

"From Easter that year," she recalled. "We went to the mall photo studio. We could barely get you to sit still. Only one photo turned out with all of us smiling at the same time."

"Yeah … that's the one. I was, like, four years old. You think I'd remember sitting on Mom's lap. Or Dad standing behind us. Nope. Not a thing. My only memory of that picture is looking at it with you and Leah, with Nana and Poppa. Hearing stories about that day. I remember looking at it when we were little and thinking it should be important to me. Memorable in some way. But when I think about Dad, when I try to remember any little detail, all I remember is Poppa. Same thing about Mom. All I see is Nan."

"We were lucky we had Nan and Poppa. Other kids in our situation, a lot of them wind up in foster care, most likely separated."

"Yeah, we were lucky," Jack said. "You couldn't get away from me that easy." He laughed softly as he stood, kissed his fingertips, and placed them on top of the headstone. When he turned his head again, the madness was gone from his eyes. "You know, I came out here to be alone. But I'm glad you came. In all seriousness, I'm glad Trev and I have you guys—you and Leah."

"We'll always be there for you, Jack. I hope you've always known that. We've always had each other's backs, right? We've had to, ever since we were little."

He looked like he was going to head back toward the house, but he stopped short of leaving. "Do you believe in evil?"

"What, like people doing evil things, or do you mean Satan-type stuff?"

"I don't know. Can you have one without the *other?*"

"Are you being philosophical, or are you becoming religious?"

"I wonder ... the evil humans ... why do they do it? Are they born that way? Are they damaged in childhood? Or are they influenced by ... something, I don't know, other?"

"You're talking about devils and demons."

"I don't know what I'm talking about. It's just, sometimes, when I feel Nan close by, like she could reach out and touch me if I allowed it," he said, shivering despite the afternoon's warmth, "what I feel isn't *her*. It's darkness. It's ... it's *evil.*"

"Well then, if you think it's her, you're clearly mistaken. There wasn't a mean bone in her body."

"I know. I know."

"So if you feel she's close by, what I think is that you feel guilty about how she died. You came for a visit and she—by sheer coincidence—happened to die that weekend. You think you could've stopped it, but you couldn't have. You need to figure out how to forgive yourself."

Jack listened intently, parsing her words like he were deciphering some mysterious code. He nodded, as if something had sunk in.

"I bet that's it. You know, I think you're right." Jack hurried to her side and planted a kiss on her cheek.

She winced at the bristles, but he didn't notice. He was already heading back toward the house. "You're welcome?" she said.

"I'll talk to you later, Krista. Thanks for listening!"

"What are big sisters for?" she said softly.

She chuckled at the drastic change in Jack's attitude. She didn't know how she helped him, but that didn't matter. Sometimes all you needed was someone to listen.

She stood from the fallen log and gathered the pile of weeds Jack had pulled from around the gravesite, and tossed them into the woods.

"Oh, Nan, I miss you …" she whispered. "So does everyone … God, Jack could sure use your strength right about now."

Krista felt silly speaking to the empty air. She had never been religious, had never believed in spirits or the afterlife, but if there were pearly gates somewhere, her grandma would surely qualify for entrance.

"I wish you were here. I need to know what to do about this map. I need to hear you explain to me why Poppa would've kept so much from me." She blinked through tears, her gaze rising from the gravestone to the thin tree branches overhead. "I need to know what to do."

"What you need to do," a soft voice called out from the woods, "is get over yourself."

Krista couldn't pinpoint the sound. It could've come from anywhere. She heard rustling in the underbrush nearby and turned to face it.

"Who is it?" she said.

The voice sounded familiar, but it hadn't been Nan's. She closed in on the sounds of movement; a squirrel hopped into view before disappearing up a tree.

"I've been waiting for you," the voice called out again, spinning Krista around.

Red hair like rust. Sprays of dark freckles across each cheek and the bridge of her nose. Demure and innocence in her composure, yet wild, with leaves and twigs dangling from the wisps coming from haphazard, braided pigtails. She sat on the log, legs crossed at the knee, hands clasped and resting on her thigh.

"Breann?"

"Hi Krista."

The words weakened Krista's legs. Her knees began to buckle. The blood in her brain seemed to have turned into molasses. Her vision began to dim and she stumbled over to the log. She sat down next to the dead girl to keep from face-planting next to Nan's grave.

"I'm not supposed to talk to you," Breann said, barely a whisper. She looked first one way, then the other. "I don't have much time."

Krista braced her elbows on her knees and took several deep breaths until she felt like she wouldn't pass out. She turned to her long-ago friend.

Breann hadn't changed one bit. The redhead cocked her head to the side like she always had, staring at her with open curiosity. When Krista didn't respond right away, the dead girl absently ran her tongue over the tip of her crooked eyetooth.

"Oh my God, it's you," Krista said.

Her hand lifted, spanning the short gap between them. She touched the warm soft skin of Breann's shoulder, could smell coconut-scented suntan lotion and cherry Kool Aid.

"Of course, it is, silly."

"I … I never thought I'd ever see you," Krista said, finding it difficult to focus her thoughts. "I wanted to say I'm sorry."

"Sorry? For what?" Breann arched one eyebrow.

"For everything. For being stupid. For not understanding about Sandy Armstrong."

"You know she was using you, right?" Breann said. "She didn't like you, but Nan always drove you anywhere you wanted."

The attitude, the snide tone … how could this *not* be Breann?

"I didn't know," Krista said, lightheaded. "I … I'm so sorry, Breann."

Before her friend could say anymore, Krista wrapped her arms

179

around her. The dead girl, so small. A tiny mass of frail bird bones beneath thin, freckle-spotted skin. She felt something else, something void, something akin to living shadow. She inhaled deeply, the cherry Kool-Aid and coconut beginning to sour.

Krista held her at arms' length but didn't let go.

"How are you here? Why are you here?"

"I'm not here," Breann said. "Not really. Just like I wasn't in the spare room playing with your Nan's quilt the other night." She laughed.

"But you are. You're right here. I see you, feel you."

Krista inhaled, the smell becoming stronger, more unavoidable.

"It's a trick of light and shadow. I had to see you. Had to have you see me. Before it's too late."

"What ... what do you mean?"

"I need your help."

"Anything," Krista said without thought.

"Find me." Something crackled in Breann's throat. Cartilage perhaps, twisted and torn under pressure. Bruises appeared on her neck, ringlets of red welts that quickly deepened to purple and black.

The dead girl had become something spoiled, something rotten and decayed, her many smells saturating the air, cloying within Krista's nose. She wanted to run away, to vomit, but she couldn't. Not when Breann was here and now.

"Of course, I will. But how? All these years ... Where have you been?"

"I don't know," she said wetly. She coughed, spraying black blood over her lips and down her shirt.

"My grandpa, he knows something about this." Krista glanced toward the house. She could see the angle of the roof, flashes of brown from the east-facing wall. "I'll go ask him. I'll have him tell me everything."

The skin of Breann's cheeks began to sag with rot, to pull away from the brittle bone beneath. Black oozed from the widening wound to gather on her lashes. She blinked, and dark blood splashed the grass below.

"He knows more than you, but nothing important." Breann's

body was collapsing in on itself, as if clamped under immense pressure. Blood flowed freely from her eyes, nose, mouth, and ears. She struggled to breathe, though she no longer needed to obey that instinct reserved for the living. "He knows the man with the beautiful blue eyes took me … took the others, but that's about it."

"So, what am I supposed to do? How can I help you?"

"Only one person knows where to find me."

Breann fell to her back, blood leaving her body in rivulets. Her knees pulled close to her chest, remained pinned in place. Her arms wrapped her legs, and her entire body squeezed ever closer. Her eyes, now nothing more than open bloody wounds, let out a soft squelching noise as her orbs burst within her head.

Horrified, Krista backed away. She felt the urge to shout for help but remained mute.

"Find me …"

Blood bubbled up from what was once a mouth, coating the remains of her face, silencing her. Breann's body twitched, shrinking in on itself, collapsing with a machine-gunning of shattered bones until there was nothing left but a stagnant puddle of gore.

Krista couldn't take it anymore and closed her eyes. Her mind swam, ready to pass out. The scent of blood and rot filled her nose. She only opened her eyes when the scent began to fade, replaced by that of subtle sweet cherry Kool-Aid.

She was alone. Not a single blade of grass stained red. When she inhaled, even the memory of cherry was gone.

CHAPTER 24

Clara was nearly home.

She sipped from a water bottle before returning it to Poppa's satchel. Motes of dust danced on the sunlight streaming through the tree branches. She held up the charm Breann had found at the end of Poppa's map. At first, she thought the charm and chain were made of black metal, but the simple links caught the light, revealing hints of silver beneath heavy tarnish. She licked her thumb and rubbed the smooth surface of the heart-shaped charm until she discovered cursive lettering.

"What do we have here?" she whispered, furrowing her brow.

The world around her pulled away as she worked to free the words from the encrusted grime. The birds hushed. The wind ceased to blow. She focused hard, rubbing her thumb until the friction warmed the pad of flesh.

She uncovered one word: BEST

Undeterred, she used the hem of her shirt to scrub the heart. She tried to recall what had preceded her falling down the pile of rocks. Breann had been so mad, and for reasons Clara didn't understand, and for reasons Melody didn't seem willing to share.

A sensation of falling backward, then blinking in bright sunshine, her head woozy as she stared straight into the forested sky. She'd been flat on her back, and when she rubbed her aching temples, the little tarnished heart thumped against the side of her face, the chain interwoven with her fingers.

The two girls had left her alone in the middle of the woods.

The two girls ... are they even girls at all?

The thought was pure insanity and she tried her best to move past it. Of course, they had merely been two girls. Two wild, bizarre girls who seemed to confine themselves to the woods and a narrow band of the Little Whisper's beach.

She revealed a second word on the heart charm: FRIENDS

After another few scrubs, the third word became legible: FOREVER.

BEST FRIENDS FOREVER.

Clara's heart ached and she didn't know why. Perhaps because she didn't have a best friend to call her own. Perhaps from the sadness of finding the heart buried in the middle of the woods. She started off again down the trail, soon reaching the lawn surrounding the summer house. She paused when she saw Aunt Leah and her cousins playing with croquet mallets. They didn't seem to abide any rules but were having fun nonetheless.

Instead of interrupting their game and drawing unwanted attention, she hurriedly cut across the side of the house and then down the hill and around to the back. With weary legs, she trotted up the steps to the deck and slipped inside, breathing a sigh of relief when she slid the door closed.

She again looked at the charm—BEST FRIENDS FOREVER.

What question would that answer for Poppa? He had been waiting so long to find out, and yet she was reluctant to bring it to him.

She remembered Breann's near-hysterical torment when she unearthed the jewelry box from the pile of stones. No good answers could ever come from something causing such emotional pain. But she'd promised Poppa ...

Overwhelming fatigue settled into her muscles. After cutting across the kitchen, she listened for anyone she might encounter before reaching Poppa's bedroom—all was quiet. The hardwood floor creaked, too loudly, as she made her way down the hallway. She stopped outside his door, knuckles poised an inch away from knocking. She chewed her bottom lip before screwing up her courage and opening the door.

Clara craned her head inside the doorway. Her great-grandfather

184

was asleep, propped up high on a number of pillows. His skin an ugly gray. His cheeks drawn.

"Poppa?"

She breathed a sigh of relief when his chest moved and his eyelids fluttered open.

"Clarabelle ..." The pain etched on his face faded as he forced a smile onto his lips. "Come in, come in."

Clara stepped inside and closed the door, hesitating to go any farther. She held her hands clasped behind her back, the heart-shaped charm incredibly weighty dangling from her fingers.

"You look like you had some adventure." His smile widened, no longer forced. "Take a look for yourself."

Clara stepped in front of the mirror on top of Nan's old dresser. She almost didn't recognize herself. Her lightweight blouse had become untucked and sported smears of mud in varying states of drying. Her tan shorts weren't much better. She could do little outside of taking a shower. She tried to straighten her hair, a nest of unbound curlicues. She removed a small leaf from a lock of hair, and when she patted her hair to look for more, the back of her skull throbbed from when she had fallen down the hill.

"I ... I did, Poppa. I really did." She didn't know when she had started crying, or why, but her emotions were building and releasing, building and releasing, one wave after another.

"Oh, Clarabelle, what's wrong, dear?"

"Poppa ... I'm scared." She paused to see his reaction. His bushy eyebrows tightened, but he said nothing. "I'm scared, but also excited. Is that even possible?"

"Anything is possible if you can imagine it. Tell me, Clarabelle, what's troubling you?"

"I found *this*." Clara held up the chain and the little heart swayed beneath it. Sunlight flashed when it caught certain angles. "The map led me to it."

"Why, that's a pretty thing, isn't it?" He looked truly surprised. "Can I see it?"

He reached out, his hand trembling.

She didn't immediately hand it over, not until his eyes shifted from the little tarnished charm to his great-granddaughter, his eyes steely and expectant.

"Please?"

She slipped the chain off her finger and handed it to him.

"I wonder whose it is?" he said in a frail voice.

"I thought you would know. That's why you sent me out there, right? To answer the question at the end of the map?"

"I didn't know what you would find. Not really. But certainly not this." He blew at the heart and it twirled in a circle.

"What is it?" she asked.

"A girl's charm."

"Obviously. But whose charm is it?"

Poppa stared at the heart, as if hypnotized.

A name popped into Clara's head and she blurted it out without a second thought. "Melody ... is it Melody's?"

Still transfixed, he didn't seem fazed by the name. "I don't know."

This worried Clara. "Or is it Breann's?"

"How do you ...?" He finally looked at her. "Did you see ...?" he said, short of breath.

"They helped me find my way. I was lost. I'd fallen down a hill. The girls found me. They brought me to the place where the heart was buried."

"They're not there. These girls ... they shouldn't have done that. That's troubling."

"What do you mean?"

"Those girls, and there are others—probably a lot of others—they are confused, caught between here and there."

"What ... like, ghosts?" A chill ran through her.

"Something like that. I've seen ... glimpses, now and then. Not of *these* girls, necessarily. But I've seen Nan. I don't know what you'd call it—reanimated memory, fragments of forgotten emotion. I don't know, and I don't care. Every time it sends me to the moon and back knowing some part of her is so near."

"Poppa, I don't understand. How can this be? Ghosts aren't real."

"I know. You're right. They're not real. But they still exist. As do demons. As do angels." He sat up taller against his pillow, took a deep breath, as if to bolster his energies. "Have you ever heard of the alien abduction myth? You know, little gray men with dark eyes come to earth to run medical experiments on us lowly humans?"

"Yes, I've heard of it. It's kind of weird."

"It is, isn't it? Well, there's a theory those little gray aliens don't exist, but are also real."

"How can that be?" Her head was starting to hurt.

"It's theorized those memories of abduction have nothing to do with aliens, and everything to do with our own births. So, like I said, real and not real, simultaneously."

"So, what about ghosts, demons, angels …?"

"They are neither here nor *not* here. They are lingering echoes that never fade away."

"And why … why are these girls—Melody, Breann—why are they … haunting me?"

"Good question. But I wouldn't say they're exactly haunting you. Perhaps they're able to communicate with you to a higher degree than other people. Maybe they see you as an ally. Someone who can help. Someone they can trust."

"Help them do what, exactly?"

"Find peace?" Poppa turned his attention to the locket. "The map I drew for you, I never travelled the route it indicates. I got this from someone … someone I'm sorry I ever knew."

"The man who put the charm in the pile of stones in the first place?"

"I'm afraid so."

"He did it, didn't he? He … killed them."

Poppa nodded. His eyes were bloodshot and watery, but he didn't cry. He didn't look like he still possessed the ability to do so.

"Did you think I would find bones at the end of the map?"

He stammered and his eyes widened, as if he just realized how young she was. "I … I don't know."

"And how … how did you know this man?" Clara asked.

Poppa looked away, but not before she noticed deep remorse twisting his features.

"Poppa …" she whispered, but he wouldn't face her. "Poppa!" she shouted. "You know who did this? Who killed Melody and Breann? It's Edgar Jenkins, isn't it?"

He shot a glance her way. "How do you know his name?"

"Am I right?"

She would never forget the name her mom had mentioned on the drive to the summer house. The man who was also the reason she had never returned until this trip.

"Yes," he said in a low whisper.

"Who is he?" she pressed.

"He's a monster." Poppa rubbed his eyes and groaned. "He's a monster who took children. Some from here in Michigan. Others in Wisconsin, and most likely in Indiana and Illinois. He hurt them, let them die slowly."

Bile rose in Clara's throat. "How did you have his map?"

"I always wanted to know where to find Breann. I … I started writing a book, hoping I could use it to be able to see him face to face. After months of pleading and negotiations with his attorney, I was granted an interview. This led to eight visits to the prison where he's to live out his life for killing three other girls. So he dictated the map to me. He told me it would lead to Breann. He told me it would set her free …"

Poppa closed his eyes and his chest hitched.

Clara sat on the bed and placed her hand on his shoulder. He looked at her with agony, guilt, and remorse. She nodded, imploringly, hoping he would continue.

"I wanted to know … why *them?* Why *here?*" he said. "But also, I wanted to figure out what would make someone do those things in the first place."

"What did you find out?"

"Absolutely nothing. I found a monster doing monstrous things for no other reason than he was acting within his nature. Just like a coyote taking down a lame fawn. And I was never able to learn … I was never able to bring home your mother's friend. Breann …"

So many things suddenly made sense, even though Poppa had never found Breann.

Poppa, his face an utter ruin, looked beyond the breaking point. His bulging eyes shed a single tear that trailed down the crags of his withered face. He nodded, and the tear fell from his chin to the sheet covering his lap.

She didn't know what else to do, so she climbed onto the bed and snuggled next to him.

"Poppa?"

"Yes, Clarabelle?"

"Why didn't you ever follow the map? Even when you weren't … sick, even then you could've followed it."

He took a ragged breath before saying, "I just couldn't take any more pain. Looking back, I can see how selfish that sounds. What's my pain compared to the ongoing pain felt by Breann's family?"

"Where are they? Her family?"

Poppa clutched Breann's heart charm against his chest until his knuckles turned white and his hand trembled. While Clara wanted to show her mom the charm, she wanted to bring it to Breann's parents, no matter where they were located.

"I lost track of the McCorts after they moved, a couple of years after Breann disappeared. They'd only bought the neighboring house after one of Brandon's investments in a tech upstart netted a big return. Unfortunately, their luck didn't last, and it didn't take long before they struggled paying for both their house in Indianapolis and the summer house here on the Little Whisper. Even after they moved away, I couldn't escape the idea I could've done something more. That I could've stopped him before he took her. I've been so tempted to track them down, just to hear their voices, to hopefully hear *healing* in their voices."

"You shouldn't be so hard on yourself, Poppa. That was so long ago."

"You sound just like my Francie." He chuckled. "I hear your words, Clarabelle, but *hearing* and *doing* don't always follow one after the other."

"Can you at least try?" she asked.

"I guess I can try. For you." He held up the heart charm, smiled sadly as he stared at it.

"What are you going to do with it?" she asked.

He pursed his lips. "I'm not exactly sure. Like I said, I don't know where the McCorts are, and I don't know if sending this necklace would do more damage than good."

"What about giving it to Mom?"

"I'd rather not waken any more pain. Those memories are old, but still raw. I can see it in her eyes." Poppa undid the clasp. "How about you become its caretaker? You'll take good care of it, right?"

"Of course. But why me?"

Even though she was uncertain about wearing Breann's charm, Clara leaned forward, almost subconsciously.

Poppa placed it around her neck and refastened the clasp.

"It just makes sense, right?" Poppa said.

Clara didn't reply, the charm resting below her collar bones. It felt substantial, and in some fashion, *alive.*

CHAPTER 25

When Krista left the graveyard, she noticed Clara cutting along the side of the yard, heading for the back of the house. She looked filthy and tired from her hike, and in a hurry.

At least she's okay.

Krista clutched Poppa's binder against her chest, giving the forested walkway a couple of glances as she went across the lawn. She saw no evidence of Breann—either in her youthful, wholesome appearance, or her bloody, decayed incarnation—as she neared the house.

"Hey, Krista, you okay?" Leah called out.

Leah was gathering the croquet equipment as Trev and Robby raced to grab the last few wickets.

"Yeah, just …" She couldn't help it. She looked back at the graveyard one last time. "Never mind. I'm just feeling a bit sad."

Krista went up the porch steps and was somewhat annoyed when Leah followed her.

"What are you doing?"

"You're going to see Poppa, right?"

"Well, yeah, I guess. I also wanted to check on Clara. She just got home."

"Well, I haven't seen Poppa since this morning, so I'm going to see if he needs anything."

Krista rolled her eyes. "Fine."

When they reached Poppa's door, Krista wasn't sure if she should knock, in case he was sleeping. She set Poppa's binder on the floor and opened the door as quietly as possible.

Poppa turned, smiling when he saw the two of them enter. He didn't look to be in much pain, just exhausted.

Clara was curled up at his side, asleep.

"Is she okay?" Krista asked.

"More than okay," he whispered. "She's exhausted from a grand adventure."

"Okay." She wanted to confront him about what she'd learned in his manuscript. Wanted to know more than anything why he'd kept so much from her. But his tired, satisfied smile held her back; that, and the gruesome sight of Breann decaying before her very eyes.

She shuddered at the memory.

She watched her daughter's posture, an echo of all those glorious years spent at the summer house. Poppa had always been there, not only for her, but everyone in their family. He had been there to comfort and console, to teach and impart wisdom. If there had been anything important to convey to her, he would've done it. Now, without question, she understood.

"Poppa …?" Clara said softly.

"Yes, dear?"

"I love you."

"I never tire of hearing that. I love you, too. The both of you."

Krista and Leah stepped away from the room, closing the door behind them. Krista picked up the binder, finding unexpected strength from the words held within.

"What was *that* about?" Leah asked.

"What?"

"You looked like you were going to rake him over the coals or something."

"I know he knows more about Breann than he's letting on … but … I just couldn't confront him about it."

"That's probably for the best."

"But I also haven't given up on finding Breann's resting place."

"It sounds like you've given up on the idea that she's still out there somewhere, living a regular life."

"I had to."

Leah looked at her sister closely, arching one eyebrow. "You've *seen* her, haven't you? You've seen Breann?"

"How ... how did you know?"

"It's so perfectly obvious now. So it's true?"

"Yes. I saw Breann. She asked me for help. She told me only one person knew where she's buried."

Leah gasped and fought back tears. "I think I knew in my heart the whole time ... you know, that she was dead."

"I know, me too."

"So that one person, it's not ...?"

"Yes," Krista said. "It's Edgar. I need to talk to him."

"How? He's in prison. He's never getting out, thank God."

"I'll just have to visit him, then, won't I?"

Krista began formulating a plan as she made her way back toward the den. It was a crazy plan if she were to consider it with an unjaundiced eye. But it made so much sense.

"What are you doing?" Leah asked as she followed a step behind.

Krista found her purse on the end table and removed her cell phone. She pulled up the search engine and within a minute tracked down the phone number for Allen Dougherty, Esquire. It took another minute or two of hesitation, of beginning to dial and hanging up, before she finally let the phone make the connection.

"I'm calling Edgar's attorney."

"Now *that's* a conversation I couldn't have predicted."

"And that's not the worst of it. I also have to figure out how to tell Neal I'm going to talk to Edgar."

CHAPTER 26

Jack wondered that perhaps the ultimate twist of madness was thinking Nan had turned evil upon her death. How could he have believed that possibility? Nan was an angel, and only some outside influence could've turned her disposition so quickly on its head.

He gathered a tackle box and fishing pole from inside the garage before cutting through the house to the back deck. From the dust and beginnings of rust on the equipment, Poppa hadn't fished in quite some time.

Jack would've expected advice on spiritual matters to come from Leah, not Krista. Leah was the sibling who saw auras, felt future turns of fate in her bones. Krista had always been the *practical* sister, the stay-at-home mom who married an on-the-cusp lawyer. Even so, Krista had opened his eyes. If Nan's spirit had been corrupted in some nefarious way, then Jack might be able to save it as well.

He stepped out onto the deck, his gaze frozen at the top of the stairs.

A flash of memory: Nan's outspread arms, Nan falling forward, Nan letting gravity take her in its grip. He had to look away to catch his breath.

As he slid the door shut, sunlight poured into the room as someone entered through the front. Jack melted back into the shadows as Leah and Krista headed for Poppa's room.

He hurried past the spot where Nan had taken the plunge down the stairs. The metal spinners, antique cork bobbers, and hooks rattled inside the tackle box with his movements.

Dark clouds rolled in over the wooded horizon. Rain was in the air, wet and warm.

Jack swore under his breath when he reached the boat, realizing he'd forgotten about the oars. He gripped the lip of the boat and tugged up once, twice, and on the third heave the momentum tipped the boat right-side-up. He reached under the bench seat, fumbled around thick spider webs that broke under his touch.

"Haha, yes." He found two oars stashed beneath, both in good condition. "Good luck for once."

"Hey there, Jack," Neal called out, approaching from the direction of the water. "I didn't know you were heading out."

"Yeah, I thought I'd get in some night fishing."

"We haven't even had dinner yet."

"That's all right. I packed a sandwich."

"You did?" Neal looked inside the boat.

"It's in the tackle box."

Jack placed the fishing pole and tackle inside the boat. He hadn't thought ahead about what he was doing. He hated lying to Neal, but he needed to do this alone.

"Well, okay," Neal said, looking concerned. "Give me a minute and I'll grab another pole from the garage. We've been talking about taking the boat out since we got here."

"Maybe tomorrow? I need to ..." Jack looked toward the water. His mind flashed to the sight of Nan's spirit chasing him out to the anchored dock. Her and the dead children, glowing, their eyes vacant, all reaching for him. Out there, in the middle of the lake, was the strongest he'd seen her spirit; if he was going to make contact with her, deliberately, it would be out there. "I need some time to clear my head. That okay?"

"Yeah, sure. Just be careful. Looks like rain is coming in. If you see lightning, come right back."

"For sure, for sure."

Jack grabbed the rope and tugged until the boat slowly shifted in the sand.

"Hold on." Neal went to the back of the boat and gave it a push until Jack built up the momentum to drag it to the water.

Jack waded in up to his mid-thighs. "Thanks, bro," he said, and hopped inside.

Neal smiled and gave a small wave, which did nothing to erase the concern Jack saw staring at him as he paddled away from shore.

Jack barely had a game plan. The Nan he'd seen wasn't the Nan he remembered long ago. She had changed. No, more accurately, *something* had changed Nan. Something vile and sinister. He couldn't let it pass. He couldn't allow her soul, her spirit, her whatever-still-lingered in this world, to be corrupted by something evil.

Oars in hand, he braced his sandaled feet on the floor of the boat and leaned all the way forward before pulling back, slicing the water. He quickly put distance between him and the shore, even after his bum shoulder ached after only a dozen or so strokes. Sweat beaded his forehead and trickled down his back. It felt good to exert his muscles, to strain his body and see his efforts measured in the growing distance from shore.

A steady wind braced his back, cold and portending rain and an early sunset. He pulled even harder on the oars, his momentum taking him easily past the anchored dock. When he reached the middle of the lake, his lungs burned. The boat drifted on the last of its inertia, twirling in a slow arc by the lake's nearly invisible waves.

"You didn't fall, did you, Nan?" he asked the water, the lapping waves. "You *threw* yourself down those steps. You had that dead-eyed stare. That's the worst part of it, you know, remembering how your eyes looked right before it happened. You threw yourself down those stairs, but it wasn't you, was it?"

Lamps blazed inside the summer house in the distance, shining like lighthouse beacons calling all to the safety of the shore. Trev would be tagging along with Robby and Leah. He pictured Leah raising his son, someone with a kind and generous heart and no ulterior motive. He closed his eyes, picturing Robby and Trev bonding like brothers. It didn't fill him with a sense of loss; Trev would be better off living with his sister. Imagining him otherwise seemed wrong.

"Whatever happens," Jack said, "Trev will be looked after."

When he opened his eyes, the skies had darkened. Thunder rumbled. The chill wind heaved the storm through the surrounding woods, sending birds skittering aloft in search of dry perches. Rain pattered the far reach of the lake and expanded steadily across its surface, until he knew the second before it would touch his skin.

"Nan, speak to me." His voice strengthened against the building storm. The rain soaked his shirt within seconds. "I'm here. You know I'm here!"

Jack again closed his eyes. He saw Poppa standing next to Nan's coffin. The old man's skin was tan, his cheeks no longer gaunt. He carried a good thirty pounds more than he did now. Looking both healthy and shattered, he placed his palm against the auburn coffin, and his tears, which had been under control for the last hour, came back in full force.

Of course, Leah had been there to console Poppa. As the casket lowered into the empty grave, Leah turned him away and wrapped her arms around him. Poppa wept like a child.

Jack could do nothing to help, and so he had backed away from the graveyard alcove. The dry rasp of dirt falling onto the casket lid sounded too utterly final.

Later on, when the burial and brief service had ended, Poppa found him sitting on the front porch steps. Jack had wanted to run away, to hide, but the old man had already seen him.

"Thank you for coming," Poppa said, climbing the stairs and clapping him on the back.

Poppa groaned as he eased onto the porch swing.

Jack couldn't trust himself to speak. His emotions would betray him. He would say something he wouldn't be able to take back. He waited, hoping Poppa wouldn't say anything.

"Your Nan ... you never saw her dark days."

"Dark days?" Jack turned to face his grandfather. "Nan was never depressed, if that's what you're saying."

"She hid it well. Even from me. But as age caught up to us both, more of her days than not were bleak, governed by storms I could never see, let alone understand."

"That can't be true. I don't believe it. I *won't* believe it."

Poppa nodded, as if to acknowledge some inner dialogue only he could hear.

Leah and Curtis, hand-in-hand, came up to the porch after leaving the service.

"We're going to get the casserole in the oven," Leah said.

"Thanks, dear," Poppa said.

Jack's upper lip curled. "Make sure you don't burn it."

Leah rolled her eyes and went inside.

"Don't worry," Curtis said. "I'll keep an eye on things."

"Well, bro, that doesn't put my mind at ease."

Curtis laughed, not realizing he was serious. Jack had never trusted Curtis from the time he'd met him.

"It wouldn't do any good to tell her I'm not hungry," Poppa said.

"Yeah, I think you're right." Jack again tried to picture Nan overcome with depression. Couldn't get the puzzle pieces to fit together.

Something didn't add up. Either he didn't know his grandmother as well as he once believed, or his grandfather was spinning tales about her emotional state.

Poppa waved goodbye to Ezra Philips and his wife, Debra, the only non-family members Jack recognized. Before his retirement, Ezra had been a professor of Biology at Grand Valley State University. When his path crossed with Poppa's during his lecture circuit days, after *To Heal the Land* became a runaway bestseller, they became fast friends. No other outsiders had come to Nan's burial, which Jack found odd. Nan had always been so gregarious, so full of life.

A chill from the rain brought Jack back to the here and now.

Cold rivulets coursed down his scalp, his neck, his torso. He kept his eyes closed and tried to recall more details from a day he'd once wanted to put well out of mind. He was on the middle of the Little Whisper, a storm lashing the woods and drumming water upon the boat, but he could still hear the creaking porch swing as Poppa slowly moved to and fro, could taste the burnt tomato and macaroni casserole of long ago.

Grief-stricken, Leah had accidentally burned the casserole. And Curtis had acted his Curtis-like self and allowed it to happen, even though he said he wouldn't.

The rain-battered lake sounded alive.

"Nan ... what happened that afternoon?"

A shiver rolled through him, and Jack opened his eyes. On the front bench of the boat, no more than two feet away, stood a full bottle of dark liquor. Rain had soaked and ruined the label. He lifted the bottle, heavy and real, as more of his sanity slipped away.

The label came apart under the slightest pressure.

The shore seemed so far away, miles upon miles, as if he were now stationed in the middle of Lake Michigan. In the distance, tiny sparks of light filled the summer house windows.

"So be it."

Jack twisted off the bottle's cap and sniffed the contents. His eyes watered and his sinuses cleared. Whatever it was, this liquor was strong.

Jack tipped the bottle, the liquid fire pouring across his tongue to splash the back of his throat. He swallowed, though instinct wanted to heave the poison from his system. Warmth spread throughout his body, instantly slurring his faculties. His brain fogged and he felt sleepy, despite the storm's increasing intensity.

A flash of light as Jack blinked, a flash of movement. He blinked again, and just before his eyelids touched, he glimpsed glowing light within his reach, within the boat itself.

Human-shaped.

He opened his eyes to an empty boat.

Jack swigged again from the bottle, the telltale burn ravaging his sensibilities. He didn't blink this time, merely closed his eyes to half-mast, and through this limited view, through tangling eyelashes, a shape resolved and came into focus sitting across from him on the bench seat.

"Nan?" he muttered.

When he opened his eyes wide, she faded from view.

He again squinted, bringing her into focus. The Nan he remembered, wholesome and warm. She wore a simple flower house dress that fell to her knees, and a smile as wide as he remembered. He wanted to leap across the boat, to embrace her, but every time he tested the limits of his vision, her image blended into the dark expanse of storm-wracked sky.

"I don't have much time," she said.

"Nan, oh, I missed you so much."

Tears filled his eyes, immediately diluted by the rain.

She leaned forward, imploring, and reached for his hand. "I didn't want to leave you." Her touch was so frigid that he felt the urge to pull away, but he didn't, not wanting to lose contact. "I need you to see. I need you to understand …"

A gentle pressure radiated from her hands into his. It travelled his arms, a cold wave chasing away the liquor's blanketing warmth.

The pressure reached his heart, travelled higher still, settling in his brain. A taste of tangy mustard on his tongue, ham, fresh bread. He was again sitting on a stool at the island counter and enjoying the homemade lunch. He remembered the plate. Poppa's food. Nothing good would come of Nan bringing him his lunch. She stood near the counter, the prepared plate ready to go. If only Jack could get the plate to Poppa … that simple gesture. He hurried from his stool and picked up the plate, thought of running past Nan, but she was there, in his path.

"Oh, thank goodness you noticed his plate," Nan said, reaching for it.

He clenched the plate so hard he imagined the ceramic shattering into a million pieces, but Nan's hold was incredibly strong, supernaturally so.

Her eyes narrowed. "Let go of the fucking plate. You don't understand!"

"I can't let you do it, Nan. I can't."

"You must, and you *will*, Jackson!" She tugged on the plate and muscled it from his grip. The flowery scent of her perfume—*Unforgettable*—had soured on the air, tasted stale on his tongue, spoiled even. She glared at him before turning away to deliver the lunch.

He trailed after her to Poppa's office.

Numerous research books surrounded Poppa in unstable towers. A ream's worth of papers was strewn around the desktop, while some had tumbled to the floor. Wadded throwaways littered the floor near the trash can in the corner.

Poppa sat with his palms pressed flat into an opened book in the middle of his desk. He rocked forward and back, but his hands never left the book, as if an odd magnetism kept him glued to the pages. His eyes rolled in their sockets, fluttering, spastic.

"Honey, here's your ..."

She dropped the plate, which shattered near Jack's feet.

He'd never heard the plate break before. Not the first time it happened, nor the time Nan first brought him back to this tragic day.

She ran to Poppa's side and took him by the arms. Reluctantly, his hands tore away from the pages. He was muttering incoherently, foam gathered at his lips.

"Oh, God, don't you take him from me!" She kneeled at his side, hugged him fiercely. "You will not have him!"

"Nan, don't," Jack said, knowing in some way what would happen next. "Don't do it!"

She was unaware of his presence. Completely oblivious.

"Dear lord, I'm not ready for you to take him," she prayed.

Poppa's head lolled and she managed, barely, to help him to the floor. She grabbed the phone from the desk and dialed 9-1-1.

No dial-tone, Jack knew.

She put the phone to her ear, jiggled the receiver.

"He always unplugs the phone when he's working," Jack said.

She didn't hear him, then, perhaps not even now.

She dropped the phone and went over to Poppa. He looked to be in the middle of a full-on seizure, his body gyrating against the floor, hands curling against his chest.

"Please ... just take *me*," she pleaded, tugging on his arm, as if urging him to stand.

"Nan, no!" Jack shouted, but he was powerless to change the past.

"Take me and leave him be." Nan's flowery perfume had turned completely, taking on the scent of death; it soaked the air, heavy and pungent.

The wooden slats on the windows vibrated and thrashed against the sash, as if caught in hurricane-force winds. The mess of papers littering Poppa's desk and floor swirled into the air.

Jack blinked, and then everything was back in its place. No papers were any more out of place than normal for Poppa's work area. The plate was no longer shattered across the floor. It sat on top of a pile of books on the desk, the sandwich half-eaten. Poppa sat stiff-backed behind the desk, his head lowered as he followed his finger across a page in the book he was reading.

"Thanks for lunch, Francie," Poppa said. "I don't know what I would do without you."

Nan, dead-eyed, turned away from his desk. She merely grunted a reply as she left the room, heading for her terminal fall down the deck stairs.

Jack wanted to wrench Poppa around, to take him by the shoulders and scream for him to stop her. When he tried, he couldn't move within a handful of inches of him. Poppa continued to study, to follow his finger across the page, only pausing long enough to turn the page.

"She's going to die!" Jack shouted to no avail. "She sacrificed herself. She's going to do it again, and you're sitting there. Just sitting there!"

Jack lunged at Poppa, using every ounce of energy to try to propel himself forward.

Pressure built behind his eyes, darkening his vision. He blinked, struggled against time and history. Rain peppered his face, cold and bracing. Thunder rumbled through the surrounding woods. The boat once again drifted beneath him, the gales heaving it across the choppy water.

Jack understood, both what had happened on the day of Nan's death, and what he would need to do now to save her. He wondered if he were brave enough to make that sacrifice.

Jack sat up, the boat unsteady beneath him. His fingers gripped the liquor bottle's neck. "You can't have her!" he yelled into the rain. He pulled his arm back then heaved the bottle into the dark water. "Take me instead!"

The lake gave no reply. The rain continued to pepper his face. He swiped his hand across the beard stubble on his cheek. As he went to sit on the bench seat—resigned once again to failure—his foot slipped in the puddling water at the boat's bottom and the back of his leg clipped the bench seat, and he tumbled overboard.

He heard a chorus of children's laughter as he broke the surface. As he gasped for breath and flailed for the boat, something took hold of his legs, his arms. Something insistent and strong. It pulled him under, and once under, the darkness filled him.

CHAPTER 27

Krista stood next to the Volvo, ready but full of apprehension to leave for the ferry. She spun the keys around her index finger, liking the rattle and crash when she caught them after a full revolution. She couldn't look her husband in the eye.

"I know you feel like you have to do this," Neal said. "I totally understand, but I want to come with you. You shouldn't have to face this alone."

"Nothing would make me happier," she said. "But I need you here. Jack isn't himself lately." She spun the keys around her finger again. "You said so yourself. He's out on the lake, alone. He's troubled. By what, I don't know, but I'd feel better if you stayed to keep an eye on things."

He took hold of both her hands, pulled her close. "Leah's here. She's reasonably level-headed." He tried his most charming smile, but it wasn't working.

"Leaving her to watch over four kids and Poppa? That's downright cruel."

Neal shook his head but seemed to understand. He'd taken the news rather well, but that was typical of her husband. He would support her no matter the endeavor.

"Believe me, I want you to come with me, but I need you here. All of us do. I'll be back the day after tomorrow."

"Two days?"

The question was loaded. Two days was a significant amount of time when considering Poppa condition. Did he even *have* two days?

When she first brought up visiting Two Rivers Correctional Facility, Neal had tried to argue that she should chase this line of questioning down the road, when they weren't so up against the clock. But she'd been insistent and, of course, Neal had supported her in the end.

"I love you," she said. Her feelings were stronger than those three simple words, and they only strengthened by the day. She wished she could express how important he was to her.

"I love you, too," he said and kissed her forehead.

"Bye, Mom," Clara said from the porch.

Krista waved to her daughter, stunned at how much she'd changed since their arrival. Clara feet were dirty and bare, her hair unbrushed and wild. There wasn't a book under her daughter's arm, or in her hand, which seemed incongruent from reality. They hadn't told her, or anyone else besides Leah, where Krista was heading. Even so, Clara had a knowing look.

Krista hated keeping anything important from her family; she whirled the keys around her index finger so hard they flew away.

Neal caught the keys in midair, like some kind of magic trick. He smiled broadly and gave her hands a squeeze when he handed them back. "Looks like a storm is coming, so drive safely. And call me when you get to Wisconsin."

"I will." She pecked him on the cheek and climbed in behind the wheel of the Volvo.

He leaned over the doorframe. "Don't worry about anything here."

"I'll try my best." She clicked her seatbelt into place. "Love you."

"Love you, too." Neal closed the door, shoved his hands in his pockets, and walked back toward the summer house.

Neal and Clara stood side by side on the porch. Krista returned their waves before pulling away. For some reason, a weight lifted from her shoulders, although nervous butterflies fought a flash of guilt as she wended away from the summer house.

Am I glad I'm leaving my family behind?

No, she realized; it wasn't who she was leaving behind, but who she would soon *confront* that excited her senses. Not that she was

206

excited to see Edgar Jenkins, but if she could finally put to rest the questions regarding Breann's final location, it would be well-worth the trip.

The Volvo hugged the country roads that curved away from the Little Whisper. Though she had a short drive to the pier in Grand Haven, it would take four hours to cross Lake Michigan, so she wouldn't be able to make it to the prison before visiting hours ended. Knowing this, she had already booked a room at a Super 8 near the prison, though she doubted she would be able to sleep. How could she sleep when she was about to see Edgar Jenkins?

She tried to occupy her mind with the radio. Chatty talk did nothing to quell her thoughts. Neither did pop music, which usually compelled her to sing along—as long as she was driving alone—after a couple songs. She stabbed the power button off in frustration.

A torrent of trees whirred by as she sped along, the reflection of their grasping branches bending as they slid across the windshield. The sky darkened, and soon a steady rainfall obscured the road.

Krista and her siblings had been too young to follow the trial of Edgar Jenkins. She only learned about him after a man named Applewood, an FBI agent out of Wisconsin, came all the way to Grand Rapids—in the middle of a snowstorm, no less—to question Leah, Krista, and Jack. While Nan hovered nearby, nervously toying with the hem of her apron, Applewood had shown them a high school graduation photo of a bright-eyed young man. Though Applewood was an old man, with a heavy paunch and unkempt gray mustache, his voice was soothing and warm. Krista remembered wanting so badly to be able to answer his questions: Had they seen this man loitering around the beach at the Little Whisper? Had they seen him along the stretch of shops downtown? The photo had conjured no memories for her or her siblings.

Krista could still picture Edgar Jenkins sitting at a haughty angle, his baby blue Polo shirt crisp and unwrinkled, his smile captivating, his eyes piercing but without a trace of malice. Even now, as she drove out to confront him, she remembered the ugly paisley couch on which she sat when she first saw his photo, could still feel the presence of Leah shaking her head no, and Jack too young to understand the weight of the situation.

She could never rid her memory of Applewood's look of dejection after none of the kids were able to provide any useful information. The man looked defeated.

Later on, Nan had answered the children's questions of what his visit had been all about, why the detective had been in such a hurry and with seemingly little energy. It had shocked Krista at the time, and had lingered, placing the term 'child killer' on someone who had looked so innocent, so All-American.

Edgar was finally caught six months after Breann's disappearance with enough evidence to put him away for the rest of his life. He'd taken the secret of her disappearance with him, and he'd remained mum on the subject ever since. Krista thought he would take those secrets to the grave, but reading Poppa's manuscript was proof enough that he just might crack.

Rain battered the windshield in drumming waves as Krista slowed at the ticket booth. She waited until the ticket seller acknowledged her before she lowered the window. Lightning flashed, revealing the ferry moored at the bottom of a slight decline in the road beyond. Red taillights winked as cars wedged themselves onto the ramp and aboard the ship.

"One way or roundtrip?" the woman asked without making eye contact. She looked bone-weary, as if she were wrapping up a forty-eight-hour shift in the tiny booth.

"Roundtrip. I'll be returning the day after tomorrow on the morning ferry."

"$129, please. Good thing you got here when you did. The last boat leaves in fifteen minutes."

Krista dug through her purse. Rain splattered inside the window. As she rummaged around, a car pulled up behind her, effectively boxing her in. Even if she wanted to back out now, she couldn't. She handed the woman in the booth her Visa card.

The woman stamped a ticket, ripped off a receipt, and handed everything to Krista.

"Place the ticket on your driver's side dash. There's a coffee shop on deck. The coffee is crap, but the cheese Danish ain't too bad."

"Thanks."

"You have a good night." The woman closed her window against the rain, ending the conversation.

The gate opened and Krista drove inside the fenced area enclosing the pier. A man dressed in yellow raingear guided her over the ramp. Another man motioned where she should park. She followed his gestures, inching close to the van in front of her. A green sedan pulled in behind her, making the ferry feel like a sardine can. A corrugated metal roof covered the deck, but gaps and dings in the metal allowed a steady trickle of water to splash the windshield.

When she turned off the engine, she was overcome by a sudden bout of tears.

She missed Neal and Clara and the rest of her family. But she also missed Breann, and seeing her at Nan's grave had brought so much buried emotion to the surface. She couldn't fight the tears, so she let them fall. She not only missed the Breann of her youth, but also the adult Breann she'd never meet.

After a few minutes, Krista sniffled away the last of her tears. A sign on the nearby wall read: *The Best Views of Lake Michigan Right This Way!* with an arrow pointing toward a stairwell leading to the deck above. Another sign read: *Come for the Views, Stay for the Coffee!*

She decided she didn't want to see the storm. The idea of crap coffee didn't hold much appeal either. More than a few drivers in the neighboring vehicles had decided to wait out the rain and she thought that was a good idea. She had hoped to get out and stretch her legs, but she didn't want to get drenched in the short distance from the car to the coffee shop. Even though she'd soon be on open water, she was glad she was on the ferry. The huge ship felt sturdy beneath her, and certainly safer than driving all the way through Indiana and Illinois to get to Wisconsin.

Krista eyed the binder on the seat next to her. She opened the window a crack and finally took her foot off the brake pedal. Her foot had nearly fallen asleep; she didn't realize how hard she'd been pressing until now.

As the storm settled over the area, the clouds continued to darken, making the late afternoon appear like night. She turned on the car's dome light, opened Poppa's manuscript on her lap, and began to read where she had left off.

> "So, Edgar—"
>
> "Eddie," he said, cutting me off.
>
> "Excuse me?"
>
> "I like Eddie better. The papers, they've been calling me Edgar, but nobody calls me that. Not even my mom."
>
> "Okay, sorry ... Eddie, speaking of your mother, how would you describe your relationship?"
>
> "I get it. You're digging, searching for something that ain't there. My moms, she was normal, treated me normal. Not too mean. Not too touchy-feely."
>
> "I wasn't trying to imply anything, Eddie, I—"
>
> "The hell you're not," Edgar cut in. "You got an idea in your head and you want to firm up the details so you can publish your book."
>
> "Okay ... okay, let's back up a bit. Why don't you tell me about the day you got caught? What was going through your mind? Those sorts of things."
>
> "The day I got caught? I no way intended to get caught. Not like some people, hoping to get stopped, you know? But good god-damn, I'm glad it happened the way it did on the ferry boat."

Someone knocked on the window, startling her. An old man with a patchy gray beard gesticulated for her to roll down the window. He wore a red rain slicker and matching red rain hat covering most of his face. At first, she didn't understand, but then he pointed to the *U.S.S. Wolverine* emblem on the breast of his rain slicker.

Krista rolled down her window partway.

"Hello?"

"I'm sorry, ma'am, but I'm going to have to ask you to leave your vehicle."

"Why, what did I do?"

She felt like a policeman had come to question her for some violation.

"Oh, I'm sure nothing at all but staying in your vehicle after we leave port. For safety reasons, I'm going to have to ask you to go up to the coffee shop, or if you're the adventurous sort, the viewing deck."

Krista looked around the parking deck. No one else had remained inside their vehicles. A young couple were heading over to the stairwell, the man holding an umbrella half-opened above them, ready to unfurl it when they reached the deck.

"Oh, of course. I've never taken the ferry. And with the rain—"

"Don't worry, young lady. I hate to rush you into the rain, but I can't make exceptions. Not on my salary." He smiled, revealing coffee-stained teeth and probably more warmth than she deserved.

"I just need to gather my things."

"Enjoy your stay on the *U.S.S. Wolverine*." The man tipped the floppy bill of his rain hat, dribbling water down his front. He raised his flashlight and started off down the row of cars, looking for any other malingerers.

Krista hurried to grab her purse and Poppa's binder. She tossed her keys into the purse, and after opening her door, remembered to snag the umbrella Neal kept stashed under the seat. When she climbed out, the air was cool and heavy with moisture. She wished she'd brought a coat or even a sweater, but in her haste to get on the road, the idea had never occurred to her. Even with LEDs blazing from every I-beam along the way, it felt like she was walking through dusk as she made her way to the stairwell.

Krista paused at the bottom of the metal stairs, long enough to ready the umbrella. Feeling like she was being watched, she looked back at the cars, but only saw the lone ferry worker walking farther away, occasionally flashing his light into vehicles.

The ferry.

Edgar had been captured on the ferry from Michigan during a return trip back to Wisconsin. For all she knew, he'd been caught on this exact boat.

She climbed the stairs, the treads of her shoes holding fast to the metal grating. A light mist greeted her as she rounded the corner for the last stretch. Cold droplets peppered her face before she could employ the umbrella. She hurried to the warm lights glowing in the coffee shop window. The deck lurched as a wave furled beneath the bulk of the ship. She was no longer on dry land, no longer tethered to the substantial.

Her family was behind her, and before her ... before her she had no idea what she might face. She only now regretted leaving her family behind.

What could I possibly learn from this trip?

A man inside the coffee shop opened the door for her. He wore a tan overcoat and smelled of wet cigarette smoke. He nodded and said, "Nice night for a boat ride, hmm?" Before she could respond, the man turned away to stare out into the rain-drenched sky.

"Yes, thank you," she said and took a seat at the counter.

The boat shifted beneath. Nausea bloomed in her gut.

She ordered a coffee from the waitress. While she waited, she took a deep breath, opened Poppa's manuscript and read:

> "I don't know how it happened, but I was sure relieved when it did. I was leaning out over the railing on the viewing deck. I can tell you for certain what I was thinking when those cops came circling around me: I watched the thin white line of waves curling away from the front of the boat, thinking how I had no idea how something so heavy, so bulky and full of metal like that boat, could not only float but carry cars and trucks and a hundred people. Crazy, right? But I remember that's what I was pondering when

someone clapped me on the shoulder with a meaty palm. I turned. The copper asked me my name. Asked if he could search my van. I told him, sure. Handed him the key. Four cops hovered around me, looking fierce, like they wanted me to agitate or run. But I did neither. I didn't say nothing. Just looked out at the waves cut by the ferry's bulk.

"It weren't more than five minutes before they all came back at me, slammed me face-first into the deck and clamped some cuffs on me. Broke my nose, they did. One of them 'accidentally' kicked me in the ribs when he hoisted me to my feet."

"They found the last suitcase, right? The one with Tanya Williamson inside?"

"Yeah, afraid so. You know how slow ferries move compared to cars or trains? Well, imagine how slow it felt with those cops itching to punch my teeth in with that poor girl getting colder by the minute." Edgar snorted, trying to contain his laughter.

"Eddie, do you have any questions for me?"

"How so?" He raised one eyebrow.

"Haven't you wondered why I'm writing this book?"

"You're a writer, aren't you? You write books. My story is a good damn goldmine. If it weren't you, it'd be somebody else in this gray room asking me if my mom fondled my ballsack or ignored me or whatever bullshit."

"You could be right, I suppose. But not really."

Edgar leaned forward, glared into my eyes. He looked like he'd aged five years since our first interview two months prior. The lines were deeper across his forehead. His hair had receded into a widow's peak.

"Breann's family needs to know where she is. They need to heal, to find peace. We *all* do."

"I don't understand …"

I waited for the cogs of Edgar's brain to pick up speed. I set down my pen. Checked to make sure my audio recorder was working properly. Took a sip from my water bottle.

"So it was you, right? You saw me parked by the lake."

I gave the slightest nod.

"That was the first day I saw them, those three little girls frolicking on the beach. And then I saw you coming toward me, walking with clear intent, straight for my van."

"That's right."

"And you, what, *tracked* me?"

"In a fashion. I had my suspicions. My gut made me aware of your presence, made me aware you were a danger to my family."

"Those cops that nabbed me on the Ferry … you pointed me out to them, didn't you?"

"Very good, Eddie. I'm glad you finally understand. Now, I need you to answer me that one question: Where's Breann?"

From deep down in his belly Edgar began to laugh. It rumbled up his throat and he laughed so hard and long his cheeks verged on purple.

"Eddie? Eddie, come on," I said, attempting to talk over his cackling. "You said you were *relieved — relieved* — you were caught. You didn't want to hurt any more kids. You said as much in your first trial. You said you were glad there wasn't a death penalty so you'd have a nice long stretch of years to consider why you did what you did. You had some small fraction of remorse at the time, and I bet it's only increased since then."

I was shouting, but I couldn't help it.

CHAPTER 28

Clara stood outside the kitchen doorway, listening to her dad and Aunt Leah. She was worried about her mom, not just because she was out in the downpour, but because she wasn't usually so nervous, so ready to jump at shadows.

"This is ridiculous," her dad said.

Clara shifted slowly, chancing a quick look around the corner.

Her father shrugged into one of Poppa's old rain slickers. The sleeves were too long, so he rolled them over once before pulling on a matching floppy rain hat. He looked like the guy on the box of fish sticks she liked—the Gorton's Fisherman. He looked so miserable that Clara had to suppress a chuckle as she ducked away, pressing her back flat against the wall. She waited a beat before peeking around the corner.

"Of course, it is," Aunt Leah said. "It's because Jack is involved. Right now, he's missing, so that means we need to find him." She handed her dad an umbrella.

Lightning flashed, followed by a rumble of thunder.

"He's not missing. He went out on the lake. I saw him, even helped pushed the boat into the water. At this point, I don't know if there's much I can do. We don't have a second boat. I'm sure someone from around the lake has one, but tracking one down in this storm is pretty much out of the question."

"But ...?" Concern ticked her voice an octave higher.

"But I'll see what I can see. Okay? No promises."

A shiver ran through Clara, and when she crossed her arms in front of her, her elbow ever-so-slightly bumped the wall. She held her breath, hoping they were too caught up in worry to notice the muffled thud.

"If I can't find him—" Her dad stopped in mid-sentence and turned the corner so he was a mere six inches from Clara. "And what do we have here?"

"I want to go with you," Clara said as she entered the kitchen. She looked to Aunt Leah for support, but her arched eyebrow and sidelong glance weren't promising.

He shook his head, looking goofy in the floppy hat. "Out of the question." He pressed the button on his flashlight, flicked it off again.

"But Dad, I can hold another flashlight, another two, even, which will only help."

"I don't want you out in this storm."

"I don't want you out in it, either," Clara said defiantly, tapping her foot.

"She's got a point, Neal. Maybe we should call the police instead of waiting."

The door slid open.

"Waiting for what?" Uncle Jack said, stepping inside, clothes dripping on the doormat.

"Jack!" Aunt Leah's eyes widened with a mix of relief and anger. "What the heck?"

Uncle Jack smiled and shrugged. "What did I do?"

"You had us worried," she replied.

Clara wasn't used to seeing Aunt Leah angry. She was normally so laid back and reserved. It was sometimes difficult to see the family resemblance with her mom, but with her face flushed and her eyes livid, the family ties were obvious.

"What were you thinking?" Aunt Leah said.

"I was out on the lake. The lake is small. Where else would I have been?"

Clara's level of disappointment over not being able to go out in the storm surprised her. Before coming to the summer house, she would've never desired to venture out in that mess.

Trev ran into the kitchen and threw his arms around Uncle Jack's waist. "Daddy! Eww, gross. You're so wet ... and cold! Like a dead fish."

"I am a bit cold," Uncle Jack agreed. "I'll go change into something dry."

"What were you doing out there?" Aunt Leah asked. "You saw the storm coming in."

"Yeah, I thought it would pass right over. There's usually good fishing at the front edge of a rain storm."

"I guess you didn't luck out," her dad said.

"Not at all, bro. Not at all." Uncle Jack laughed and shook his head like a dog. Water flew from his sopping mop of hair, sending Trev running away in a fit of giggles.

Aunt Leah clucked her tongue. "Not cool, Jack." She snagged a towel from the handle of the refrigerator and tossed it to him.

Caught off-guard, the towel smacked him in the face before falling into his hands.

Uncle Jack smirked and wiped his face dry, rubbed his hair until it wasn't dripping everywhere. He tossed the towel back at Aunt Leah, looking refreshed for the first time since his arrival at the summer house. His eyes glimmered, the pupils wide black voids. He tipped his head back and laughed. No one else seemed to be in on the joke.

Thunder rumbled angrily and the lights flickered, sending out shouts of fear and excitement from Robby and Heidi, who were watching the storm through the front windows in the den. The lights flickered again.

Uncle Jack stopped laughing, leveling his darkened gaze to Clara. He raised a quizzical eyebrow and then the power went out.

"Mommy!" Robby called out from the den. His feet pounded the floor as he ran toward the kitchen. "The lights went out!"

"I know, sweetie," Aunt Leah grumbled, mostly to herself. "Hopefully, it won't be long."

Robby flew into the kitchen, ran smack into Aunt Leah's midsection, his arms squeezing her tight. Heidi followed a second later, arms crossed in front of her, apparently not as frightened as her brother, but not by much.

"Here, champ." Her dad turned his flashlight around, offering Robby the handle.

"Thanks, Uncle Neal." The boy took hold, pressed the power button, and with the shining beam of light under his control, his fear dissipated almost completely.

"Candles?" her dad asked. He pulled off the overlarge raincoat and hat, draping them over a stool.

"Top cabinet above the stove," Aunt Leah said. "There's also some hurricane lamps, flashlights, that sort of thing. It's not unusual to lose power out here in the boonies."

"I'm on it," her dad said.

"I better change out of these wet things," Uncle Jack said, "before Leah sends me to bed without dessert."

"You're pressing your luck," Aunt Leah said, only half-angered.

Uncle Jack pulled his soaked T-shirt over his head, and Clara saw the heart-shaped tattoo over his heart with Trevor's name at its center, and as he walked past her, the raised surgical scar on the back of his shoulder that ended his baseball days.

"I'm going to check on Poppa," Aunt Leah said. "Robby and Heidi, mind your Uncle Neal." She walked out into the darkened hallway. "Geez, Jack, water's all over the hallway!"

Her younger brother's laughter reverberated down the hallway.

Rain battered the windows and roof, a rising white noise that seemed even louder since the power outage.

"Hey, look, I'm a Jedi!" Robby sliced the beam of light across the floor, then up across his sister's torso. "Hey, you're dead, Heidi. You're dead, ain't nothing you can do about it!"

Heidi ignored her brother, even as the beam crisscrossed her body.

Clara's dad handed her a heavy-looking Maglite. She pressed the power button and it gave off a weak cone of yellow light.

"Batteries are a little low, but I don't see any more in this cabinet. Why don't you ask your mom where we can find some more?"

"Okay," Heidi said. She looked conflicted over leaving their company for the darkened hallway.

Clara hoped she didn't ask her to go with her.

"She can't leave," Robby said. "She's dead!"

"Robby, tone it down a notch, will you, bud?" Her dad flashed a charming smile.

Robby practiced Jedi stances, the flashlight held like a lightsaber.

That was enough to chase Heidi out into the darkness. She padded away in a huff.

Robby went over to Trev and pretended to slice him open from stem to stern with his flashlight's beam. Trev fell dramatically to the floor, silently, and tried in vain to keep his invisible guts from gushing out across the kitchen floor. The boys rolled around on their backs, laughing without sound.

"Dad?" Clara whispered, not wanting to break his concentration, but unable to hold back.

The boys clamored to the back window and pressed their faces against the glass, taking turns shining Robby's flashlight into the storm.

Her dad gave her a quick glance as he brought down a cardboard box with various candles piled inside. "Yeah, honey?"

"Do you think Mom's okay?"

He set the box of candles on the island counter and looked at her fully.

"Of course, she is."

"She's probably still on the ferry boat in the middle of this," Clara said.

Rain battered the deck's broad windows. Violent gales shook the tree branches, scattering wet leaves.

"Yeah, you're right ..." He trailed off, a hint of concern reaching his eyes. "But they wouldn't leave the pier if there was any danger."

"Can you text her?" she asked. "Just in case?"

"I sure will." He took his cell phone from his pocket. "Ask and you shall receive." He sighed in relief. "She texted about five minutes ago; I must've not heard the notification." He looked up from the screen. "She's fine. Just fine, dear. She's going to text again when she finds her hotel room."

"Why did she leave? Why did she have to go to Wisconsin? Is it to see him? To see Edgar Jenkins?" Clara felt more empowered than any other time in her life to speak up. She didn't feel more mature—she'd always been emotionally mature for her age, or so her parents often told her—but something had changed in her the last few days.

"How do you know about Edgar?"

"I heard Mom talk about him before we got here. On the ride up ... she was so upset. And her friend ... Breann—"

"I thought you were sleeping," he said.

"I kind of wish I had been."

Aunt Leah entered the kitchen and said, "Poppa's resting."

Heidi, at her side, added, "He looks so ... small."

An uncomfortable silence filled the room.

"What?" Aunt Leah said. "What did we miss? Everything okay?"

"I asked about Edgar," Clara said, glad the subject was now out in the open. "I still don't know why Mom went to see him tonight." Clara looked from one adult to the other. "It could've waited. For any number of reasons, it could have waited."

Aunt Leah grabbed a shoebox from a high shelf in the pantry and pulled out fresh batteries for Heidi's flashlight. The girl's apprehension went away when she turned it back on to push back the darkness.

"She had to, honey," Aunt Leah said. "This whole thing has been weighing on her for a long time, since long before you were even born."

Clara wanted to press with more questions, so ready for answers.

Aunt Leah, as if sensing her, said, "Hey, how about we play a game!"

"Boring!" Trev said. "How 'bout we go run in the rain?"

"Yeah, right," Heidi said. "You're too chicken, Trev."

"Am not!"

"I'll go with!" Robby added.

"There will be *no* going out in this storm." Her dad's voice rose above both the children's voices and the squall outside. "We will all gather together as a family and play a game."

"All of us?" Clara asked.

"Yes, no better time for it," her dad said. "What should we play? Monopoly? Yahtzee?"

"Yuck!" Trev pretended to throw up.

"How about *The Knowing*?" Heidi asked.

"What's *The Knowing*?" her dad asked. "I don't think I've played it before."

"Oh, it's just ... it's something I made up."

Aunt Leah looked away, as if embarrassed. "We can play something else," she said. "There's even a big five-hundred-piece puzzle in the front closet."

Uncle Jack joined them, having changed into a white knit shirt and black jeans. His mop of damp hair was combed, his eyes unfazed, steady, assured. "I heard something about a game?"

"I suggested a puzzle," Aunt Leah said.

Uncle Jack's face wrinkled, as if he'd eaten something spoiled. "A puzzle, no way!"

"I agree!" Trev said.

"I want to play *The Knowing*," Heidi said.

"Me too," Robby said. "Come on, Mom, let's show them!"

Aunt Leah looked around the room. Everyone waited expectantly, eager for her decision. "Okay, fine. But you can't make fun of it."

"Would I make fun of you?" Uncle Jack said.

"I'm going to regret this, aren't I?"

"Most likely, sis. Most likely." Uncle Jack wrapped his arm around Aunt Leah's shoulders and squeezed.

And then he did a surprising thing, something Clara had never seen before. He closed his eyes, contented, and tilted his head until it rested on the crown of Aunt Leah's. It wasn't a sarcastic motion, but sincere. Clara didn't have siblings, didn't think she would ever understand the give and take, the love-one-second hate-the-next aspects of such relationships.

When he broke the embrace, Aunt Leah slugged him in the arm, but a slight grin played across her lips.

Her dad clapped his hands together, grabbing everyone's attention. "So, how do we play this game?"

"Well," Aunt Leah began, "it's only as fun as your belief is strong."

GLEN KRISCH

Jack scoffed. "This sounds like one of your new-agey performances."

Aunt Leah rolled her eyes. "Why do I bother?"

"Mom!" Heidi cried. "Please!"

"For the kids, Jack?" her dad said from the corner of his mouth.

"I'm sorry, Leah," Uncle Jack said. "Go ahead with the game. It's better than staring at the walls."

"Or some dumb puzzle!" Trev added.

"Okay, everyone, gather around the island," Aunt Leah said.

While she explained the rules, Clara listened intently, thinking it wasn't any sort of game at all, but a form of magic.

Within a few minutes, the family had gathered around the island, spreading chairs around to allow them all to sit and hold hands. They placed a trio of hurricane lamps on the counter.

Aunt Leah looked at each of them in turn. "Do you all remember the phrasing?"

"It sounds more like a chant," Clara said.

"Well, I guess it is. The words themselves don't mean much, but the focus, the connection you feel with the other people in the circle, that's the key."

Uncle Jack smirked, his eyes gleaming in the darkness. "So chanting, spooky candle light, a crazy storm outside—this is witchcraft, isn't it?"

"No, brat," Aunt Leah said, obviously annoyed at her younger brother. "Go someplace else if you're going to poke fun."

"Dad, come on," Trev said. "Stay. Please?"

"Okay, Leah. I'm sorry. Proceed."

"So, *everyone*, make sure you're holding hands with those on either side of you," Aunt Leah said, looking around the circle. "Don't let go, or you'll ruin the circuit."

Their shadows danced on the walls, thrown into marionette-like gyrations by the guttering flames at the center of the island.

"Okay, now everyone, close your eyes. Picture a ball of heat in each of your palms. Picture it flowing both out from you and into the person next to you. Picture the circle gaining strength, energy. Picture this energy projecting toward the center of our circle."

224

Clara's hands broke out in clammy sweat. It was either that or sweat from Heidi and Robby on either side of her. Perhaps a little of both. Heat bloomed in the center of her palms. She almost broke contact, but held fast, curious about the cause of the phenomenon.

"Trev, you need to keep your eyes closed," Aunt Leah said, then added, "and Robby, you know better."

"Sorry, Mom."

"Okay ... does everyone feel the bond of our circle? It's power?"

Everyone echoed affirmatives, even Uncle Jack, who didn't sound snarky in the slightest.

"Let's begin," Aunt Leah intoned. What do you see, what do you know?"

"What do you see, what do you know?" everyone repeated, not altogether in sync.

"What do you see, what do you know?" she said again. "Heidi, what do you see?"

Clara's cousin's hand jerked in her own, gripping tighter from surprise. Everyone else started to hum as Aunt Leah had instructed.

"I see ..." Heidi said and trailed off. "I see a boat on a lake. A lake on the earth. The earth in the universe."

Adding the details, Aunt Leah had explained, amplified the circuit's focus.

"Some vision," Trevor scoffed. "It's the Little Whisper."

"Trevor, no interruptions," Uncle Jack said.

Clara wanted to open her eyes, but she kept them clamped shut. The heat diminished in her palms, as if the flame of their collective had died from lack of momentum.

"Okay. Sorry, Dad."

"You see a boat on a lake. A lake on the earth. The earth in the universe," Aunt Leah said. "Now that you see, what do you know?"

"I know the universe is as big as anything you can imagine. I know the earth is special, full of life. I know the lake ..." Heidi paused to collect her thoughts. "The lake is a pit ... that it's bottomless," the girl's voice cut off, as if choked. She cleared her throat.

"Are you okay, honey-bean?" Aunt Leah said.

"It's empty and dark," Heidi said, "it's full of ... de-de-*despair*."

"No wonder I didn't catch anything!" Uncle Jack said.

Everyone opened their eyes.

Every step of the way, Clara had been able to picture Heidi's vision. That's why, when she looked into her cousin's eyes, she knew she was lying. Heidi didn't mean to say *despair*, even if it was a close approximation for what she had seen, what she had felt. The word she had been unable to say was *death*.

"Oh, Mom." Heidi wrapped her arms around Aunt Leah's waist.

Aunt Leah shushed her and rubbed her back. "It's okay, honey-bean. You just glimpsed something you shouldn't have."

"What does *that* mean?" her dad asked.

"This lake is old," Aunt Leah said, "older than human habitation, most likely. Any number of things could've impacted her vision."

"Sounds like a game not suitable for kids," Uncle Jack said.

Everyone sat in silence, looking around at each other. Shadows continued to dance across the walls; the darkness cast an ominous pall over everything.

Clara wished she could turn on the lights.

"We can't end like this," Heidi said, holding her mom at arm's length.

"I think we should put *The Knowing* on the shelf for a different day," Aunt Leah said.

Robby slapped his palm against the island's countertop. "Mom!"

"Hey, I thought it was fun," Trevor said.

"Is there a way to," her dad said, "I don't know, steer the game a bit?" He didn't look like he cared if the game continued, but he couldn't help mediate tensions and find middle grounds.

"Well, I guess ..." Aunt Leah said.

"Then it's settled!" Uncle Jack said.

"I thought you said it's silly?" Aunt Leah said.

"It is, but I also felt something, you know, in my palms. Heat. Like it was really working. I could clearly picture Heidi's vision. Like I was there, seeing every detail."

"Me, too," Trevor said.

Robby nodded agreement.

"Does anyone *not* want to continue the game?" Aunt Leah asked.

"Just remember, that's all *The Knowing* is: a game."

Clara looked around the circle; everyone wanted to play.

"Okay ..." Aunt Leah sighed. She couldn't back out now. "Everyone, *again*, hold hands and close your eyes. Picture a ball of heat in each of your palms. Picture it flowing both out from you and into those next to you. Picture the circle gaining strength and energy. Picture this energy projected at the center of our circle."

Clara felt the heat building in her palms, but this time it didn't relent; the heat quickly became nearly unbearable, close to scalding. She held fast, and as far as she could tell, so did everyone else.

"Let's begin," Aunt Leah said. "What do you see, what do you know?"

"What do you see, what do you know?" everyone repeated, this time as one voice.

Everyone hummed as before.

"What do you see, what do you know?" she repeated. "Neal, what do you see?"

"Um ... hmm, well, I guess ..." Her dad paused while everyone else continued to hum rhythmically. "I see a book on a shelf. A shelf in a room. A room in a house on the Little Whisper."

"What's inside this book? Go ahead, reach out. Take it off the shelf."

Clara felt herself swaying forward and back, slowly, and couldn't do anything to stop it. In her mind's eye, she saw the volume on the shelf in Poppa's library. It had gilded edging and was bound in worn brown leather. She could read the title, so clearly, yet obscured by the language of origin: *Terrenum Quidem Monstrum*.

"I ... I'm not sure. I see ... I see words on the binding, but they are, I think, Latin."

"Monsters," Clara blurted, surprising even herself. "*Terrenum Quidem Monstrum*," she whispered, and it felt like the weight of the air absorbed her words.

"Yes," her dad said distantly.

The heat left her palms, rushing out to the center of their circle.

Clara opened her eyes.

The candle flames guttered, sending shadows in a violent fury across the walls. Everyone else continued to hum, continued to sway, eyes still closed. She tugged her hands and Heidi and Robby reluctantly released their grips. No one said a word. No one reacted to what she had said, either. They all remained entranced as they hummed and swayed.

The deck door sliding open drew her attention. A shadow swept inside, as if something sinuous and enormous passed just outside the door frame. But the darkness continued to manifest within the kitchen, blocking out the view to the woods beyond.

"I see pages of writing," her dad said, his swaying picking up speed. His forehead wrinkled as he concentrated.

"Tell us what you see," Aunt Leah said. "Yes, tell us everything."

"No!" Clara shouted, but to no effect.

"*Et assumam monter locum occupando ponte crebra vivorum et mortuorum*," her dad said, and Clara was somehow able to translate the words: *And the monster will take its place, the bridge between the living and dead.*

The whirling darkness filled the borders of the kitchen, absorbing the dancing shadows cast by the hurricane lamps.

"Dad, wake up. Snap out of it!" Clara backed away from the circle, horrified. This could not be happening. It wasn't rational. It wasn't even close to being sane.

Her dad spoke again, in Latin, and again, she was able to translate his words, verbatim: *And it will harness their darkness to its bidding, gaining strength beyond measure.*

Tendrils of shadow lashed out at Heidi, coiling around her wrists, prying her up and out of her chair. The girl never opened her eyes as she fell back, as if unconscious. The darkness took her cousin in its embrace—with something resembling maternal gentleness—and lifted her above the broken circle. The darkness wound so tightly around Heidi that it left indentations in her skin, like a boa constrictor strangling its prey.

"Heidi!" Clara screamed, until her throat was raw and her voice cracked. As she backed away, her legs bumped into the counter by the sink, and there she remained, paralyzed, a witness to this waking nightmare. "No!"

228

More amorphous appendages slithered away from the larger mass; they wrapped around Trevor, then Robby. Again, her cousins didn't react as they were lifted from their chairs. The constriction began, the narrow bands of shadow tightening until furrows deepened in the unconscious children's skin.

Clara snapped out of it. She hurried over to her dad, to shake him from whatever spell had taken over the game, but a dark tendril shot out at her, slamming her square between the eyes. The darkness shattered before reforming in a single sheet to cover first her face then the rest of her body. The curling dark coiled around Clara's arms and legs, burning her exposed skin with icy coldness.

She whimpered blindly, "Daddy, please!"

The darkness shot out, funneling between her parted lips. It writhed and snaked through every inch of her, leaving a bitter broken trail in its wake.

Clara no longer felt the ground beneath her.

The humming of Aunt Leah and Uncle Jack continued, a steady vibration reminding her of bees in springtime. Her mind retreated as the dark specter ravaged her mind, the very nature of her being, down to the cellular level.

The last thing Clara heard was her dad speaking in Latin: "*Et ambulate in aeternum. Maledicta, maledicti sunt daemonium vestra. Daemon tui; domine.*"

As she lost consciousness, her mind followed its instinct and translated the words, finding their meaning, plumbing them for their every etymological wrinkle: *You will walk forever. Cursed, cursed to serve your demon. Your demon; your Lord.*

CHAPTER 29

The storm settled in over the Super 8 and remained into the early morning. Krista tried to sleep but gave up when she realized it was a wasted effort. She was still awake when the steady static-hum of rainfall slackened to a silent mist around 3 A.M. She spent the long hours until sunrise sitting in the padded office chair, staring at an elaborate spider web sprawling across the exterior of the window frame. A little black spider scuttled along rain-dappled silk, cleaning and repairing every square inch. She marveled at its tenacity, but then, of course, the web was its life.

What would you do if you were that little spider?

Fatigue weighed heavily on her senses, making her maudlin and short-fused. She shut the heavy curtain and headed for the bathroom; ready or not, she would start her day.

After showering and changing into jeans and a modest white blouse, she gathered her travel suitcase and headed down to the lobby.

She twirled her car keys around her index finger, remembering with a smirk how Neal had magically caught her keys.

Was that just yesterday?

The dull green carpet in the hallway smelled like urine. She held her breath and hurried to the lobby.

She felt isolated and alone—better, sure, because she didn't want to subject any of her family to what she was about to do—but she wasn't the go-it-alone type. She wanted to put this day to rest, even though it was just beginning, and she was facing it with no sleep.

GLEN KRISCH

She gripped the keys. It would be easy to turn around and head back to the warm embrace of her family. No one would question her for coming home so soon.

But Breann ... Her friend had risked so much at Nan's graveside just trying to make contact, to reach out to Krista for help.

Not heading immediately back to the ferry was only confirming her growing madness.

Before leaving the sun-washed lobby, she filled a travel cup with complimentary coffee. No sugar packets. A house fly sat on the sugar shaker's spout. Her eyes burned with fatigue, and the sunlight glared as if she'd been drinking all night.

"I guess I'll take it black," she whispered in exasperation.

"Ma'am?" a voice called out, and Krista turned with a start.

A young woman, worn beyond her years, came in through the front door in a cloud of cigarette smoke. She swiped her hand through the air and stepped behind the high counter.

"Yes?" Krista said.

"Are you checking in?" the woman asked as she typed into her computer.

"No, just getting some coffee before I head out. I left my room key on the counter."

"I hope you enjoyed your stay," the woman mumbled. She didn't wait for a reply before swiping her cellphone's screen and propping her elbows on the counter.

Krista gave the woman an unseen thumbs-up and secured the lid on her coffee. She left without another word, stepping out into air both heavy from the storm and acrid from the clerk's freshly smoked cigarette.

The prison was pretty much what she had expected. The building was broad and brooding, brown bricks capped with gray cement bulwarks topped with ringlets of razor wire. A guard gate secured the employee parking lot. She left her car in the out lot and followed a narrow sidewalk walled off on either side with twelve-foot-high fencing. The sidewalk led to a small building that acted as the central hub. Access to the large windowless building beyond was only possible through the entry building.

She passed through a set of double doors, visible security cameras recording her from every angle. From inside a glassed-in booth, a doughy man with beady eyes looked up, as if expecting her.

Of course, he knew you were coming; he probably saw you on a dozen security screens.

"Good morning," Krista said when she reached his desk.

"Can I help you?"

"Yes, I, um … I'm here to see Edgar Jenkins. I talked to his lawyer and he was supposed to clear it with you."

"Let's see." The man's eyes narrowed as he pecked at his keyboard with his index fingers. "All right. Are you Mrs. Forrester?"

"Yes, Krista Forrester."

"ID please."

She slid him her driver's license through the slot below the bulletproof partition.

He took her license, typed some more, and then stood from his office chair. He scanned her ID and then clicked some more on his computer.

Krista suppressed a mad desire to explain why she was here.

No, I don't sympathize with the child killer. No, I'm not here to profess my love to Edgar and propose marriage.

She wondered what she must look like on those security cameras, and then decided she didn't want to know.

"Thank you, ma'am." The doughy man slid Krista's identification back through the slot. "Kind of unusual," the man said, throwing her off-guard.

"Pardon me?"

"Jenkins's lawyer, he's not here. That's just, I don't know, unusual."

Krista returned her driver's license to her wallet and her wallet to her purse. "I don't think anything can be *usual* when you're talking about a killer like Edgar Jenkins."

The man cleared his throat and raised his eyebrows. He looked like a scolded child. While he might be used to being surrounded by evil men, working at a prison wasn't something Krista could ever imagine being 'normal.' She might've offended him, but she didn't really care at this point, just as long as she got a chance to face Edgar.

"Someone will be right out to see you," he said, and pointed to the wooden bench near the door. "Have a seat."

She sat on the bench and checked her cell phone. A new text from Neal:

Love you like crazy

The message was exactly what she needed right now, but she couldn't bring herself to reply. Not now, not when she was so close.

A door next to the glassed-in booth opened and a young prison guard with a tense glare and peach fuzz on his lip stepped through. He was massive, at least six-foot-five. He looked suited for the football field. A wooden baton hung from his belt. The holstered gun looked far too big, like it could take down an elephant with one pull of the trigger. His presence lessened her apprehension, but only slightly.

"Mrs. Forrester?" he asked.

Krista cleared her throat, which had gone suddenly dry. "Yes?"

"I'm Officer Burkhart." He didn't offer his hand, not that she expected him to; even so, he didn't exactly look pleased to see her. He unlocked a small locker embedded in the wall.

"I need your purse and other belongings. Sharp objects, dangling jewelry. Anything that might be fashioned into a weapon."

She removed her watch and stashed it inside her purse. She placed her purse inside the locker. She patted her pockets and along her neckline, but she didn't have anything else that might be fashioned into a weapon. Or so she hoped. Burkhart gave her a nod.

"If you follow me, I'll escort you to interrogation."

"Interrogation?"

The word was intimidating. She knew the meaning, but not the origin, which Clara would no doubt know off the top of her head. Krista missed her daughter something fierce.

"Don't let the word get to you. We set you up in a quiet room. I'll be right outside the door." He tried smiling to set her mind at ease, but it wasn't working.

"I'll be *alone?* With *him?*"

"That's what I've been told." He gestured down a side hallway. "After you."

She already knew this, but it was still shocking to hear. Edgar's only requirement to meet her was for it to be one-on-one. His lawyer adamantly opposed the idea, but he eventually backed down. She imagined having at least one prison guard standing at her side, ready to wallop the sonofabitch if the need arose. It was hard to ignore the urge to turn and run, far and fast, and never return.

Their feet were loud in the enclosed, featureless tunnel.

"I can see you're nervous, Mrs. Forrester, and I understand." He loomed next to her and tried to match her shorter strides. "I'll be right outside. Plus, he's already handcuffed to the table. He can't move more than two inches from where he's sitting."

They turned a corner and Krista followed him down a long hallway with cinderblock walls painted a shade or two darker than the institutional beige floor. They passed through another set of doors that locked behind them. Three doors were off to the left, three to the right. Another stood at the end of the hallway; through the small glass window were at least two sets of prison bars. Transfixed, she nearly ran into Burkhart, who had stopped outside one of the rooms.

"You need anything, I'm right outside this door. Just call out for Damon and I'll be at your side before you can finish saying my name."

"Okay." She felt small, a child venturing where she knew she shouldn't.

Burkhart unlocked the door and stepped inside first. Krista followed on his heels and felt reluctant to leave his considerable shadow. The sterile gray room was bare except for a heavy metal table between two folding chairs.

"Edgar? You be a good boy, you hear?" Burkhart said.

Edgar's head remained dipped low, none of his face visible until Krista stepped around the prison guard. His hands were flat against the table top, and when he lifted his head, he clapped so hard it echoed in the tiny room. His wrists moved a little more than the two inches Burkhart promised. Manacles around chained him to a heavy loop secured to the table.

"Oh, don't you worry about a thing, Officer!" Edgar's eyes gleamed, alert. He smiled at the two of them.

"I mean it."

"I know you do. And so do I." Edgar lifted his manacled wrists to their limit. "What am I going to do, besides?"

Burkhart leaned in to Krista, whispered, "Are you okay?"

She nodded.

"Like I said, just say the word."

"Thank you." She couldn't take her eyes off Edgar.

Burkhart stepped outside, closed and locked the door behind him. He peered through the door's tiny window and nodded to Krista before blotting it out with the bulk of his back.

As she approached the table, she noticed the cameras at the upper corners of the room. Could she speak openly without sounding crazy? She took a deep breath, took strength from the fact her family was intact, loving, and eagerly awaiting her return.

Edgar stared at her every move, curious.

Krista willed her hands to steady before she reached out for the chair. When she finally sat across the table from Breann's killer, she realized Edgar was little bigger than she was. She had always pictured him large, broad, a physical menace.

"The old man, he's dead, isn't he?" Edgar's smile was lurid, somehow suggestive. He clasped his fingers together. Waggled his eyebrows. Waited.

CHAPTER 30

Rain trailed off to a fine mist sometime before dawn.

Clara awoke from a deep sleep, without warning, segue, or outside provocation; at least that's what it felt like when she sat bolt upright. Her heart galloped along, as if she'd sprinted the length of the sandy beach.

The dream was so entirely consuming that every moment felt real—walking along the sand near the lake, kicking angrily as she plowed a path, water lulling close by.

That much she remembered. Like photographs long studied.

Does eidetic memory work with images from dreams?

She swung her feet around to the floor, fully expecting to find sand clinging to her soles. She found nothing of the sort, but the emotions from her dream remained.

Heidi hadn't stirred in the bed next to her; she let out a barely-there snore.

The light outside shined weakly through banks of gray fog, the windows rain-dewed. She only now remembered the storm, how it had knocked out the power.

Clara picked up her flashlight from the bedside table. She'd fallen asleep with the light powered on. The cone of dirty yellow light did little to push back the shadows. She pressed the power button.

"Hey, Heidi," she called out.

Her cousin stirred but continued to slumber.

Clara shook Heidi's shoulder, startling her awake, blinking, scared.

"Sorry. I didn't mean to scare you. The sun is up."

"Really?" Heidi said. "What ... what time is it?"

Clara looked at the alarm clock, but its numerals weren't lit. She tried the light switch and it too didn't work. "Power is still out."

Heidi sat up and rubbed her eyes. "Can you believe the crazy storm?"

"Sure. Storms happen all the time," Clara said, feeling an instinctive urge to downplay the previous night.

"But what about ... what about all the other stuff?" Heidi pulled the covers to her chin, obviously scared of something.

Clara's mind flashed to last night, playing Aunt Leah's séance game, *The Knowing*. She remembered everyone's shadows dancing around the outside of their circle, cavorting along the walls. And then ... and then, she couldn't remember.

"What stuff?" Clara felt a sudden chill so she slipped into her robe and cinched it around her waist.

"The weird stuff your dad was talking about. That book. The pages. The words, they were in Latin. Remember?"

Clara looked at the knotty wood floor. She remembered the shadows cavorting, and then ... the door leading to the deck slid open, and ... and then a cold darkness crept inside. She suddenly remembered everything.

"The shadows," Clara said with wide eyes. "They snaked inside. They swirled and danced. They ... they took you, yanked you away from the island. Robby, too."

Heidi gave her an unsure look and said, "Come on, Clara, stop trying to freak me out."

"You don't remember?" Clara recalled more details, in more depth.

"No. Sorry," Heidi said. "I'm starving. Let's go eat." Heidi bounded over to the door, opened it, and skipped into the hallway. "Coming?"

Clara flipped the light switch on and off. Still no power.

"Yes."

She paused at the doorway and had to brace herself against it as a vivid image came to mind: her dad chanting in Latin, her broken knowledge of the language translating in fits and starts. *You will walk forever. Cursed, cursed to serve your demon. Your demon; your Lord.*

"Clara, come on," Heidi called out from down the hall. "Let's make breakfast!"

Clara shook her head, trying to regain her sense of *now*.

"Okay," she whispered. "Okay," she repeated, as if to reassure herself.

Before leaving the bedroom, she glanced back at the beds. She had no memory of going to bed. She had no memory of changing into pajamas. She had no memory ... no memory after Aunt Leah's game. In fact, she couldn't even remember the game finishing.

She made her way down the hallway, trying to piece together what had happened. When she reached the kitchen, Poppa was sitting at the island, sipping orange juice from a glass.

"Clarabelle! So, I heard it on good authority you're going to make me breakfast." Poppa winked at Heidi and she smiled in reply. He looked spry and much healthier than he had since the day she arrived. His dark blue polo shirt and tan work pants seemed to actually fit his emaciated form.

"Sure ... I guess." She watched as Heidi gathered ingredients from the cabinets. "I don't really ever cook."

"Why not?" Heidi asked.

"It's just ... I don't know. My mom always does the cooking."

"I guess you can be my helper then," Poppa replied.

"Can we cook with the power out?" Clara asked.

"It's a gas stove," Poppa said, "so I'll need a match to get it started. I guess it all depends on what you're making."

"Pancakes?" Clara said. "That's all I know how to make."

"I'm sure they'll be delectable," Poppa said.

Heidi smiled and returned to gathering ingredients.

Clara remained in the doorway, her mind slipping into the comforting churn of word dissection.

dih-lek-t*uh*-b*uh* l: delightful; highly pleasing; enjoyable.

Once she had the word mastered, her mind relaxed, and last night receded like a fading memory. *Nothing bad had actually happened, right? So what's the purpose of stressing over it?* If anything, her mind had merged memory and dream. *Last night … last night hadn't been weird or frightening.*

"Where is everyone else?" Clara said, helping Heidi gather cooking supplies.

"Your dad, Uncle Jack, and Trevor, are out on the lake fishing," Poppa said. "Leah and Robby are out front. I think they're playing croquette again."

Heidi said, "We better get cooking. They're going to be hungry."

"Okay!" Clara said.

"What do I need to do first?" Heidi asked, dumping cups of flour into a big metal mixing bowl.

"We need eggs," Clara said. "Oh, and milk from the fridge."

"Don't dawdle or you'll let out all the cold air," Poppa said.

"Okay, Poppa." Clara went over to the refrigerator, trying to picture where everything was before opening the door. She hurriedly grabbed the egg carton and a milk jug. She kicked the door shut, having gathered her supplies in just under two seconds, and smiled at Poppa. "Pretty fast, huh?"

"Nice one, Clarabelle!" Poppa said.

The front door opened and Robby let out a blood-curdling scream. "Help! Please, someone help my mom!"

Clara nearly dropped a carton of eggs before setting it on the counter. By the time she turned around, Heidi was already running toward her brother, and Poppa wasn't too far behind.

Robby stood in the doorway. Tears streamed down his tan cheeks. Snot bubbled from one nostril. The front of his shorts was stained dark with urine.

"What happened, Robby?" Poppa asked.

Heidi charged outside, calling for her mom.

Poppa struggled to one knee to meet Robby's eye level.

"She's … she's at the grave. Nan's grave. She heard …" The boy fell into a fit of tears that choked off his words.

"What is it? What did she hear?" Poppa said, his voice a reedy rasp.

Heidi's voice faded as she got farther from the summer house.

Robby cleared his throat and when he spoke again it was in a frail croak. "She heard … Nan. She heard Nan and she's trying to dig her out."

"What in the world?" Poppa gasped.

Heidi screamed in the distance.

Poppa took off as fast as he could for the front door, Clara and Robby a step behind.

Clara easily overtook Poppa and sprinted in the direction of the graveyard. By the time she reached the tiny alcove, her lungs were burning.

Heidi was weeping as she pleaded with her mother. "Mom, please … please stop!"

Aunt Leah stood waist-deep in a muddy hole. She glanced at Heidi before returning her attention to the grave. While she didn't say anything, the look of madness in her eyes said plenty. She was using a gardening trowel to scrape at the widening hole. Rain from the night before had certainly helped loosen the soil, but it wasn't effective to dig with such a meager tool. Mud streaked her face and upper torso and caked her hair, as if she'd been rolling around in slop. The whites of her eyes flashed—unhinged madness. Abrasions and gashes littered her filthy knuckles and hands. Blood trailed from a number of wounds, mixing with the mud.

"Aunt Leah," Clara whispered.

Heidi noticed her arrival and practically fell into her arms.

"Aunt Leah!" Clara shouted, gaining her voice, even as she tried to console her cousin.

"What do you want?" Aunt Leah said, and turned toward the girls with a snarl.

A twig snapped as Poppa entered the alcove. "What are you doing, dear?" His voice was gentle and warm, but his eyes were full of worry.

"She's here. *Alive.* I heard her," Aunt Leah said with a tremble in her voice. "She asked me to get her out. She wants to be free. She wants to feel the sunlight on her skin." She turned back to the widening hole and made another scraping pass with the trowel. While she still attacked the task at hand, she began to cry. "I have to get to her. She needs me."

"Oh, my poor girl." Poppa reached low and placed a hand on her heaving shoulder.

She jumped at his touch. The madness filling her eyes softened.

"Poppa? Poppa, what's wrong with me?"

She fell over at the waist at the lip of the hole, her head resting near his feet.

Poppa shushed her like a baby woken by a nightmare and patted her back.

Poppa turned toward Clara and said, "I need you to get your father and uncle. Okay?"

Aunt Leah allowed Poppa to help her from the hole. He wasn't manhandling her by any means; he was far too weak to offer her anything besides a gentle guiding hand.

"Yes, of course," Clara said.

"Make sure you tell them how imperative it is they come here right away."

Clara nodded.

Robby ran to his mom and wrapped his arms around her neck. "Mommy, I'm so scared."

"Please, Clarabelle?" Poppa said, his eyes showing deep worry.

Clara nodded again and started sprinting across the front lawn and around the side of the house. A cramp quickly built up in her side. She barely felt her bare feet as they slapped across the grass. Her robe loosened as she reached the sand. She wanted more than anything to rest her hands on her knees and catch her breath, but noticed her dad and uncle dragging the boat ashore. She started off again, waved her arms above her head and called out, but they didn't notice her.

By the time Uncle Jack saw her, cramps stabbed her ribs in two places.

Uncle Jack pointed her out to her dad. They both ran to her.

"What is it?" Uncle Jack said. "Did something happen?"

Clara dropped her hands to her knees, sucked in as much air as the cramps would allow.

Her dad touched her shoulder. "Clara, you're scaring me. What happened?"

"Aunt Leah …" She paused to draw in more breath, "she's … she's digging."

"What?" her dad said, confused.

"Nan's grave..." she wheezed. "She thinks she hears her, that she's alive and needs to get out. Poppa, he's with her." Saying the words made it sound insane.

Uncle Jack took off, kicking up sand.

"Are you okay?" her dad asked, rubbing her shoulder.

"Poppa said it was …" she said and sucked in more breath, "that it's imperative you come as fast as you can. I'm fine. Just a little cramp."

Her dad gave her a quizzical glance.

She panted, catching her breath. "Really, I'm okay." She waved at him to leave, and he followed in Uncle Jack's footsteps across the sand to the side of the house.

By the time Clara reached the front yard, everyone had returned from the graveyard. From the mouth of the alcove, she saw the crazed defiling of Nan's grave and felt soul-sick. She couldn't imagine what had driven Aunt Leah to such madness, but there could be no other explanation than some kind of mental break. She turned away, haunted by her aunt's crazed digging and ranting about trying to save Nan. When she reached the front door, her father stepped outside.

"Is she okay?" Clara asked.

He paused before saying, "I'm not really sure."

"What happened?"

He shook his head. "I don't know, but she needs help. The cell service is still down. The land line isn't working either."

"What can we do?" Clara asked.

"I'm going to drive her to the hospital in Grand Haven. She's calmed down quite a bit, almost like whatever had come over her had never even happened. But she still needs looking after. Heidi is coming with to help keep her calm. Your aunt seems in much better spirits with Heidi nearby."

"What about Mom?" Clara pressed.

"There's not much we can do if we can't call her, right? So I want you to stay here with your uncle and Poppa. Watch after Robby and Trev. Okay?"

She wanted to plead to go with him, but she knew it was better if she stayed. She wasn't an adult, but with Poppa being so weak, and Uncle Jack acting flaky, someone had to keep an eye on things.

"Okay, Dad."

The front door swung open and Aunt Leah stepped outside. Heidi stood next to her, acting as both guide and crutch as they made their way to the car. As she walked past, Heidi made eye contact with Clara. Her cousin looked beyond scared.

Clara had seen that fear before. It reminded her of Breann's panicked expression just before she snapped and went digging into the mound of rocks. Clara touched the heart charm through her shirt, which brought her a small amount of comfort.

Poppa joined them on the porch and put an arm around her. Together they watched her dad load Aunt Leah into the front passenger side of her Hyundai minivan. Faded bumper stickers covered the rear bumper: *Bernie or Bust, Got Tofu?* and *Namaste*.

"She'll be all right." Poppa sounded uncertain, as if he were trying to convince himself.

"I hope so," Clara said.

Her dad closed the door for Aunt Leah. As he hurried around the back of the car, he gave them a harried wave.

Clara felt a mad urge to run up to him to give him a hug. She was being foolish, but she had an overwhelming feeling she might not see him again.

"She'll be fine," Poppa reiterated. "She's just ... really tired."

They watched the minivan pull away. When they were certain it wouldn't just turn right around, they went inside.

"Poppa ..." Clara broke off into a sob as they neared the kitchen. "I'm so sorry, but ..."

"What is it, Clarabelle?" Poppa placed a hand on her shoulder. "What's wrong?"

"It's stupid. Just *so* stupid. But I don't know how to make

244

pancakes, and you must be starving."

While the tension in Poppa's expression eased, it didn't altogether leave his wrinkled face. "Don't you worry. I know how to make them. How about I teach you?"

"Aren't you tired?" she said.

"All the time, sure. But teaching you how to make pancakes? I can always nap later."

Poppa smiled and Clara couldn't help following suit. She walked with Poppa's arm wrapped over her shoulder as they made their way to the kitchen.

Uncle Jack and Trevor were sitting at the island. Upset over what they'd witnessed, Trevor sipped a tall glass of ice water while Uncle Jack tipped back a can of beer.

"That sure was something," Uncle Jack said.

"Not another word about it, Jackson," Poppa said. "Not now,"

"It's just that—"

"We are making breakfast. You can either help out, or go off some place to drink yourself into a stupor. In either case, not another word."

Uncle Jack nodded but didn't say anything. He crushed the can in his palm and tossed it in the recycling can. He went over to the cabinet, and with the help of Trevor, set the table.

In no time, Poppa taught Clara the rudiments of making golden brown pancakes.

CHAPTER 31

Edgar repeated, "So, the old man, he's dead, right? That why you here?" His lips curled into a grin as he examined her reaction. He sucked on his front teeth, as if trying to dislodge a bit of food.

The question hung in the air, and when Krista couldn't immediately find her voice, she felt a surge of panic. She looked back at the steel door with the small viewing window. Burkhart's broad back blocked the thick pane of glass. She was on her own.

She took a calming breath.

"No, he's not." She finally turned her gaze to him, meeting his cold blue eyes with an unwavering stare. She pulled out the chair across from him and sat. When she clasped her hands in front of her on the table, she noticed him looking at her fingers. He arched one eyebrow.

Is he smirking about my wedding band?

She felt uncomfortable being so close to him. No, not just uncomfortable, but sickened. She lowered her hands to her lap.

"He's not dead, but he's not well, either. Right?"

She wasn't expecting the intense knowing projecting from his eyes. It was unnerving.

"What does it matter?"

Edgar laughed, as if he'd pieced together the entirety of Poppa's plight by parsing her few words. "I miss good ol' Pierce. He's always been good to me. Kind. Understanding. I don't see much of that in here most days." He again sucked on his teeth, easing back against the back of his chair and slumping until his chest was level with the table. He didn't look like a killer, more like a janitor, or perhaps a post office clerk.

"He told me," she said, trying to catch him off guard, "about you and Breann."

"I don't know no Bree-ann."

"Yes, you do. You killed her. She was my friend, and you killed her."

Edgar pointed an index finger and clicked his tongue as he cocked his thumb forward, as if firing a gun. "You know, I remember *you*. You have the same eyes as when you were nothing but a lithe little girl. I see the rest of you has changed. You've become a beautiful woman. Comely, they call it, right? But those eyes ... Just like back in the day."

He stared at her, but Krista wouldn't look away, even though she wanted to cry, even though it was hard not to vomit.

"You killed my friend," she said, slowly, deliberately, "and I want to bring her home. I want to bring her peace. She never hurt anyone."

"I know. That's why I took her—"

"You said you didn't know her," Krista cut in.

"Yeah, well, I lied. I wasn't ever good at jokes. But guess what? I'm imprisoned for the rest of my goddamn life, and I fully admit to my crimes as a serial kidnapper and child killer. One of the only honest people in this joint. So, yeah, I knew little Breann McCort. Knew her *real* good. I knew she was nice, just as nice as you and your sister."

"What, were you spying on us?"

Krista knew this from reading Poppa's manuscript, but a fount of information was opening and she wanted it blown wide. Not only was she sitting across from Breann's killer, he was speaking unguardedly.

"To a point, I guess you could say. I had to study until I figured out which of the three of you would be going for a ride in my van."

"But why us? Why at all?"

"That's a complicated story," he said with a sigh.

"But Breann ... you liked her pain. That's why you chose her over me?"

"You're asking a question, but it sounds like you already know my answer." Edgar leaned his forearms against the heavy table, stooped as far across the divide between them that his manacles would allow. His eyes narrowed. "Did Pierce ever finish his book?"

"I ... I don't know." She screwed up by revealing information she could've only learned through Poppa's manuscript. She'd wanted to project an air of innocent ignorance about the broader information regarding Breann's disappearance.

"But you've read it. I can't imagine him talking to his granddaughter about our private conversations. He never came across as someone who'd talk about my proclivities, my ..." he broke off in a chuckle, "... *demons*."

"Yes, I've read some of it. And yes, you're right. Poppa *is* sick. Almost gone, really. To be honest, he doesn't know I'm here. He doesn't need to know, either. I don't think I could trouble him at this point, not with how sick he is. I just want answers. Please ... Mr. Jenkins."

Edgar's smile faded, his humor gone. He crossed his arms and leaned back against the chair again. "It's a shame."

"What's that?" she asked.

"I never got to see it completed."

"See what?"

"My masterpiece. Just one more piece to the puzzle, and it would've been complete. But Pierce put an end to all that. Dropped that dime and put my ass in here."

She had a million questions, but hesitated. She didn't want to risk him clamming up if she said the wrong thing.

"What did your 'masterpiece' do for you?" she finally asked.

"Working on it fixed me. Like new. Like, the demons inside me were no longer there, had never even been there."

"So, your killing set you free?" she asked, confused.

"Yes. I'd killed before I came to your neck of the woods. I'd been angry since I was a tyke. So goddamn angry all the time. But all that changed. Even as I started collecting pieces for my masterpiece. The anger had gone. And the shame of it, not being able to see it completed really is a shame. But, I suppose I'm better off for the bargain. Now, imprisoned 'til my last breath? I consider myself a free man."

"Nothing could change who you are."

"That's where you're wrong. The urge to kill, it's gone out of me. That's what I'm talking about. The urge is quiet."

"The children ... they were a sacrifice?"

"I suppose they were," Edgar said and crossed himself.

"Tell me, how did it all start? I mean, what makes someone decide to do what you did?"

"When I was young ... Jesus ... when I was young, I didn't know what I was doing. You know, with the killing. It was totally random. Messy. Inelegant."

"But something changed?"

"I needed guidance. Understanding to my outbursts. I always focused on strong girls. Kind girls. But *flawed* girls. Girls with underlying pain."

"And, Breann?" Krista asked, trying to steer him.

"She fit the mold, totally. The potential of my ... obsessions, when they were on the cusp of adulthood, that's what I sought. To find someone strong, and to snuff them out."

"What was your relationship with your mother like?" she asked, hoping to provoke.

"What does that have to do with anything?"

"Apparently, everything."

"Don't you fucking talk about my mother." He stood so quickly that the chair tipped backward and rattled against the tile floor.

Krista eyed his manacles, took a steadying breath.

"I'm sorry, but I just want to understand. Why did you take Breann? Where is she? Where is my friend?"

"She's dead," he said, leaning forward with his palms against the table. "I wrapped her in plastic, hung her feet from a meat hook. I sliced her throat to drain her dry. Then I cleaned the blood off her freckled fucking face."

"Where is she?"

Edgar burst into hysterical laughter.

"Where is Breann?" she said between gritted teeth.

He tipped his head back as laughter wracked his body.

Krista felt her rage rising. This little man no longer frightened her. She came around the table and he turned to face her. He was no more than an inch or two taller. Her fear nearly returned because of his closeness, but she kept it in check. She grabbed his shirt collar and shook him as hard as she could.

She glanced at the window and noticed Burkhart watching her. Their eyes met. He might have given her a slight nod, or maybe she only hoped as much. Regardless, he turned away as if disinterested.

Edgar's head whipped forward and back, but he continued to laugh.

This set her over the edge. She wheeled back and slapped him hard across the face. Edgar's eyes boggled and his laughter died off, but his wide smirk remained. She'd forgotten how close they were, but it became evidently clear when he grasped both of her forearms. He tightened his grip as their eyes met.

"You're a pathetic piece of shit," she said, glaring at him.

Burkhart was half a second away, but she didn't want to end this visit, not when she hadn't gotten the information she had come for.

"I know." His grip on her arms weakened and his hands dropped away.

"Where is she?" Krista said, hating how pathetic she sounded.

He shook his head, wiped his lips on his sleeve, still with that damn smirk on his face.

She shot out her knee and caught him in the balls.

Edgar let out a choked sob and leaned over to brace himself against the table.

Krista checked the window in the door, but Burkhart hadn't moved. The little red lights on the video cameras continued to shine. If someone was monitoring the feeds, her visit would soon come to an end, and she would most likely wind up arrested. Either that, or they enjoyed watching her punishing a child killer and so had given her some leeway.

She gripped his right ear with her left hand and twisted until it verged on tearing from his skull. Edgar cried out hoarsely, barely above a whisper, and didn't fight back. Through his pain, he met her gaze. And smirked. Krista again slapped his face, this time so hard her hand stung with pins and needles.

Krista wrenched him by his ear, forcing him to his feet. "Why do you look so happy?"

"Because it's over." His smile, now flecked with blood, widened.

"What's over?"

She shoved him hard until he fell back into the chair.

"The work I was set to. It's complete by now, for sure. What, with you here. With you here and unable to protect that sweet little girl of yours."

"What are you talking about?" Krista said, feeling faint. She paced the room, trying to steady her wobbly legs.

"Your daughter, of course."

"How do you know about her?" She stopped pacing and glared at him.

"The old man, he stopped me, in a fashion, from completing my work. But all he did was put pause to my final actions."

She came close to clobbering him again, but a low buzzing started in her ears, and she didn't know how much longer she would be able to keep her wits together.

"What can you do to me or my family if you're locked up for the rest of your life?"

"Not me. It was never *just* me."

"What? Did you have a partner?" She had never considered the possibility, and now that it was in the open, the notion horrified her.

"Not exactly. Sure, I had my urges, my perversions you might call them. Sure, I did things I still won't admit aloud. Horrible, horrible things. But those horrible things brought me a sense of calm, let me sleep at night. Once I lost my way and found myself near enough to the Little Whisper to feel its gentle pull ... it took me under its wing. This darkness, this vileness, became my own. I reveled in it. Oh, Lord, how I reveled in it."

"You're saying you weren't responsible for your actions? That girl, the one they found in your suitcase ... Tanya Williamson ... you didn't kill her?"

"Every action was my own, sure. It was me, sure, but ... amplified. Supersized. I was a … a host, I guess you could say. A host for a demanding guest. Pierce removed me from the equation, but the guest remains."

"What, like a ghost?" Krista felt a sudden overwhelming sense of dread.

"I don't know the proper name of things such as these. All I know is that its powers of persuasion are exquisite. And it finds its own playthings, just like I found mine in those damaged little girls. This … guest wheedles its way inside, turns everything sour, corrupt. Noncompliance can be … fatal."

The door opened and Burkhart filled the space with his tremendous bulk.

"Everything okay in here?"

He must have noticed Edgar's swollen face, the trail of blood from his nose down to his lips, but he didn't acknowledge it.

Burkhart stared at Krista.

"Yes, everything is fine," she said. "We're just talking."

"Edgar, everything square with you?"

"Of course! Like young Krista here said, 'We're just talking.'"

Burkhart looked from Edgar to Krista and back again. He knew something was happening between them, but he obviously didn't see the harm in it continuing.

"I'll be right outside." It sounded like a warning to the both of them. He closed the door and glanced through the window before blotting it out with his back.

"Is my family in danger?" Krista asked, her voice a whisper.

Again, that cocky smile. "Are they at the Little Whisper?"

"Yes. They're staying at my grandfather's summer house."

"Then of course they're in danger."

Terror coiled in her gut.

"What? How …?"

"I'm done talking. If you want real answers, go ask your Poppa."

With her pulse throbbing at her temples, Krista waited for him to continue, but he merely turned away from her and stared at the wall, as if transfixed by the rough cinderblock. After it was evident he wouldn't say anything more, she reached for the door.

Edgar chuckled, and said, "While you're there, make sure you thank the old man for me."

Burkhart gave Krista a wide berth as she exited and slammed the door.

Edgar's laughter echoed long after she left the prison yard.

CHAPTER 32

Night fell faster than Clara expected. One moment seemed to be the earliest minutes of dusk, and the next pitch-black skies blanketed one horizon to the other.

A wavering brightness drew her attention from the window in Poppa's library, from where she watched the driveway. Her copy of *The Hobbit* remained open in her lap. She couldn't focus on the words when the sun was still up, and now it was beyond pointless to try in the dark.

Uncle Jack entered with two candles. He set one on the table next to her.

"How are you holding up?" he asked.

"I'm worried."

"Me too, kid." He looked like he'd exhausted the topics they could share. "Do you have a flashlight?"

She pressed the button on the heavy flashlight resting on her lap. Turned it off again.

"Your Aunt Leah will be okay. Your dad is with her, and you know nothing can go wrong when he's around." Uncle Jack tried to laugh, but it fell flat.

"I know," she said, noticing the candle light reflected in his eyes. He looked different. Sharper, perhaps. More alert. She hadn't seen him have a drink since the beer at breakfast. Perhaps she hadn't seen him sober before now.

"Trevor and Robby are playing Connect Four in the kitchen. You can join them, you know."

"I know." Clara sighed. "I'm just waiting for my mom."

"Okay, kid. Do you need anything?"

"Just quiet." She immediately regretted her tone. "*Please.*"

"Sure thing. Poppa's resting. Probably out for the night. I need to go take care of something. Something a long time coming."

"Do you need any help?" she asked.

"Thanks, but this is something I need to do myself," he said. He stared at her for a long intense moment, as if he were memorizing her features. Finally, he smiled. "Good night."

Candle in hand, Uncle Jack walked away, halving the visible light with his absence. Clara stared out at the driveway, feeling lost, like a stranger in her own skin.

Someone shook Clara's shoulder, but sleep was reluctant to let her go. Her eyes flickered open. Robby and Trevor stood shoulder to shoulder, watching her wake.

"What is it?" she asked, her voice thick and groggy. The boys remained mute, their eyes wide with fright while, their mouths agape as if in mid-scream.

She forced her mind through the morass, forced it to focus. The boys swayed together from side to side, their posture bending to and fro like dune grass caught in a capricious breeze. Their eyes spasmed and rolled back to full whites. Foamy spittle gathered on their lips.

"Robby, Trevor, what is it?" She stood from the chair and her book fell to the floor, forgotten. "You're starting to scare me."

She grabbed the candle from the table next to her and brought it close to Robby's face. The muscles beneath his cheeks quavered, as if he fought to control his movements.

Both boys began chanting jumbled words through parted lips.

No, not jumbled, she realized. *Backward.* And they came so quickly she couldn't decipher them.

The boys took one stride in reverse, then another, as if rewound.

Clara followed them as they stepped in reverse, until they backed into the kitchen. They sat at the island and began to intone the methodical humming from their séance game the night before. The boys swayed and hummed, swayed and hummed.

Clara's candle revealed shadows that should not be there. Silhouetted bodies danced across the walls—*a half dozen, a dozen, more*—even as the boys' mesmerized humming picked up in pitch and intensity. The silhouettes leapt from the walls to the center of the island where they swirled, funneling, drawing all the air from the room until Clara struggled to breathe.

When she thought she couldn't take any more of this madness, the swirling shadow shot out at the sliding deck door, pried it open, and streamed out into the night. The door slammed shut, and the boys tipped over on their stools until they fell to the floor, unconscious.

Clara hurried to them as someone desperately knocked on the back door. She crawled around the island, using it for cover.

Two people stood at the threshold.

Clara gasped and pulled back, hoping she hadn't been noticed.

"We know you're in there, Clara," Breann said.

Trevor began to shake, and then Robby. She had never seen a seizure in person, but couldn't think of anything else it could be. Their bodies vibrated, arms curling up toward their chests, and more sticky foam leaked from between their lips.

"Please come to the door so we can talk," Melody said.

"I … I don't know who you are," Clara said.

What she truly meant was: I don't know what you are.

She didn't know what was happening to her cousins, but she felt a helplessness that terrified her. She felt penned in, incapable, and for the first time in a long time, exactly her twelve years of age.

Breann chuckled, but with little mirth. "We're your *friends*, silly."

"You left me in the woods." Clara's voice cracked on the last syllable. "Anything could've happened to me."

"We couldn't help it," Melody said. "We … we had to leave you, or you would've been in terrible danger. It was for your own good."

A sudden anger rose through her. She wasn't about to cower from the unknown, and so she stood and turned toward the sliding glass door, then clamped a hand over her mouth, stifling a scream.

Breann's skin was so bloodless-gray that even her freckles had faded. Both girls had black bags under their eyes, and the eyes themselves shot through with lightning bolts of black veins. Their throats had been slit, and their gaping wounds pulled wide, exposing flesh, bones, and cartilage ...

"We didn't want you to see us like this ... how we really are," Melody said. "It takes so much to hold the darkness at bay."

"You need to let us in, Clara," Breann demanded.

"Why ... what are you going to do?" Clara glanced at Trev and Robby. At least their seizures had faded. They gave off an occasional twitch, nothing more.

"You know what we need to do," Breann said. "What we *all* need to do."

Clara gasped.

Faces of other dead girls filled the windows, children with wounds identical to those of Melody and Breann. They clamored at the glass, scratching with splintered fingernails, whining for entry.

"Is it Poppa?" Clara asked. "Is it Poppa you need?"

She removed Breann's heart-shaped charm from around her neck. She considered giving it back to Breann, that perhaps she would go away, that they would all go away, if she made that simple offering.

"Isn't it obvious?" Breann said. "Your Poppa saw the monster and didn't act. At least, not right away."

"What monster?" Clara said. "Do you mean, Edgar?"

"Yes ... and something else," Melody said, her voice low, "his guiding hand."

Tears trailed down Clara's cheeks.

"Poppa's sick. He's dying. There's no point."

"It's the only way we can move on," Melody said. "It's nothing more, and nothing less."

"You don't know that," Clara said. "You can't possibly know that. You're just angry, and you want to place blame."

"You can't stand in our way," Breann added.

Clara felt torn between cowering on the floor with her cousins and rushing to Poppa's side to protect him. She wrapped the charm's chain around her wrist, then twice, and a third time, until the heart rested in her palm.

"I don't understand!" Clara shouted through tears. "What did he ever do to you? He's just an old man. He wouldn't hurt anyone."

Moans and gasps issued from the milling spirits, but it didn't seem like they were reacting to her words. Little fingers tapped against the window panes, as if to warn her.

Melody's eyes went wide as she called out Clara's name.

"What is it," Clara said, confused. "What's wrong?"

"You been here this whole time," Uncle Jack said from the doorway leading to the front of the house. "The whole fucking time ..."

Clara jumped at his voice and reluctantly turned her back on the dead girls.

While it looked like Uncle Jack, his posture was too erect, and his eyes twin pools of pitch glimmering in the candlelight.

"I didn't even realize you are exactly what I need," he said, his voice deeper, full of menace. "Thank goodness for the curiosity of children. Sometimes they open your eyes to what's standing right in front of you."

"No!" Breann shouted, and banged on the glass.

Other children joined in, forming of chorus of discontent.

"Uncle Jack, what's ... what's going on?"

The kitchen island was to her back. The ghosts stood at the threshold to the deck. She had nowhere to run, and even if she did, she couldn't leave her cousins, unconscious and defenseless.

"Your loneliness ..." Uncle Jack whispered, stepping closer. "You never realized how alone you were. Not until you came to the summer house. Not until you experienced life, exhilaration, nature passing beneath your feet. *That* was your awakening."

"Please, Uncle Jack, you're scaring me," she said, her muscles tensing.

"You *should* be scared."

She made a break for the hallway, but he shifted into her path and gripped her around the throat with one hand. She bucked against him, but he held fast. She could barely catch a breath.

"Your pain ... it's exquisite." Uncle Jack leaned in close until their noses nearly touched. "It's just what I need. Just one more soul. One more soul bursting with pain ... beautiful, beautiful pain."

"Melody ... Breann ..." she gasped. "Please help me."

Uncle Jack chuckled, the wide span of his fingers pressing hard against her throat, dimming her vision, sending her into a spastic panic. She kicked out her legs, but couldn't connect with anything.

Uncle Jack ... Uncle Jack is killing me.

With a heartbroken crack in her voice, Melody said, "I wish we could help you. Oh, how I wish I could."

Breann laughed morbidly, the sound slurring, distorting.

ok-si-juhn ... Clara's mind drifted, fogging. *I need oxygen ...*

The candle flames seemed to retreat, to dim to nothing. The only details that had yet to succumb to the shadows were the glowing faces of the dead girls.

Clara's limbs weakened, and before she could collapse into unconsciousness, the hand at her throat lifted her off the ground. Her vertebrae shifted and loosened, as if her neck might snap with the slightest additional pressure.

"Puh ... puh ... Please ..." she choked out.

Blood throbbed in her head. Her face and her lips pulsed from the blinding pressure.

"That's it. Go to sleep, little one," he whispered into her ear. "We have much to learn. So very much to learn. But first, you must go to sleep."

Clara's arms became so heavy she could barely get them to twitch at her sides. Her mind fogged as she felt her body lifted parallel to the ground. Her head and feet dangled until she was placed onto something wide and flat.

The kitchen island, she thought.

She blinked and her vision momentarily brightened as he released his grip on her throat.

"We're going on a trip, you and me." Not-Uncle Jack hefted something onto the counter next to her. A cylindrical roll. He pulled from one end, and plastic sheeting gave off an agonized shriek as it unraveled. He tucked one end underneath her body, then lifted her knees to her chest. "I need you to ... just hold, right there. Perfect."

He wrapped her body, lifting her hips and then her shoulders when he needed to roll the plastic spool under her body.

The cracking of glass, the tinkling of shards hitting the floor. The sound of a latch opening and a door thrown wide.

"Go ahead. Take the old man," Not-Uncle Jack said to the intruders. "It won't matter."

One of her cousins groaned, as if waking, and Uncle Jack let loose a vicious kick into the boy's torso that elicited a sharp cry, then nothing, not even a whimper.

Clara's vision stabilized and the spirits of the dead girls crossed into her line of view: Breann, then Melody, somewhat reluctantly, soon followed by others. So many other dead girls.

Melody stopped at her side.

Uncle Jack continued, as if unaware of her closeness, or not caring. The girl reached out with ethereal fingertips, brushed them against Clara's brow.

"Don't worry, Clara. We'll be waiting for you. At least you won't be alone ..." She drifted away, caught up in the tide of dead streaming by.

I'm going to die. They know it. They want me to join them ...

Uncle Jack hoisted her off the island counter, resting her on his shoulder like a sack of laundry. At best, she could move her head from side to side, but even that motion flared pain along her neck where he had nearly strangled her to death.

Clara tried to whisper his name, but her voice was hoarse and her throat burned, as if something inside her had burst.

"Shh ..." he said, "enough talking. Time to rest up."

Not-Uncle Jack turned toward the door, and his elbow knocked over the candlestick resting on the counter. Fire sputtered before catching and feeding on the kitchen curtains.

"Whoopsie-daisy," he said. "There I go, being a clumsy fool."

Clara tensed at the brightness.

He chuckled, said, "Lights out," and then slammed her skull against the doorframe as he stepped out onto the deck.

Sparks flew across her vision and then darkness swept over her in waves.

Clara's body rocked on his shoulder as he climbed down the steps to the beach. She heard the shrill cries of the spirits left behind in the summer house. And somewhere, out on the lake, a lone loon issued its haunted call.

CHAPTER 33

Rain rattled the windshield so hard the wipers couldn't keep up. The view ahead was a fever dream of melted forested landscape. Krista kept to the center of the road, praying she would see oncoming headlights long before she risked a collision. As she sped southward along the curving highway, back to the summer house, she once again chanced a quick look at her cell phone. Yes, the ringer was set to full volume. Yes, it was fully charged. Since leaving Edgar behind in the interrogation room, she'd been obsessed with his cryptic words.

I'm done talking. If you want any real answers, go ask your Poppa.

She couldn't imagine Poppa knowing more than what she'd already learned from his unfinished manuscript. She needed her sounding board. She needed to sort this all out with Neal. She could always count on him to see the truth in difficult circumstances, and these circumstances were more fraught with difficulty than anything she'd ever faced.

If you want real answers ...

After sending Neal three texts, she realized something was seriously wrong. The first, when she reached her car after leaving the prison: *On my way home. Miss U. Need to talk*. The second, while on the ferry from Wisconsin to Michigan: *Is everything OK?* The third, halfway home, with mounting dread: *Neal? What's going on?* It was easy to miss a single text, but three? It was so unlike Neal to not respond.

She was really starting to worry.

She readied a fourth text when she received a bulk notification telling her the first trio of texts had all bounced. She shut off the radio and slowed the car to a crawl before pulling off to the shoulder. Shadows and tangled trees loomed all around her. Rain danced on the tarmac, drummed a dull roar on the roof of the car. The rearview mirror reflected an empty road trailing behind her with no oncoming headlights. She thumbed over to dial the phone.

She speed-dialed Neal. After two rings, the phone picked up: *We're sorry, but the number you have dialed is no longer in service.* She tried Jack's and Leah's phones and received the same message.

Heart in her throat, she dialed Poppa's landline. The receiver never picked up, even after fifteen or more rings, and would've likely continued its shrill tolling if she hadn't hung up.

Krista stared at the reception bars on the phone, dumbfounded. It wavered from four to three before dropping off to nothing. The brightly lit reception graphic became slate gray: *No Service.*

What the hell?

She considered flagging someone down, to borrow their phone to call 9-1-1, but in reality, nothing bad had happened at the summer house, at least as far as she knew. She assumed it was a mixture of the weather and the isolation of the hilly terrain conspiring against her cell phone service. It had to be. The summer house was just a few short minutes up the road. She resolved to only allow herself to panic if there was something to panic about, and the only way she would know would be to get back to her family.

She tossed her phone on the center console, returned the car to the road, and gunned the engine. The wipers frantically tried to part the falling rain, but it was a thankless task; she couldn't see well enough down the road to justify her speed. After taking a deep breath, she slowed to five miles per hour over the speed limit. Even at that pace, the Volvo struggled to hug the curves as she negotiated the final tense miles.

Only after coming to a halt in front of the summer house did she realize the windows weren't lit up from within with lamps. The house was on fire. Flames roiled the front curtains of the library, the front den as well.

"*Oh, my God ... oh my God ... oh my God.*"

The car lurched to a stop.

Krista jumped out and sprinted through burgeoning puddles and up the front porch steps. She hesitated, and then touched the doorknob.

Still cool.

Warm smoky air greeted her as she charged inside.

"Neal!"

There came no reply, at least none she was aware of. Wood crackled and fire roared all around her. The wood-paneled walls were alight, spouting black smoke that whirled like living creatures enthralled with the act of destruction.

"Leah! Jack!" she called out.

Still no reply.

Krista shielded her face with her hand and closed in on the kitchen. She saw no one.

"Clara?"

The hallway leading to the kids' bedrooms was engulfed in flames and impassable. The other direction, leading to Poppa's room, was smoky, but clear.

"Poppa!"

The front door burst open and Neal stormed inside.

"Krista, my God, what happened? Where's Clara?"

"I don't know! Where is everyone?"

"I haven't been here," Neal said. "I had to take Leah to the hospital."

"Jesus, what happened?"

"Later," he gasped, wincing at the smoke. "She's safe. Heidi's with her. Let's make sure no one is still inside."

Krista said, "I'll check for Poppa."

"I'll check the bedrooms." As the fire crept closer, now licking along the ceiling, Neal looked back at the kitchen and down the opposite hallway.

She held onto his hand, not wanting to let him go. "Just ... just be careful. Okay?"

"I will. You too."

He took off into the swirling smoke, muffled by the animalistic sound of burning.

Krista covered her mouth and nose with her shirt. She squinted against the scorching air and hurried down the darkened hallway toward Poppa's bedroom. The flames had not gotten so far, the air clearer. Poppa's bedroom door stood ajar, wide enough to illuminate a sliver of hardwood floor bathed in silvery light. Not fire. No fire could be so white, so pure.

She shoved open the door and stumbled back against the doorframe.

Breann, and the spirits of a half dozen other dead girls, circled above Poppa's bed, their ethereal bodies lit up from within by a painfully white light. They shrieked and swooped, lashing him with overly long boney fingers.

"Poppa?" she said, barely a whisper.

The immediacy of the fire drifted away. She couldn't stop staring at these children, these ravening spirits, as they swept down, one after another, and took turns striking Poppa with their jagged, filthy nails.

Poppa remained transfixed, his face a rictus of utter fear. He flinched in pain at their stinging lashes, but no visible wounds appeared on his skin.

"Poppa!"

Every wailing spirit paused in flight and turned their dead-eyed gazes at Krista.

"Leave me alone," Poppa said, his face collapsed in shame. "Krista. Let me die."

"Yeah, Krista," said one of the glowing spirits, "let him die."

The other spirits joined as a chorus: "Let him die! Let him die! Let him die!"

Krista felt her hands drawing into fists. "What did you do? What did you do to Breann? To all those other children?"

"I ... I did nothing." Poppa sobbed, barely strong enough to look at her.

Krista slammed her palms into the mattress at his side. "Bullshit. Edgar told me. He said you have the real answers. So, tell me!"

"You have to get out of here. The fire ... it's coming."

Krista coughed against the smoke creeping into the room.

"I'm not leaving until you tell me."

"Please, Krista, just go," Poppa said with defeat in his voice.

Krista took him by the lapels of his pajamas and shook him violently. His head whipsawed. There was so little left of him, and he had so little regard for his own wellbeing, that he didn't even raise a finger against her. She shoved him back into his pillows and glared at him, resolute she wouldn't leave without learning the truth.

"Like I said, I did nothing," Poppa said. "Absolutely nothing."

"So help me God, if you don't start talking, we're both going to die tonight."

He sobbed, but had no tears left to fall. "I found Edgar Lee Jenkins a long time ago, when he was still practically a child and living in foster care in Wisconsin. And for years his aberrant behavior was my prized subject. If I could make sense of predator/prey relationships in the animal world, I figured I could do the same with humans."

"You let all of those kids die?"

"I thought the sacrifices would be worth it. If I could unlock what made a human predator act out, perhaps it could be stopped. I thought—"

"You thought nothing!" Breann screamed, dipping close to Poppa, raking her raised claws against his face.

Poppa screamed and held up his hands in defense.

Krista's legs weakened as she backed into Nan's old dresser.

"Somehow, he came here, to the Little Whisper," Poppa said, cowering and whimpering. "I still don't know how he found me. He might have seen me during one of my observations and followed me back here. I don't know. But he found me, and that's when ... that's when something even *more* vile took hold of him."

"What's that supposed to mean?" Krista said.

"Demons. Unclean spirits set upon the living."

"Demons?" she said, incredulous.

"Don't discount something you don't understand. Look around you, Krista. The world is not what it seems."

The spirits of the dead children hovered closer, waiting on his every word.

"Why didn't you end it?" Krista asked. Tears streaked down her cheeks as she approached the bed. She looked away from her grandfather, to the dead girls staring at her in fascination. "You could've stopped it."

"I did turn him in. Eventually. But only when he got too close to my family. And by then it was too late. I let too much pain into this world through my inaction."

"No, not by your inaction, your *complicity*." Krista raised a hand toward Breann. The spirit extended her own fingers, and Krista felt a cold tingle in her fingertips as they came close to touching. "You might as well have killed those kids yourself."

Poppa nodded, his eyes struggling to remain open.

Breann smiled her crooked smile. The anger and grotesque reworking of her features faded away, and in its place, Krista was left with the sweet image of her once dear friend.

"Thank you, Krista. For seeing me. For believing me."

"I never stopped missing you, Breann. I never stopped hoping you were safe."

"You must go, Krista. Your daughter needs you. Out by the lake. You must hurry."

Krista glanced at Poppa, saw how sincerely he wanted it all to just simply end.

"Goodbye, Poppa." Her throat constricted on the words.

She couldn't bear to see his final expression. She'd seen enough, learned enough. For as long as she could remember, Poppa had been a part of her life. Not a small part, either, but a foundational bulwark of her life. He had raised her, imbued in her a sense of morality, fidelity, the rigor that comes from strong beliefs held dear. But it had all been a lie. This whole time, he had been—if not a monster—the enabler of one of the most heinous beings imaginable.

No, she didn't want to see him now, at his end, and didn't know if she wanted the memories to remain, which she'd long held so dear.

The spirits set upon the old man like hyenas on an injured wildebeest.

So many thoughts assaulted her as she rushed out the door, toward the roaring flames and blistering heat. Krista covered her mouth with her hands to both fend off the smoke and to stifle sobs that, if let loose, would break her spirit. She sprinted down the hallway, hoping she wasn't too late to save Clara.

She could sense the dimensions of the house, but with the gathering smoke, she became disoriented when she reached the wide entryway foyer. The smoke thickened, and she couldn't hear any signs of life. For all she knew, Neal had already succumbed to the fire, and Clara, and her cousins, and—

My God, I've lost them all. My whole family is dead …

She swooned with dizziness, yet her head cleared the instant a cold hand gripped her shoulder. When she turned, Breann's fierce smile greeted her.

"We have to hurry. Clara needs you."

Breann took her hand in her own, her touch chilling the depths of Krista's bones, and gave her a gentle tug. For the briefest moment, Krista felt twelve years old again, chasing after fireflies with her best friend. But just as soon as memory tried to intercede, the reality of the situation shoved it away.

"Come on!"

Krista followed her long-dead friend through walls of smoke and spreading flames.

CHAPTER 34

Cold rain stung Clara's face as she regained consciousness. Long before she pieced together what was happening to her, she instinctively understood she was in mortal danger. She didn't know what was more terrifying, the fact that her brain remained fogged, or that she could barely move a muscle. Rain rattled hollowly, and something slapped and cut rhythmically through nearby water. No, not nearby—it was around her, *beneath* her. It sounded like ... oars.

Oh, my God. The lake!

Adrenaline cleared her mind.

I'm in the rowboat!

Her right cheek pressed against cold fiberglass. The choppy lake jostled the boat, sending rain puddled in the footwell splashing against her face. She tasted blood in the water and spat, realizing the blood was most likely her own. When she opened her eyes, she saw nothing but rolling murk through spattering rain. With rhythmic consistency, heaving shoulders and a curving spine worked the oars, a man grunting with the effort.

Uncle Jack?

She couldn't fathom why he'd taken her, or why he ...

He hit me. Uncle Jack hit me!

Her head throbbed where she'd been struck, and her crazy uncle was taking her out onto the open water in the middle of a rainstorm.

"Isn't the water beautiful?" he said, his voice cutting through the storm.

Did I call out in pain?

She didn't know how he could possibly know she'd woken, not with the wind and rain.

"The water ... from both above and below," he continued, "it washes away the filth."

She didn't reply, would only break into sobs if she tried, so she remained silent. Huddled with her knees drawn up tight to her chin, she decided her best way out of this was to leap from the boat. She wasn't the best swimmer, but Uncle Jack might not see her in the darkness. She might have a chance. Throwing herself into the lake's storm-lashed waves seemed like a safer choice than waiting to see what he had in store for her.

My God, how is this happening?

Her Uncle Jack had always been a sweet man. Someone who would rather trap a spider and release it outside than step on it.

Clara tried to move, shifting from her side to her back, but her limbs were completely immobilized. Her senses reached out, hyper-vigilant, as panic stirred through her.

She suddenly remembered the sound of plastic sheeting unspooling from the roll. How he had used it to cocoon her.

Uncle Jack looked over his shoulder, a sharp gleam in his eyes.

"Don't worry. It'll soon be over," he said.

This wasn't Uncle Jack. His humanity was gone, and his compassion, and in their place was something vulgar, something mean.

Her lips trembled from both fright and cold. "Wha ... what's going on?"

"Oh, sleepy head," he said and chuckled, "I thought it would be a good time for a night swim."

"I ... I don't understand."

Clara writhed, still unable to free herself, and only succeeded in bumping her head against the side of the footwell.

"I guess it didn't have to be you." His voice became deeper, more resolute. "It could've easily been Heidi. After all, I came close to choosing her mother all those years ago."

Stri-dĕnt, she thought. *Loud, harsh, grating.* His tone was definitely strident. She shook her head to help clear it before she automatically broke down the word's etymology.

"Your aloneness," he said, "that's what sealed my decision. That form of pain is more exquisite than anything besides physical injury." He gave her a wink and turned back to pull against the oars, his effort heaving the rowboat through a rough, white-capped swell.

"Who are you?"

Claustrophobia swept through her, as if the plastic sheeting constricted tighter with her every exhalation.

He laughed and pulled the oars once more. When he completed the stroke, he carefully brought the oars to their resting positions along the gunwales. He turned to face her, swinging his feet around until they settled with a splash in the water puddled around her. He leaned his elbows against his knees, cocked an eyebrow.

"Who *am* I?"

"You're not my uncle," Clara said.

Her hands were partially numb, but she continued to test the strength of her bonds. As she pressed out with her elbows, trying to stretch the plastic sheeting, something scratched painfully across her wrist. She wondered if a fishhook had somehow found its way into the plastic sheeting, but she didn't think so.

"Well, there's some truth to that, I suppose," he replied. "It won't matter once my masterpiece is complete."

"Masterpiece," she whispered, not wanting to know the answer.

Her fumbling fingers discovered what had scratched her wrist.

The charm. Of course. The heart her mom had given to Breann.

It all made sense.

"It'll be easier on you if you don't struggle. Struggling makes time slow, makes it so you'll feel every ounce of water as it sears your throat and lungs. And it'll burn twice as much when you puke it up. And you will. There's no shame in it; everyone does it."

The boat drifted in the rain. The man who had once been her Uncle Jack leered at her, his features twisting into a grotesque mask.

Clara managed to grasp the heart charm between the knuckle of her index and middle fingers. She coiled her wrist and a sharp edge snagged the tough plastic skin, and there it remained, buried and of little use. She wanted to cry out in frustration, but held it back.

"*What* are you going to do to me?" she asked.

"If I had more time? Complete exsanguination. Do you know what that means?"

For once she felt within her element, and with a shudder she replied, "It means the total draining of blood."

"Very good!" He seemed startled by her reply. He leaned in close, brushed the hair out of her eyes. "I'm so glad you're the one." He looked out at the dark water and sighed contentedly.

"So ... so, you're going to drown me?" she said, trying to prolong her remaining time. She worked the heart charm, and with some effort, pulled it free from the plastic. With her knuckle she felt a small rent in the plastic, little more than a dimple—the smallest hope, but all she had, so she clung onto it as she again attacked the plastic. "I've never done anything to you!"

"Just know, when you join the others, a cycle will be complete. And once it's complete, I will regain dominion over this human form." He tilted his face toward the sky, and the rain trailed down his cheeks like a thousand tears. "I will, again, be human."

"What are you?"

The charm tore through the plastic as she feverishly slashed against her bindings. She tried so hard to keep her voice steady, her face as calm as possible.

His eyes hardened, subsuming the last trace of Uncle Jack. He grabbed the plastic enshrouding her and easily lifted Clara waist-high.

"*Nonononono!*" she begged.

"Thank you for this gift, Clara," he said, and heaved her into the water.

Chaotic darkness descended over her. Water invaded her nostrils and seeped into her lungs. She coughed as the panic of drowning stoked her heartbeat.

The sound of the rain intensified when she broke the surface, but only briefly, before her body again sunk beneath the water.

Clara held her breath and worked the charm against the plastic. She tore enough to punch her fist all the way through the many layers. Her wrist afforded little movement to help widen the hole. Still, she tried, with all her might, she tried.

Her burning lungs began to spasm as she fought the instinctive urge to take a breath. She couldn't see anything, neither the direction to the surface nor the depth in which she thrashed.

She wedged her arm outside, forcing the hole wider, but it was of little use.

Her heart throbbed in her ears, and a shadow of a shadow soon enveloped her. Her efforts became futile and began to ease, no matter her sense of urgency. The straining in her muscles drained away. A trickle of water breached her lungs, and though she sputtered against its invasion, it was easier to allow it to happen than to fight any longer.

The heart charm slipped from her fingers, drifting toward the bottom of the lake. The tarnished metal somehow caught the light, or maybe emitted its own light from within, and seemed to shrink as it floated down, twinkling in the darkness. The last air bubbles jetted from between her lips, and she too began to sink into the darkness at the lake bottom.

CHAPTER 35

Krista could barely see Breann through the smoke as she was guided away from Poppa's bedroom, squinting through the heat of the fire. They hurtled through the kitchen, but when Krista dug in her heels to avoid slamming into the sliding door, Breann slipped from her grasp and floated without pause through the pane.

Breann placed her palm against the glass separating them. "*Krista!*"

A wall of fire separated the kitchen from the front of the house.

"Neal!" Krista called out.

The only reply was the roaring of the fire. A section of the ceiling collapsed, sending sparks and ash swirling into the air.

Breann's voice wavered inside Krista's head.

"*Hurry, Krista.*"

She coughed against the searing smoke, fumbled for the door pull, shoved it open, and fell to her knees on the deck as she gasped for fresh air.

Tears coursed down her cheeks. Despair weakened her limbs. She couldn't face the world. Not alone. Not without her family.

"*Clara needs you, Krista.*"

The dead girl kneeled next to her. When Krista lifted her gaze, she saw the trees through her friend. She was losing substance, her hold on this world.

"Why did you come back for me? Why aren't you in there with the others?"

"*Because,*" Breann said, tears filling her eyes. She smiled, revealing crooked teeth. Her skin glowed from within, a pure white. *"You're my best friend. You've always been my best friend."*

Breann offered her hand, and Krista took it, gaining her feet.

"I never got to live, but you did. And so did your daughter. And the both of you still have so much more living to experience."

"Where is she? Where's my Clara?"

"Down at the lake. The spirit that took me … that took all the girls … it has her. And we need to get there, like, right now."

With fear and adrenaline pushing her close to a panic attack, Krista followed Breann hurriedly down the deck stairs. Somewhere between the deck and rain-swept sand, though, Breann had vanished. Krista was alone.

She felt a profound sense of abandonment, but pushed it aside. She couldn't think about losing Breann again. Not when her daughter's life still hung in the balance.

Krista scanned the lakeshore and it was immediately apparent where she would find Clara. A white ball of light glowed in the middle of the lake, from *beneath* the lake.

Whatever it was, *whoever* it was, it better not harm her daughter. Krista sprinted toward the light, sprays of sand kicked up with her every stride. Without a second thought, she dived into the water, and as she kicked away from shore, the cold darkness took her in its embrace.

CHAPTER 36

Alone in a dark void. Drifting ...

Warmth gathered in Clara's center spreading outward, until the heat touched her from toes to fingertips. Then she opened her eyes

(or have they been open this whole time and only now has my sight returned?)

and found herself immersed in a ball of liquid light. Free of her bounds, of that stifling plastic shroud, there was an even brighter light, this one small and shimmering, just outside the limits of the ball encircling her. She swam toward it, ever deeper, but it remained elusively beyond her reach, taunting her. The more she kicked and paddled through the warm viscous light, the more this beacon took shape and definition. And it all made sense.

The heart charm.

"*Don't go, dear. Stay with me,*" a voice called out from behind her, but still somehow *within* her, halting her movements. "*Stay with me and fight.*"

Clara floated, immobile, within the light, seeking the source of the voice.

Wearing a black funeral dress fringed with delicate lace, the woman was beautiful and beaming, the great-grandmother she'd never met.

"*Nan?*"

"*Take this,*" Nan spoke within Clara's mind, holding the heart charm out to her, the chain looped around her wrinkled hand.

Clara looked from the charm to the object she'd been chasing; the bright beacon flared brighter before extinguishing like a blown candle, if it had ever been there in the first place.

"*But ... I thought ...*" Clara thought, returning her gaze to Nan.

"*That's not the light you want. That light leads to damnation. And you have so much more ... so much more everything to do in your life.*"

The ball of liquid light encircling them began to shrink, to dim.

"*Take it, Clara,*" Nan said. "*It's yours.*"

Clara reached out slowly, as if tempting a tarantula's caress.

Nan nodded as Clara's fingers neared.

The heart charm glowed warmly, and a feeling of security and love seemed to emanate from it, as well as from her great-grand-mother. Clara took hold of the heart. She had nothing to fear from this woman who'd so indelibly shaped the lives of those she loved. Nan hugged her close as the light continued to dim, and when Clara blinked and opened her eyes, she could no longer see her, could no longer perceive the light that had brought them together.

Something tightened in Clara's throat and she began to choke. Cold water filled her mouth, her lungs, and she could taste the lake on her tongue as it tried to kill her.

"*Stay with me,*" Nan said, her voice weakened within Clara's mind. "*Fight for me, Clara. For your mom.*"

Clara rose from the cold depths of the lake, the lake water streaming up her throat. She imagined her spirit continuing up to the heavens until the earth itself became a distant blue beacon of its own.

She breached the surface of the lake, vomited long and hard. Choppy waves washed across her face, again threatening to drown her, for she remained entombed in plastic sheeting.

Nan helped her remain afloat, looking down at her with a beatific smile.

CHAPTER 37

Krista had never been a great swimmer, even during her summers spent on the Little Whisper as a child, but she somehow found the strength to power through her awkward form and untested stamina. Within a handful of strokes, the rowboat, fighting the storm-wracked waves at the center of the lake, seemed not so far away.

Nothing ...

better ...

hurt ...

her ...

She repeated the mantra over and again as she cut the distance to the boat. As she came within twenty feet, she began to tire. Cramps exploded along her ribcage, and the muscles in her shoulders screamed in agony.

Nothing ...

better ...

Krista slowed, but barely. She saw no signs of anyone aboard the boat as she closed in, only a nebulous ball of white light coming from the water's surface. She squinted against the glare.

Clara!

Her daughter was inside the light, looking tiny and so young.

And Nan ... her very own grandmother, held Clara's head above water.

Is she moving? Is she alive?

"Nan ...?" Krista gasped.

The spirit of her grandmother turned toward her with agony

written into her features. The white light was nearly gone, and so was she. The lake was visible *through* Nan, as if her substance were the final scrim of ice melting come springtime.

"My dear, Krista," Nan said weakly.

As soon as she spoke Krista's name, the last of her grandmother vanished; Clara bobbed, constrained somehow, her face dipping below the surface.

Krista reached her daughter and lifted her face clear of the lake. Her entire body, except for her head, was wrapped in plastic, as if cocooned. Krista tried to rip it free, but she was slippery and bound tightly. Freeing her was an impossible task while treading water.

What the hell?

Water drained from between Clara's lips, but she didn't cough or flinch or show any other signs of life.

"My baby, *please* ... Clara." Krista sobbed as she struggled to keep them both afloat.

Thunder ripped across the sky as the rain intensified.

"Please, Clara. I can't lose you."

"Krista! Need a hand?"

Jack leaned with his palms against the gunwale of the boat.

Isn't the boat empty?

"Help us, damn it!" Krista said as water splashed into her mouth. She coughed, but kept a tight grip around Clara with one arm, while continuing to keep them afloat with the other, legs kicking tirelessly.

"Sure thing, sis," Jack said, lifting an oar.

His face darkened as he swung it down against Krista's shoulder.

A crack of bones breaking, her scream puncturing the night, and then Krista's head dipped below the water, silencing her. Excruciating pain radiated from her shoulder, nearly making her forget the dangers surrounding her.

She flexed her good arm, thankfully feeling the weight of her daughter still within her grasp. When they surfaced, Jack had already raised the oar a second time.

Krista kicked away from the boat. The oar passed over head, chopping the water mere inches from her face.

"Jackson!" a clear voice called out, cutting through the storm.

Nan stood onboard the boat, a pale white light emanating from her skin.

"Nan ..." Jack said, struggling to say the single syllable. His expression drained of anger—temporarily—and he looked again like the boy who used to swim these waters twenty years ago. "I'm ... sorry ... I thought I could save you, that you'd finally be able to rest with one final sacrifice, if I sacrificed myself, if I gave myself over to the dark spirit ..."

"Oh, Jackson ... you always had the most loving heart."

Jack shook his head, as if to clear it. His eyes steadied, darkened, once again filled with anger. He raised the oar high above his head to strike at Krista.

Nan wrapped her arms around his waist. He struggled at first, as if he'd been embraced within a giant molten fist. His eyes boggled and ropey veins stood out ridged from his neck. But Nan held fast, even as her brother let out a low whine of pain. His eyes turned red with bloodshot, then darkened to cinders.

Krista watched as she struggled, sometimes from above the water, sometimes from below. She kicked, and even though it was agonizing to move her free arm, she pumped it through something close to a full stroke. She nearly passed out from the pain, but then she attempted another stroke, broken bones grinding.

Nan's white light enveloped Jack as Krista gained distance from the boat. The longer Nan maintained her embrace, the less he struggled. The light brightened briefly, then both Nan and Jack fell overboard.

The rain erased their splash.

Their light dimmed to nothing.

They were gone.

The summer house glowed with flames in the distance, charting a beacon's path for Krista through the dark water. Her sole focus was to keep a firm grip on her daughter, to get through the next stroke. Each pass through the frigid water brought them inches closer to shore. Each pass was the most agonizing pain she'd ever experienced. She inhaled, swam some more, exhaled slowly. After a while, Krista's pain became a distant thing, an echo, a memory.

As they neared the shore, Krista's toes brushed the lake bottom.

Clara coughed in her arms—which awakened a strength in Krista she didn't know she possessed—and started vomiting, more than she thought possible. Krista wanted to wash her daughter's face, to clear her throat, but they were so close now.

Clara's eyes fluttered open as Krista's tired legs found purchase. Krista tried to carry Clara one-armed out of the water, and collapsed with her onto the shore.

"Mom ... you made it," Clara whispered. "Nan, she said you would come. And you did."

"Oh, my God, Clara, I thought I'd lost you."

Krista tore through the plastic sheeting blanketing her daughter. She could only use her right hand; her left arm hung at her side, practically useless. She couldn't raise her hand above her head, so she had no idea how she managed to get Clara to shore.

Someone groaned nearby, and they both turned to the sound.

"What was that?" Clara asked.

"Can you walk?" Krista said.

"Sure ... I think so."

Krista stood, pulled the last of the plastic away, and helped Clara to her feet.

Again, they heard the groaning. They followed the sound, which came from somewhere near the tree line at the base of the deck stairs. A small body was cloaked in darkness, curled up in the sand next to the lean-to, soot-stained and semi-conscious.

"Robby!" Clara called out and rushed to the boy's side.

The house atop the Little Whisper burned, the sky glowing with false-dawn brightness.

Exhausted, Krista fell to her knees, sending a jolt of pain grating through her shoulder. Tears streaked her face. Clara was safe, and she had never felt a happier moment since the first time she held her in her arms after giving birth. And yet, she couldn't help feeling the weightiest despair. She couldn't live without Neal. She doubted she would be able to forge ahead—a broken shell that would never heal.

She sobbed uncontrollably. She couldn't help it.

"Krista?"

That one word, spoken by that singular voice, scattered the dark cloud before it could fully engulf her. It gave her strength to stand.

Neal stepped away from the final wooden stair. He carried another body in his arms: Trevor. The boy's dangling arm was blackened with burns. Fire had melted away part of his hair behind his right ear. His skin was a landscape of blistered and suppurating wounds.

"My God," she said, as more tears filled her eyes.

Neal was crying as well. She wanted to hug him, to feel his closeness, to have their embrace chase away every horrible thing in the world... but she couldn't. One hug wouldn't fix the broken child held in her husband's arms. Krista reached out, touched Neal's cheek.

"I thought …" She trailed off and shook her head. "I thought you were gone. I thought you were *all* gone."

Robby groaned in Neal's arms as life twitched through his spindly limbs.

Krista's tears fell afresh. But these were tears of joy. Before long, Clara came over and wrapped her arms around Krista's waist. Krista reached out and one-arm hugged Neal. Their collective tears were as quickly shed as washed away by the continued rain. Robby joined them, bumping into their collective embrace, hugging them all as much as his tiny arms would allow.

"And Poppa?" Krista asked.

Neal said nothing, just shook his head with his eyes downcast.

CHAPTER 38

THREE MONTHS LATER

Clara stood within the alcove cut into the woods near the road leading to the summer house. She couldn't bring herself to look at Uncle Jack's headstone. She didn't blame him for what had happened, but it was hard for her to see past their final night together in order to remember the sweet man he'd once been. Perhaps, in time, things would change.

She brushed a fallen twig from the top of the other new grave.

"I'm going to miss you, Poppa," she said, fending off a tear. "I don't know exactly what you did, or why you did it, but I know you were a good person. I have no doubts."

The simple stone stood next to Nan's. While she'd never *known* her great-grandmother, not in any real sense of the word, she would miss her, too. Without her, Clara wouldn't be alive. Without her, the evil that had overcome Uncle Jack would have lived on. And in so doing, that spirit would have regained human form.

Huh-loo-suh-ney-shuhn. Even now it was hard to believe the tragedies during the summer had been anything more than a horrible hallucination.

An unfounded or mistaken impression; that was far too simple an explanation for everything she'd experienced. Besides, she couldn't deny the indelible memory of Nan's smile as her spirit kept her from falling beneath the waves. That smile had been real, and she would take that memory with her the rest of her life.

Footsteps crunched over fallen leaves as her mom approached.

While she wished that so much of that last night at the summer house had been a hallucination, some things made that denial an impossibility. Besides the memory of Nan's smile, her mom had only recently set aside the sling, having sustained multiple fractures in her shoulder. Even now, with the bones newly mended, her shoulder dipped lower than the other.

They all bore their scars.

"Are you ready?" her mom said, offering a small smile.

"Sure. I guess."

Clara exited the newly erected chain-link fence surrounding the graveyard and waited for her mom to close the gate and click the padlock. When their gazes met, Clara was the one to offer a smile.

"What's going to happen to this place?" she asked.

"The property ..." her mom said and trailed off. She placed her arm over Clara's shoulders and gave her a squeeze. "The land, it will become part of the new state park. That's what Poppa always wanted."

Her mom wouldn't look at the flattened plane of newly planted sod where the summer house had once stood, but Clara couldn't help staring. It was both surprising and soothing to see the silvery shimmer of sun on the lake below.

The morning after the storm and the fire, when the police had been called and the place swarming with dozens of emergency responders from three counties wide, a fireman found Uncle Jack face down in the water, about thirty feet down shore.

Within days, a dredging crew had been brought out to search the lake. They found the plastic-shrouded bodies, eleven all-told; each was situated on the lake bottom like numerals on a clock's face. All that had been missing was the final numeral.

When they reached the Volvo, Clara turned to her mom and said, "I'm so sorry."

"Sorry for what, honey?"

"Everything. What happened to Uncle Jack, Poppa, Breann ..."

"Oh, honey, there's nothing for you to feel sorry for. I'm the one who should be sorry for ever bringing you here."

"But Mom, we *had* to come here. Breann, Melody ... all those other kids ..." Clara sniffed back a tear, "Nan ... all of them. They're at rest now. That wouldn't have happened if we didn't come back to the summer house."

Her mom leaned over and kissed Clara's forehead. "You, my dear, are far too wise. I feel horrible that you went through what you went through, but I'm glad to hear that perspective."

Clara smiled a real smile, one not forced or small.

"Are my two ladies ready to get home?" her dad said.

"More than anything," her mom said.

"Me too." Clara looked back through the rear window as her dad pulled away from the shoulder. The copse of trees surrounding the graveyard got smaller and smaller, until it disappeared as the car climbed a hill into the surrounding forest.

"Mom, so did you ask Dad?"

"Ask me about what?" her dad said, and Clara could see the glimmer in his eye and that her parents had already discussed it.

"My birthday, silly," Clara said with a giggle.

"You have a birthday coming up?" her dad said.

"In two weeks. You didn't forget, did you?"

"No, of course not." He looked at her in the rearview mirror and gave her a wink. "And the answer is yes. Your Aunt Leah and all three cousins are coming out for your birthday."

"Are you sure there's room?" Clara asked with a touch of worry.

"It's going to be a tight squeeze, but it'll be easier next year."

"Neal, you said we shouldn't mention anything—"

Clara's dad smiled and shrugged. "What can I say? I can't stand sitting on good news."

Clara leaned forward between the front seats. "What are you guys talking about?"

"We're thinking about moving. Somewhere with more room. The suburbs maybe?" Clara's mom said.

"Just imagine, a place with a big back yard with plenty of trees. A bedroom for everyone. Maybe one of those mother-in-law cottages for Aunt Leah."

"Really?" Clara said, elated. "The whole family in one place?"

"We were going to talk about it more when we got home ... but yeah," her dad said.

"Is that okay with you?" her mom said, hesitantly, as if she feared Clara's response. "I know you're used to having your own space—"

"Absolutely!" Clara said. "Can we get a tire swing?"

"Sure," he said and her parents laughed and exchanged a glance. "Anything you want. See, Krista, that wasn't so bad, was it?"

Her mom kissed her fingertips and pressed them against his cheek. Clara smiled and her mom pulled a sheaf of papers onto her lap. "Now, Clara, I know you want to jump right back into your Spelling Bee list."

"Mom," Clara said, meeting her dad's eyes in the rearview mirror.

"Top ten is outstanding," her mom continued, "but with enough practice—"

"Honey?" her dad cut in.

"Yes?" Her mom looked up from her papers and arched an eyebrow.

"Listen to your daughter," he said with a wink.

"Clara, what is it, honey?"

"Mom … I want to just, I don't know … stare out the window for a while."

"Hmm … yeah, okay," her mom said, nodding in understanding. She put the papers back into the folder. Her dad reached out, and her parents held hands as the car cut through impenetrable forests shedding their leaves to the season.

Clara touched the heart charm hanging from the chain around her neck. She stared out the window and let her mind wander.

ABOUT THE AUTHOR

A native of the Chicago suburbs, Glen Krisch hopes to add to his list of ghosts he's witnessed (two), as well as develop his rather pedestrian telekinetic and precognitive skills. Besides writing and reading, he enjoys spending time with his wife, his three boys, simple living, and ultra-running.

OTHER WORKS

BY GLEN KRISCH

NOVELS

The Nightmare Within
Where Darkness Dwells
Nothing Lasting
Arkadium Rising: Brother's Keeper Book One
Little Whispers
Echoes of Violence
Gleaners: Brother's Keeper Book Two

NOVELLAS

Loss
The Hollowed Land: A Brother's Keeper Novella
Husks
The Painter from Piotrków

COLLECTIONS

Through the Eyes of Strays
Commitment and Other Tales of Madness
No Man's Dominion
Filth Eater
The Devil's Torment

Made in the USA
Middletown, DE
23 June 2019